UNIMAGINARY

UNIMAGINARY

PATRICK TYLEE

CAMEL
NEEDLE &
ASSOCIATES

Copyright © 2016 Patrick Tylee

Published in 2016 by Camel Needle & Associates ®.

www.patricktylee.com

ISBN-13 Paperback 978-0-9905498-9-5

ISBN-10 Paperback 990549895

To those who believe there's more to
reality than that which we can sense.

Chapter One

This time they won't catch me, she thought. *I won't let them bring me back to the Joining.*

"The Externals are of no concern to us," the Elders warned. "We exist apart from them." Obsessed with the concept of mortal beings, Ahnim's depression deepened. Eternity delayed a death by boredom. She sought escape from her life, her people, the Joining.

"Listen and heed our words, child," they said. "We of the Immini express our lives within. Focus on construction of your inner self. Reject the urge to seek gratification beyond the limits set by nature."

Ahnim wanted more. Desire gripped her. She fed it, and gave herself to its haunting pull. She dreamed of new beings, strange entities, discoveries. Memories of the blue planet flashed in her mind.

There must be more to my life, to any of our lives. Why do they ignore what's truly out there?

The mature Immini reproached her, restrained her from outward expression of individuality. From the first 'no' to the last 'do not', every chastisement piled high upon her mind. Each unfulfilled wish stacked upon another until it verged on toppling. But in deep space nothing falls. Frustrations tumbled inside her, weightless, irritating.

If they don't let me go, they'll regret it.

Gathered into a massive sphere as large as a moon, the Joining soared across remote stretches of space between the star systems in the galaxy. It condensed a community of over twelve thousand, their ship-selves bound together. Each vessel carried the living soul of the one who abode within. Immini law permitted the being to create whatever life they wished. Be they masculine or feminine, demure or uninhibited, every member aligned inner mechanisms to develop according to their own imagination. The Elders encouraged personal expression, but it must fit within the boundaries of your own crystalline shell.

Like the rest, Ahnim could create and become anything— inside her ship-self.

One law gnawed away at her. No Immini may ever explore the space where planets of the Externals might be found. Immortals must remain in the stars, and leave the worlds in peace.

As one of the outlayers, Ahnim's ship-self fit into the external surface like a tile, or reptilian scale. Like many on the Joining's crust, the bottom edges of her perfect pyramid set against the fellow Immini on that side. Her underside touched the others of the interior beneath. A deep blue-green permeated her pliant surface. Flesh miles deep covered colossal mechanisms. Within her empty spaces, a black cloud of anti-photons beat with interstellar lifeblood.

Ahnim possessed a blaze array at her peak to deliver a powerful stream of red-hot plasma at any enemy. Her weapon dematerialized external elements.

A mere wish forged internal elements into any shape Ahnim desired. She toyed with internal construction, but her thoughts strayed outward.

My life is my own, and I'm not waiting anymore, she thought.

Ahnim's chance came as the Joining made a course correction to maneuver around a large asteroid floating far from any sun. The mighty sphere loosened along her side, where she guarded the horizon. As the pressure around her eased, she let go her magnetic grasp and flew out alone, a single ship broken free of the collective.

Another Immini within his own ship-self called her back. "Ahnim! Get back into place!"

"No, Brecca," she said. "I need something else."

"What something? There's nothing out there but emptiness. Now merge back in!"

"It's emptiness I need—not being contained. I want to be… out."

"No," Brecca said, "you mustn't say that. It's not allowed, Ahnim. Besides, we may need your pull at the next star."

"They never let me help!" she said, fuming. "I can pull to a star as easy as any of those with a drive inside of us. You just always—"

"We just what, Ahnim? We keep you safe. The Immini aren't meant to rove the galaxy alone. There are dangers."

"Don't do that, Brecca. Whenever I want to test my skill, or go exploring, or discover something—a planet or anything—you have to remind me."

"I'm supposed to remind you," Brecca said. "Others

separated from the Joining to save you. They were injured doing so. You should know better by now."

They do still blame me. I didn't ask to be rescued. It's their own fault they nearly froze.

"Ahnim, I wonder about what happened," Brecca said, "why you did that before."

"What's there to wonder about?" she asked. "I found the little water world and went to see it for myself. I was fine."

"Yes, exactly—you went. You're not allowed to do that. *We* aren't permitted to do that. And consider the result, Ahnim. Four Immini detached to find you, and they suffered out there, apart from the Joining."

I have my own mechanism for inner warmth. Maybe they should've known better.

"The five of you barely made it back," Brecca said.

"We did," she said.

I didn't want to come back. I want to try being something on the outside. There are others out there who are free, living outside themselves. I'm going to try that. You'd better not stop me.

"Ahnim, don't you even care that your actions put others at risk? You must learn to be patient, to live according to the rules. We must each create our own life, our own inner story, but it must not effect anyone else."

"Why not, Brecca?"

"Why not, what?"

"What could be so wrong about my life and the life of another coming together outside?"

"That's not right, Ahnim," he said. "It's forbidden. I can't even imagine..."

I can. I think about nothing else.

"If an Immini were to do that," he said, "to merge experiences, there would be real danger of someone getting hurt. Our lives must be contained, Ahnim."

"I don't see anything wrong with trying it," she said, "maybe just once."

Ahnim coasted along near Brecca's place in the Joining. The tiny divot sparkled on the gleaming blue globe. It pressed on, revolving, on course toward a distant nebula.

"Ahnim, listen to me," Brecca said. "Merge back in."

"No," Ahnim said.

"Are you going to fly off on your own again?"

I'm going to do exactly what I choose, that's what.

The Elders ordered she be kept out of trouble. She'd brought the entire Joining to a halt in space twice already, making them turn back once.

"All who are Internals must be initiated," the Elders had commanded. "Every one of us shall be forever in the Joining. There can be no exceptions."

So few were found anymore—Ahnim the last. Her birthplace, a collapsed supernova encountered far behind them. A smaller formation of Immini made a desperate dive across the black hole's event horizon. They searched through the stream of x-rays emitted from the singularity's poles. Somewhere, hidden in the dazzling energy could be a newborn.

The star itself died. The Immini dedicated the freed soul now embodied in the crystalline shell: Ahnim (Fire), Goyo (Fills), Thalia (Bursts Forth).

Now an adolescent, she lived up to her name.

"You breaking free again," Brecca said, "is going to make it difficult to trust you."

"So, I'm not trusted anymore?" asked the intractable Ahnimgoyothalia.

"It's not about you being anything. It's about others who don't."

"That makes no sense, Brecca. Now you're just purposely confusing me."

"Your confusion comes from having already decided that I'm wrong—that we're all wrong, and you alone are in the right. Ahnim, you've got to look beyond yourself, to the needs of the Joining. There's more going on than you can see from where you are. Your perspective is short-sighted. There's a reason we prevent ourselves from doing what you consider."

Without her knowing, Brecca sent a coded message to the Elders and the other Defenders nearby. They prepared themselves for another of Ahnim's attempts to escape.

"Tell me about the little beings on the planet, Ahnim," Brecca said.

"Why?" She asked. "You don't even believe me. You think I'm making all that up."

"I wouldn't ask if I didn't. What did you see that time?"

With the barest of voice, she dared express her deep desire to be believed.

"I'd gone exploring. There was a new smell, so I followed the trail of it. I found the little orange star with its gas planets. The system moved through a cloud of stellar vapor, leaving a swirl and a wake that made it easy to track. I figured I could pull to it and still get back to the Joining before anyone noticed. That's when I discovered the water world. It sparkled, in a cold sort of way, not like other planets. I didn't want to pull to it directly. Its surface, so incredibly fragile and soft. I worried that if I touched it, or even reached to it, the water would spill off. Have you ever seen a water planet, Brecca?"

"No, they're exceptionally rare. Donthel has, though. But the frozen water made noises, he said. It crackled as the planet turned in the warmth of its sun. If he found anything, he's never said."

"Oh, I didn't hear crackling," Ahnim said. "What I heard scared me. I recognized it, inside me, where my feelings are."

"What did you hear, Ahnim?"

"Screams...screams of terror," she said.

"What would make that sound?"

"A little someone, at their last moments."

"Did you head back to the Joining then?" Brecca asked.

"No, I went closer to see if there was a little someone down near the planet."

"What did you find?" he asked.

"It was so fantastically small. I had no idea things came small like that. You know, real things. That living someones could even exist at that size—I mean, there's hardly anything there to hold together."

"Was it on the water world?" Brecca asked. While she told him the story of her last unauthorized adventure, Brecca received the response from the Defenders. They readied to corral her, if necessary. If she moved further away from the Joining, they would stop her.

"Not at first," Ahnim said. "It stayed close to the planet,

flying just over the surface. I didn't want to frighten it."

"What did it look like—the tiny someone flying down near the water world?"

"It was pointed at the front, and had a wing on each side. The wings pushed down on the blue coating of the planet, helping it to fly. But one of the wings turned to black smoke. That's what made it start."

"Made what start, Ahnim?"

He isn't listening to me. They never listen to me.

"I told you...the screaming," Ahnim said.

"Was it a machine?" Brecca asked.

"Yes and no," she said. "Like I said, super tiny. But the living parts were inside the mechanical part. Inside-out from us, I'd say."

"How can that be real?"

"I know. Nobody thinks it's real," Ahnim said. "That's why none of you believe me."

He thinks this is just another one of my dreams. As if I don't know the difference between what's real and my imagination. There are Externals out there, beyond the Joining. Maybe they know about us.

"Don't get defensive now," Brecca said. "The story is just getting good."

"Our enemies make that horrible shriek," she said, "when they fly past and threaten the Joining. But this was different, a sad screaming. Like they wished it wouldn't happen, but it was going to anyway."

"What happened?" he asked.

"There were more than one—many, I think. Different tiny

someones, all somehow together in the pointy flier with the missing wing. The gravity took them straight at the water instead of over it. The flyer thumped, like when we trade places in the Joining. That ended the sad noises."

"Ahnim?" Brecca asked.

"Yes?"

"Did you ever actually see the tiny someones, or just the pointy flyer?"

"I *knew* you wouldn't believe me! I am so—I fell for it again."

"Wait, now look, Ahnim—"

"No, Brecca—you look. Or better, try feeling something for once, or listening. No, I did not see them. I heard them. They were there."

Ahnim shut down her gravity. She drifted away from the Joining which continued to soar through space. Those responsible to secure her became aware of her distance. A dozen Defenders, each shaped in the typical mountainous pyramid, broke free on the far side of the Joining. They remained hidden from Ahnim, poised to swing around and capture her again.

Brecca struggled from his layer, one below the surface. He pressed himself out to the edge and disengaged from the Joining. He flew back to where Ahnim rolled brokenhearted in the nothing between the stars. Larger than Ahnim and more like a cube, he possessed mass and stability, but not an interstellar gravity organ as she did. He kept up with her, as long as she didn't pull to a star or a nearby planet.

"Ahnim, wait! Please stop yourself. Please don't make the Joining have to slow for you again. I really didn't mean to upset you. Please!"

I'll show you what really upset looks like.

Ahnim righted herself in an instant, charging at Brecca. She flew to him by pulling the mass of the others behind him. So fast, her image stretched to catch up to her. As she stopped, her tip came close to his retreating surface.

"Do you honestly believe I would've stayed if I hadn't discovered the tiny someones? I did because I know for a fact there's someone on that water world. There are many of them. Just because they're too small to detect with our regular senses, doesn't mean they can't see each other as well as you see me."

"Ahnim, I'm sorry..." Brecca said.

"Yes, you're going to be," she said.

"Why? What are you going to do?"

I know how to get back to the water planet. I can find it on my own. Maybe I'll just go and find some tiny someones, bring them back to the Joining. Then they'll see. Yes, then they will all see.

"You want proof? I'll go get it for you."

Ahnim circled behind the Joining as it continued away from Brecca. Immediately, she noticed the others waiting for her. As fast as her, their experience gave them the advantage. Twelve adults easily surrounded the unruly child. Ahnim spun and rolled between them, moving toward any opening through which to fly. They closed in.

Why won't they let me go? What's so terrible about one Immini making contact with someone out there? If I don't get away now, I'll be sent to an inner level of the Joining. I'll never even see the stars again.

Ahnim energized her blaze emitter. Her uppermost tip glowed bright with nuclear fire. The Defender above dodged out of the way in case she triggered her weapon. That left the gap she needed. Ahnim darted through. She reached to pull on a nearby star and looped around it.

Gaining speed, she whipped herself back past the Joining as the Defenders rushed in from behind.

Ahnim's soul wrenched with polarizing emotions. To abandon the others, the Joining—her family—brought waves of guilt and fear. But she would discover the truth. Others existed outside the Joining. Not everyone experienced life as the Immini, contained and guarded.

I will find someone, someone different from us. Maybe I could even meet them.

Without another word, Ahnim reached her gravity to its limit. She set course in the direction of where they'd passed the system of the little blue water world. Ahnim found a supergiant star along the path. Its strong gravity merged well with her own.

She pulled to it, and streaked away faster than light.

"Do we just let her go?" Brecca asked. "She's so young." An Elder came alongside him. Together, they contemplated the darkness.

"Ahnim *is* very young," the Elder said. "Just as we were when we tested the law."

Chapter Two

The seconds ticked up with less than one minute left. Tension, almost palpable, hung in the air of the crowded schoolroom. Seated at the table, Edwynn Dubroc slouched, a subconscious habit to mask his height. In a crowd of other high school boys, he stood two inches above the rest. He sported a lanky build, not quite athletic. Solid and lean muscles hid beneath the daily plaid button-down opened over the white t-shirt. Brown hair fell loose in random curls. Of the deepest brown, Wynn's skin and eye color came from his father's side, a mix of West African and Creole. Facial contours hinted at the mother's DNA. Regardless of the social groups at school, Wynn's black Pacific Islander didn't fit.

Oh, just shut up already, Wynn thought. *Fourteen seconds left to the end of the school year, and Mister Behrens insists on trying to teach us anything. Nobody cares. We just want out.*

Shut. Up.

At 14:29:53 Wynn scooped up his stack of compulettes. From his assigned place at the micro team table, he stood.

Mister Behrens, the classroom's Learning Facilitator, snapped his head sideways. He cast a stern glare at the student with the gall to get out of his seat seven seconds early. Before he replaced the well-practiced year end punchline to a reprimand, the clock struck two-thirty. Every one of his forty-six students leapt from their chairs. They scrambled around him to make their hasty exit of 2024's Sophomore EuroMath.

Officially summer break, the students dashed to their parent's cars or their own 'lectrascooters, leaving Mamanou High School behind them. The city's scooter trams boarded many of the students at the nearby train station's wide loading ramp, still on their rechargeable motorbikes. Parked together in the diagonal docks for the ride out to Lafayette or Baton Rouge, the students would meet their parents at one of the many stations throughout the urban counties.

Wynn escaped as far as the flagpole on the school grounds. His bodyguard rounded him up, to escort him to the bulletproof GMC Suburban. Black and imposing, it owned the No Parking area at the curb.

Not a single day this semester where I get to ride myself home, Wynn thought. *Gotta be the freak. Thanks, Dad.*

"Where's Raymond?" Wynn asked the tall and well-muscled suit with smart-sunglasses.

"Called in sick," the bodyguard said. "I am your service today."

Wynn pulled up short of the vehicle, his reaction prompted by special training. Eric Dubroc would've reminded him to never, *ever* be the last to know what's going on. His dad's personal assistant should've sent him a graphicon over his NowSeeHear, his Nish. She'd always been diligent to warn him over his personal communication device about any changes, like the schedule or pickup location—especially an unplanned rotation of the guard.

Wynn observed the man wore the usual mirrored lenses connected to the squared, military version of the NowSeeHear. A narrow metal arm ran across the temple and looped back around the ear.

"Okay," Wynn said. He searched for clues in the bodyguard's attire. "Then do you care to tell me your name, or do I have to guess? And it won't be flattering."

"Large," the bodyguard said.

"Yeah, that certainly fits, Mister Large. How about a first name? Oh let me guess...Extra?"

"Please get into the car, Mister Dubroc," Large said. He reached over and opened the rear passenger door.

"Raymond always lets me ride up front with him," Wynn said.

"Raymond may choose to ignore client protection protocols," Large said. "I do not. Please make entry of the car."

This guy's way too pushy and impatient.

Though his eyes were hidden behind the mirrored shades, Large's gaze aimed directly forward, towards Wynn.

They don't do that. They talk sideways while they're watching everyone else. His attention should be focused on the surroundings, not me.

"Of course, Large," Wynn said, "but now's when you tell me the code word so I know you're the do-right." Wynn tested him. The client security protocols included the directive that if the client ever spoke the words 'code word', the bodyguard would immediately draw his weapon in response to a perceived imminent threat the client might be aware of.

"The code word..." Large said. "The code word algorithm was compromised last night. We can't use them at the moment. They're sending me a new one right now. You can wait in the car."

Wynn struggled to contain his fear. Toshira guards can't use contractions when they speak, to prevent verbal misunderstandings. Chemically controlled by an implant in their brain, the bodyguards usually spoke like robots.

This guy just used two contractions, one after another. If this is a trap, I've got one chance.

He hooked a thumb under the shoulder strap of his backpack to swing it off. He hoped to use it as a shield or at least knock the guy in the head before turning to run.

"So, Large, why do they insist on calling it a car?" Wynn asked. "I mean, it's really a monstrous wagon after all, right?" A vicious shove in the back caught Wynn by surprise. His forehead barely missed the top of the door frame. His arm stretched out with the backpack slammed into the car door window frame, wrenching his shoulder backwards with a crack.

Large and his accomplice grabbed the teen by the feet and scooped him into the back seat. Wynn yelled and kicked, outmatched by the two heavily muscled adults. Large climbed in on top of him while the other slammed the door shut and hurried to the driver's seat.

The attacker stayed on top until they had driven out of the school parking lot, and rolled down the street. His elbow pressed into Wynn's rib cage, making it impossible to suck in enough air to scream for help.

Wynn struggled to focus. Tunnel vision signaled an approaching blackout. Never knowing such fear in his life, he sweated through his clothes in half a minute. All the afternoons spent in the gym lifting weights and practicing martial arts proved ineffective. Barely one minute and Wynn conceded.

"All right, Dubroc," Large growled into his ear, "I'm gonna let you take a breath. Don't fight me and you won't get hurt. You just lay there real quiet."

Wynn tried to nod with his head jammed deep into the gray leather of the back seat.

"What happened to Raymond?" Wynn asked after Large sat up.

"You actually care about that loser?"

"He's my friend." Wynn said.

"Yeah? Your friend should've spent more time at the gun range. He missed me three times before I split his apricot."

The medulla oblongata, Wynn remembered. Raymond told him about that being the single best place to shoot someone to instantly turn them off, to stop all muscular motor control.

At least Ray died quickly.

Without warning, Large swung around in the seat and grabbed Wynn by the throat. He shoved him hard against the rear seat cushion and pulled a black hood down over his head. Next came a hard plastic zip-tie on each wrist. Another in the middle pulled his arms together in front.

"Sit up," Large said. Then he slapped his open hand hard into Wynn's chest. "And no big ideas. You just play along and maybe you'll get to see mommy and daddy again."

"Hey, Dwayne," the driver said, "you ain't supposed to be

talkin' to the kid. Sonny's instructions were to keep our mouths shut."

"Yeah, 'wipe, and you're not supposed to use names either," Large said. "Thanks for that. More slips and we *will* have to quiet things up."

Quiet things up, Wynn thought. *That would mean killing me. I've got to survive this. Whatever dad's doing for work, for the military or whoever, it certainly can't be worth us having to go through this, not worth one of us getting murdered.*

Eric Dubroc often received spam from insurance companies fishing for recruits. He'd even busted up laughing once, sitting at his computer—his bearded face lit bright blue by the glow in the space above the desk. "Hey, do I look like an insurance agent?" he'd asked, turning to grin at his son.

Yeah, Wynn had thought then, *you kind of do.*The body odor of Dwayne Large found Wynn's nose. *Insurance agents don't get their children kidnapped.*

The Suburban rolled out of town, much farther than Lafayette. On the interstate, the afternoon sun beamed hot through the windshield.

The next big city should be Houston.

Wynn considered asking to use a restroom, but figured with the rough treatment he'd received already, there would be no chance for an opportunity to escape.

Getting me out of Louisiana is the first step. Cross the state line as soon as possible. That's where authorities put up road blocks.

He remained alert to the vehicle's turns, and when they might be on an off ramp to head in another direction. Three hours on the freeway and the warmth of the sun moved around Wynn. It rotated from the front to the right side, and slowly to the right rear.

Why Galveston? They're going to put me on a boat. On the first day of summer there'll be thousands of boats heading out into the bay or the gulf. It'd be impossible for the Coast Guard to search everything on the water for a missing kid. Odd they haven't swapped vehicles yet. Why would it be okay to stay in the Suburban? Because that's the safest place to be—with Raymond in the hardened super-limo. Nobody knows yet.

"We're at the bridge," Large said.

Wynn turned in his seat, groggy from hours of no interaction, and the soft rhythm of the tires on the super-slab. "What?"

"The two seventy-five to Port Industrial, Dock ninety, lift G. All right. Got it."

Obviously not talking to me. He must be on his Nish, getting directions. An industrial port makes no sense. There're no boats there except the sea-going freighters.

After another hour, the Suburban slowed and took an exit leading them under the freeway and off to the left. Wynn smelled the ocean air mixed with diesel oil. Under the hood, he scowled at the stench from the many decades of rotting fish parts and seagull feces.

"That's it there," Large said, pointing to the right. His heavy fingertip tapped against the thick glass.

"Yeah, up ahead," the driver said, "a big white 'G'."

The tires clop-clopped, rolling fast across wide seams between cement dock plates. The tempo slowed as the wagon swung around in a tight turn to line up for a massive open shipping container, the perfect size to hide a three-quarter ton truck, an object of an FBI manhunt. The Suburban lurched to a stop.

"We're here," Large said into his Nish. He followed careful instructions from someone who required regular reports.

Two more men armed with military style assault rifles flanked the swing-out doors of the box, opened at right angles to the three meter square. One of them put his hand to his ear. He waved the Suburban closer. Deep shadow swallowed the nose of the big wagon. Its front tires bounced up over the hard steel threshold.

Wynn suppressed a shudder of fear as the wave of darkness passed over him. His eyes had grown accustomed to the faintest light that wormed through the black fabric.

Stopped inside, the engine shut off. The cool blast from the overhead air-conditioning vents faded to the fetid warmth of the nearby fishery. He expected the door on his left to open. Instead, Large climbed up and over the seat back and grabbed Wynn roughly by the shirt collar.

"Get on your feet, Dubroc. We're going out the back."

The three seconds Wynn spent to ponder the situation were one too long. Large yanked him up off the seat. Wynn's head slammed into the upholstered ceiling of the wagon.

"I said get up and move your butt back here!" Large said.

With several harsh pulls from Large and his own blind effort, Wynn managed to stand upright behind the Suburban. Abrasions on elbows and knees would make for bruises tomorrow.

Wynn sensed Large's hand on his shoulder, guiding him sideways a couple of steps as one of the paired doors shut hard. The clunk from the latch reverberated in the metal enclosure. He stumbled as Large pushed him back against the closed car door.

"Hey, Dwayne," the driver said. "Wait up, man. I gotta get my stuff." The man grunted and cursed, straining to pull himself out through the narrow gap between the front bucket seats.

Large drew his gun out of the hard plastic holster, startling Wynn. He recognized the sharp clack. Raymond sometimes allowed Wynn to look at his service pistol.

"I've told you about using my name, *Jack*," Large said. "It's the last time you will."

Jack's voice squealed like a little girl, rising in pitch with the realization of his impending doom. "Dwa—I mean—No! Wait!"

The boom and shock wave from the barrel of Large's fifty-caliber pistol rocked Wynn off his feet. He slid sideways, falling into the man's shoulder and back into the opening at the rear of the Suburban.

The thumb-sized projectile hit square on Jack's chin. It cracked the lower jawbone in half before tearing through the upper-most vertebrae under the skull. His body slid down into the passenger side footwell, chest first, with the dislocated head hanging upside down over the back of the shoulders. Eyes wide with shock, blood filled the nostrils and spilled over. It ran down across the forehead and into the hair.

Wynn's ears rang. A cloud of gunpowder filled the air. Even through the cloth of the hood, it choked in his throat and stung in his eyes. His stomach heaved and bile soured in his mouth. If this man would murder his own partner, it'd be all too easy for him to finish off a troublesome victim.

Large took a handful of Wynn's shirt and dragged him to his feet, slamming the right-hand door closed on the gruesome scene. The two men with assault rifles shut the container doors after

Large pulled the staggering boy out of the way.

"You," Large said to one. "Lock that up and verify it gets onto the ship. You! Follow behind us as we go down," he said to the other.

With Wynn's nervous jitters, he yelped as his captor reached up under his elbow to haul him off to the left. They came to a flight of stairs. Large directed him to keep his feet moving down until they reached the underside of the dock. Hidden beneath the pier, a small motor-yacht lay anchored out of sight from prying eyes or searching helicopters.

Large and the mercenary lifted Wynn up and over the side of the boat. They dropped him onto his back on the slick wooden deck. The hard landing knocked the wind out of Wynn's lungs. His face and ears turned red with pain, then blue with lack of air beneath the bent rib cage. His pulse hammered loud in his ears. Large spoke to someone—perhaps to him or into his Nish.

A fresh stab of pain shot across his hip as the toe of a boot struck hard.

"I said get up off your butt!"

Oddly, the kick in the side helped restart stalled respiratory muscles. Wynn sucked in a deep breath of the damp coastal breeze. Before the next kick landed, Wynn rolled onto his knees and managed to right himself. The rocking of the boat surprised him. It crossed his mind to run to the side and fall overboard. Maybe make enough of a splash and a scene to attract attention.

"Don't even think about it," Large said. The grip of the man curled tight around Wynn's upper arm to guide him down into the yacht's main galley. This time, the shove in the back landed him on the cushioned lid of a wooden bench. It doubled as storage for the boat's dinette.

"You just do nothing right there, Dubroc. We're going for a little cruise."

Wynn found some leverage with his elbow against the hard wood to push himself up. Without too much trouble he sat up without discomfort. Fluorescent lights of the cabin shone through tiny holes of the hood's fabric. His head leaned back, the window sill behind the bench carried the weight of his tired head. Sloshing water and rocking of the waves escorted him to the only escape open to him.

*****

Noon the next day, Wynn jolted awake. Someone's fist pounded onto the countertop to his left.

"Of *course* it was the Bureau listening on the call!" The male voice had worn rough by anger and hate. "They think they're so smart. But you can hear the digital chop in every word. I don't even need a scanner to measure the line."

"So," Large said, "if they're asking for proof the kid's still alive, we give it to them."

"Yeah, we do. Go tell the captain to launch the skiff, and make sure the tank's full."

Large spun on his foot. The rubbery sole of the military boot squealed wet against the polished wood of the inner deck. Heavy footsteps moved across to the right, then up the four thick planks of the steep ladder leading to the stern.

Focused outside, Wynn's ears failed to detect the nearness of the one giving orders. The stink of alcohol and rotting teeth assailed his nostrils. He flinched, and banged heads with evil.

"Well, well, little Dubroc. It seems your father didn't take Sonny's advice, eh? I warned him not to call the authorities. I told him it'd be best to just upload the files to me—but no. He had to be stubborn, or weak maybe? You tell me, eh? Is your old man weak? Does mommy boss him around?"

Wynn stiffened with rage. It earned him a blind slap on the side of his head.

Sonny Conde took a handful of hair through the black hood and twisted Wynn's neck around. The kidnapper's thick words plopped out in a steady march, invading Wynn's ear, his mind, his soul.

"Nobody gets to push back on ol' Sonny. Not without it costing something extra. And you—you, little Dubroc—you get to pay up. Daddy could've sent me the file and a little cash for my trouble. But no, he had to make trouble for me, and for you."

Conde wrapped his tattooed arm around Wynn's neck. It choked off his air to drain the fight from the fit and wiry teenager. Wynn's pulse pounded in his head. Large returned to the galley, his weight creaking the joints of the short ladder.

"Isn't that my job?" Large asked. He took a firm hold on the boy's belt at the back of his pants. It nearly lifted Wynn off his feet on the way to the kitchenette in the ship's galley.

"Oh, yeah," Conde said, grunting with the effort, "but then you know I so enjoy this part."

Wynn heard the malice in Conde's voice. A surge of adrenaline made up for the lack of oxygen in his blood. A mix of fear and fire shot to his muscles and will. He fought the two men as if his life depended on it. He kicked out into the space in front of him, to hit mostly air. A few landed on a shin or a knee, none effective. With a fast uppercut of his right elbow he found Large's chin. The man's teeth clapped together hard from the blow.

"Why you little—!"

"Leave me alone!" Wynn screamed. "Let me go!"

"Aw, the pup's got some fight in him after all," Conde said. "That's good with me. I like it better when they squirm around some."

"No!" Wynn's mind raced with thoughts and images of what Conde might mean.

The two men dragged him to the counter at the kitchen sink. Large slammed his boot into the back of Wynn's legs. It buckled his knees. He slid down the front of the cabinet, exhausted and weary. Conde pulled up on the zip ties that bound Wynn's wrists together, forced his hands up and into the stainless steel basin.

While Large leaned his mass into Wynn to pin him against the cabinet, Conde drew a serrated steak knife from where it hung on a magnetic strip along the wall.

Lost and bewildered, Wynn's mind reeled. Under the sweaty sack, his eyes swelled shut from the silent sobs. He didn't put it together. Conde would amputate one of his fingers.

Searing pain at the middle joint of his right index finger brought instant clarity and panic. His strength all but spent in the fight just to get into the kitchen, he had nothing left to pull free of the torture. He could only scream.

His voice reverberated on the thin glass of the galley's windows. It wrestled past the laughter of the greedy, despicable men. Out across the waves of the sea, some fifty miles off the coast into the Gulf of Mexico, Wynn's mournful wail carried his fear. Up into the sky, into space it reached, clawing with the desperation of a child's battered soul.

Chapter Three

Ahnim allowed herself to drift along in the dark spire of the planet's shadow. With the star on the exact opposite side of the tiny water world, she floated high above the night-side of the planet. Millions of impossibly small lights twinkled on its surface, intriguing her.

Closer to Earth than the moon, she detected thousands of active mechanical devices in orbit above the blue and white. The satellites were machines, though not capable of reasoning or life. Not like the ones the Joining encountered before, so far from this solar system. These didn't mind her quiet hover while she enjoyed the marvelous beauty of the scene.

That jagged stretch of lights must be where the water meets the land. Maybe the tiny someones shine with light on this dark side. And where the rock turns faster, the waters are close, pinching the land.

She brought herself closer to the water world. Just north of the equator, the edge of the night gave way to the glow of the sun, illuminating the Panama Canal. From one ocean to the other, the waterway brought miniature machines floating on the water, cheating the barrier of land. With an adjustment to her personal gravity, Ahnim held place just above many tubular flying mechanicals. A slight twist to her reflectivity, she glowed as blue as the morning sky above her, practically invisible.

This entire rock is alive. It must be more like us of the Joining than I imagined. Perhaps the sphere itself is a Joining. The life in the sea and the life on the land trade energies. They balance each other. Water melts upward and spirals over the land to cool it, then converges again as it draws the warmth of the sun and the land back to the sea. The rock melts into the sea here, and the waters push it back up over there. Yes, this is a Joining of water and rock.

A glint of sunlight flashed on the skin of a commercial airliner. The plane skimmed along in the air below her. Ahnim remembered of the one that dove down, the tragedy, a hundred tiny someones all wishing they might live instead.

A new cry mingled with Ahnim's lonely memory. Not a retrieval of archived synapse, but real.

Like a chameleon changes color, she divided her underside into dozens of audio receptors. Each a mile and a half across, they focused on sections of the water below. Ahnim distinguished between the roar and burble of the small boats from the songs of whales in the deep. Squawks of living flyers hovered just above the water.

She sensed many mechanicals, and even more voices, some like her own and others like the voices of those in the Joining. Men yelled out—fortune. Babies cried—hunger. Women wailing—betrayal.

And screams of terror.

Just like before, when I wished to save the tiny someones.

I want to save someone, even a tiny someone. It must be a good thing, to be saved.

Her ship-self spanned a fourth of the Gulf of Mexico. She couldn't come closer without causing damage to the fragile planet. Ahnim reasoned how much of her, or which part to send to the floater on the water. But she made ready to go, her thoughts creating a portal in her shell.

It will need to be a living part, and knowing most things. It should have useful senses for this world, adaptable, with morphing capabilities.

She chose a single cell of her inner self as a probe, programmed to locate the source of the sound from below. The tall black crystal resembled an upside down ponderosa pine. Released from its place within her dermal tissues, it pressed out toward her exterior, piercing the blue-green surface at the port. Birthed from her ship-self, it fell free into the early morning sky.

Drawn by Earth's gravity and goaded by Ahnim's will, the probe tore through the atmosphere. Moist, cool air howled and whistled across the chiseled edges and knife-like sensors. Like a meteor, it left a smokey trail from the searing heat. As soon as Ahnim singled out the small craft on the water below, she put on the brakes, pulling back against an invisible tether to her ship-self high overhead. The probe slowed to a stop, but too late.

It crashed through the roof of the yacht. The pointed bottom penetrated further, opening a hole six feet wide clear through the hull below. Debris flew outward in a deafening rumble. Sea water shot up from the massive puncture to boil in mid-air as it came too near her. A cyclone appeared under the boat, where her own gravity stirred the ocean's liquid.

Large lost his footing. The floor of the yacht collapsed into the rush of turbulent seawater where it fell into Ahnim's probe. In a reflex, he clawed the air to find anything to hold him. As his flesh came within a few inches of her, she absorbed it. From his wrist on, his hand dissolved into ever smaller fractions until even they became smoke.

Conde clung to a heavy wooden beam partly torn loose from the bulkhead.

"What in God's name?" he yelled. "It's a demon from hell!"

Ahnim's probe grew spikes, like swords of obsidian. They reached out to every corner of the boat as it hung free in the air, a dozen feet above the whirlpool.

One stretched itself to Conde, piercing him through the chest, but not injuring him. Neither did it absorb him, though it tasted, and took inventory of his sins. He stared down, unable to fathom the impossibility of the moment.

Three spikes shot through Large, and on out among the disintegrating boat's walls and hull. He lifted up into the space near the crystalline probe. More of Ahnim's probing lances inspected him, testing, sampling, interrogating. One touched the stump at his wrist where the flesh cauterized, the bones powdered. Another found his open mouth, caught in a scream. She listened.

No, she thought, *this is not the one. This one has many memories of hateful actions.*

The boat continued to crumble. Its engines and fuel tanks fell into the lazy wash of confused gravity. With a mournful groan, the stern of the yacht broke away, hung in the air for a few seconds, then splashed down into the cauldron below.

The probe contacted every piece, every fragment. It found the two men and their evil lusts. One spike discovered smeared drops of blood on the counter. In the sink it found the finger, the knife, the serrations with bits of skin and bone. And a hilt that fit into the hand's recent memory of the evil one cowered in the corner. But the fearful one still hid somewhere in this fragile mess.

She reached out with more probe spikes to investigate every corner of the churning mass.

A shiver ran back to where Ahnim's thoughts had been apportioned in the probe.

There is another. He's right there.

Wynn huddled inside the hollow storage of the galley's bench.

A cupboard door fell open, books tumbling out—a service manual, magazines, a dictionary. Behind them came a digital bible with thirty-seven translations and dialects.

She absorbed the data like a breath. She'd use the languages of this planet to communicate hope.

"Ek is hier," Ahnim said. "Ja sam ovdje. Sóc aqui. Ako ania dinhi."

"What? Hello?" Wynn called. "Is someone there?"

His heart raced with hope. He strained his ears to listen for a chance at salvation.

"Oui, je suis ici!" the voice called louder, and clearer, like it was just on the other side.

Wynn yelled over the tumult and snapping of the wrecked craft and the hiss of the whirlpool. "I can't understand you, but I hear you!"

"I am here," Ahnim said.

"Oh, okay! Here I am in this box. I'm here! Help!" Wynn shoved the lid—the seat of the bench—up and open. He flailed with his hand, hoping to find the strong grip of a friend. Like an arrow, another spike shot out from the probe and through Wynn's palm. As he climbed to his feet, more spikes ran him through. They lifted him, suspending him in mid-air. The remnants of the yacht fell away to sink under the falling whitecaps.

Ahnim had come down to him, reducing herself to the smallest possible fragment of her physical being. But it worked. She saved someone, and it *was* a good thing.

She studied him closely.

What manner of creature have I found, its body so frail? The mind is exhausted, but contains amazing images.

She held him, impaled by her embrace, turning in a slow dance over the now calm water.

This is an External, a mortal. I should let him go or risk absorbing him.

"Now that I've got you," Ahnim said, "I'm not quite sure what to do with you."

Chapter Four

The door to the upstairs guest bathroom creaked open an inch. Dry hinges cried along with everyone else in the Dubroc family residence.

"Nev," Brigitte called in a hoarse whisper, "are you still out there?"

"Yeah, Mom," Geneva Dubroc replied.

"Where's your father?" Brigitte asked.

Wynn's older sister scooted from her place on the floor. Her legs ached from three hours spent where her mother avoided the agents of the Bureau of Investigative Affairs. The agent's faces carried the wordless message, 'she'll never see her son alive again'.

Nev leaned her head against the ornate trim of the door frame. She avoided eye contact with her mother. She wanted the door to remain open, to maintain some closeness. Too much shared pain right now and Brigitte would just slam it closed again.

"He's down with them," Nev said. "He was on the phone for a long time, angry. It's not helping. The more he demands they find Wynn, the less the agents talk with him."

"Have they given up?" Brigitte asked.

Nev stretched herself out over the four feet of the polished wood floor. She pushed her face to a gap between the white spindles under the railing. Three agents appeared bored already. One pretended to look up information on her tablet. The woman's fingernails tinkled over the arched keyboard of the glass rectangle.

"No, Mom, they're hard at work," she lied. "In fact—"

"Shut up," Brigitte whispered.

"Mom! Hey, what did I—?"

"No, shhh! Listen," Brigitte snapped.

Nev swiveled to rest her forehead against the bathroom door at knee height.

"Mom—what?" Nev asked.

"Listen, did you hear that?"

"No, hear what?"

The door opened about a foot to light Brigitte's face. Dark circles and eyelids swollen red hung beneath auburn bangs matted with sweat.

"It rumbled like a sonic boom," Brigitte said.

"Like a what? A bomb?"

"When your father and I lived on base, at White Sands, the jets flew over supersonic. The pressure wave rattled the windows, a sonic boom. I heard one just now." Brigitte stared up to the ceiling of the darkened room, as to peer through the roof, to confirm what her ears had caught. "It's not a bomb, but it can be heard far away, you know?"

Her daughter's reply never came.

"Nev?"

Brigitte stood and opened the door. Her daughter leaned out

over the railing. Everyone on the first floor ran out through the foyer of the house.

Nev whirled around, her eyes wide.

"Mom! They said Wynn's outside!"

The two women raced down and around the curve of the staircase. Nev leapt off the third step from the bottom to the marble tile floor. Her bare feet made a tiny squeak upon landing. Midday sun poured in through the open front door. To Brigitte's weary vision, her daughter's blurred silhouette faded into a rectangular corona. Several voices shouted out in the yard, one of them Eric, her husband.

"Oh, my son, please wake up," Eric stammered. "Oh, Lord, if you're up there, please, please save my son."

"I am here," Ahnim said from high above the clouds.

Brigitte stumbled headlong across the lawn. A half dozen people huddled together around Wynn. He laid face down in the cool grass. Single minded, the grieving mother dove between the shoulders of two Bureau agents. They knelt beside the boy's body. She landed on Wynn's back, and buried her face in his hair. Choked with sobs, she sat up. She grabbed tightly onto his arm and pulled him over, face up. His skin pale, lips blue. Nothing led her to believe he still lived.

Motherly instincts transformed from fear to heartbreak, from heartbreak to rage. Not knowing who to hate, and lacking direction to vent her wrath, Brigitte shoved the agents away. She knelt over Wynn, fists clenched at her sides.

She screamed into the sky above her neighborhood, her tiny town, and the valley in which it sat.

"Why? Why would you do this? How could you end his life

when he just got started? He's my son! He came from my own blood, and from our love. So, you up there, God or Creator or whatever you are, you can't have him! You give him back to me now!"

Ahnim listened to this new scream. Along with the anguish, fears, and longing, she sensed something new—motherly love. From a great height, a spark delivered Earthward.

In a searing gasp, Wynn's body sucked in breath. Delirious, disembodied, Wynn's mind floated in another place.

"You need to go back to your Joining," she told him.

Ahnim sent him down to the body, the heart of the boy, and into a mother's arms.

"Ahnimgoyothalia," Wynn said.

*****

Brigitte Dubroc sat next to the bed in room nine of the Intensive Care Unit, at Saint Ignace Medical Center in Baton Rouge. Her hand clasped tightly to that of her only son, warm and alive. Exhausted from worry, she'd hardly eaten for days. Wynn's attending physician scolded her. If she didn't drink four pints of water a day, he'd have a nurse stick an i.v. in her arm.

Brigitte held up the squeeze-bottle of now room-temperature water. Eric and Nev just turned to exit the room after a visit. They headed down the hall and home for the night. Liquid in Brigitte's container bent the light. Through the bottle, the view of her husband stretched upwards into the ceiling. The slim girl with straightened hair twisted around the side. One warped leg flowed behind Nev onto the floor. A laughably long face elicited a grin.

Then the two moved out of range of Brigitte's silly game.

With one eye squinted shut she panned her arm to the left in a slow arc across the room. The clear plastic bottle dangled plumb from its top. A white bin for soiled linen, the bathroom door, a chair, the nurse's shift chart, the brown recliner brought for guests. All passed into the awkward lens wide and warped. Objects raced across the middle in a squiggled frenzy, to flare out again as they fell off the other side.

All except a single black line. It ran the full height of the bottle, steady, and moving along with her arm. Brigitte moved back in the opposite direction, but the black line kept going to the left.

A wave of goose bumps scurried up her arm, over the bare shoulder and under her shirt. The bottle bounced off her knee and onto the floor with a crinkled smack.

"What the hell?"

Brigitte sensed someone else, or some*thing* else in the room. Someone besides her comatose son and the assorted inanimate objects. She scanned the breadth of the small room, from the windowed exterior wall to the wall of windows along the hall— nothing.

"You're a silly-brained woman," she spoke aloud, "master's degree notwithstanding."

"I didn't know you had a master's degree," Wynn said, his voice a coarse whisper.

In a whirl of sudden energy and love, Brigitte spun up and out of the chair to land on top of Wynn. She scooped an arm under his head.

"I do," Wynn said, interrupted by a cough, "I do get the silly-brained part."

He endured his mother's sobs for a long while. Her tears wet his pillow and the shoulder of his hospital gown. A steady drum of comfort, Wynn patted her back and rubbed up and down. Every vertebrae of her spine pressed out against the skin.

"Mom, are you okay?" Wynn asked. "I can feel your—you seem—"

"Don't worry about me, Wynn. I'm fine. You just rest and get better."

"I don't want to rest anymore," Wynn said. "I'm sick of doing nothing. It's like I've been frozen in space for the past two days."

He pushed himself onto his elbows. With his weight rolled to one side, he swung a leg off the bed to get up. His mother held him down.

"No, Wynn. You need to stay put for now." Brigitte reached for the call button. "You haven't so much as blinked in over—it's been more than two days, Wynn. Hold still."

"I've got to go pee, Mom," he said. "Let me up."

"You can't. I mean, if you have to pee, just—you're catheterized."

"I'm what?" Wynn lifted the stiff sheet. The thin tube protruded out of him. "No way!"

"That's why it feels like you have to urinate."

"Mom, why did you let them do that?" Wynn stuttered. "They stuck a tube in me! Where does it go?"

"To your bladder," she said. "Don't noodle out. It happens to many people in the hospital."

"What am I supposed to do? How do I use it?" Wynn asked.

"You don't do anything. Just relax. It takes care of draining out the urine through your—"

"Okay! Never mind, please."

After a glance at the horror foisted upon his manhood, Wynn fell back against the pillow.

"All right, " Wynn asked, "how long have I been in the hospital? And where are we, anyway?"

"We're in Baton Rouge. You've been here eleven days," Brigitte said.

"Eleven days? Are you serious?"

She nodded, now even more weary. The worry for her son to come out of coma now merged with exhaustion and relief.

"Mom," Wynn asked, his tone serious. "Is there something horrible wrong with me? I mean, besides my finger?"

"No, Wynn, the doctors can't find any—"

"Hey! They reattached my finger!" Wynn yelled. "It doesn't even hurt."

"What? Wynn, what are you talking about? There wasn't anything wrong with your fingers. Or anything else for that matter. You're in absolute perfect health, except for sleeping away the past week and a half."

"But—it—the whole thing was cut off." Wynn held his hand close to his face. He peered intently at the joint. The knife had sawn through the skin, muscle, ligaments and bone.

In place of the severed digit, a brand new one, like one he'd been born with. The skin shone bright and fresh, like that of an infant.

"Did I dream all that?" Wynn asked.

"How I wish that were true," she said.

"So, those guys, the fake bodyguard, they did actually take

me...kidnap me...whatever?"

Brigitte nodded. Just behind her, the nurse entered the room in response to the signal from the call button. The nurse's eyebrows raised at Wynn, upright and talking.

"Oh my, look at you child!" she said. A wide white smile split her face across the middle. "I best be roustin' me up a physician." She spun on her heel and strode out of the room with a pleased kick in her step.

"She could've at least checked your vitals," Brigitte said.

"Mom, I told you. I feel fine."

"I should con-a-graphy to your father and Nev. They'll be pulling out of the parking garage just now. Maybe they can get turned around."

She slipped her Nish out of a small pocket inside her lightweight jacket. With a snap of her wrist the flexible circuit unwound from its tight roll. The thin, flat membrane pressed onto her forehead and curled around her ear. As it turned on, the shiny black of the device faded to a perfect match of her skin and hair. Body heat energized the micro-thermocell. A glance to the avatar of her husband directed the processor to link up to Eric's Nish. Within two seconds, a photonic representation of his face floated a foot in front of her. It appeared three-dimensional to Brigitte, though merely a sparkling disk to Wynn.

"What'd I forget?" Eric asked.

"Oh, nothing, just that Wynn is awake and trying to argue his way out of here."

"Are you kidding me?"

"No really, check it out!"

The tip of her index finger pressed against her forehead along the middle of the membrane. Eric's view flipped from her face to outward, aiming straight at Wynn, who went cross-eyed and wagged his tongue out one side of his mouth.

"Edwynn!" his father shouted. The strong audio waves dazzled the photons coloring the air between Wynn and his mother.

"In the flesh and ready to go," Wynn responded. "They messed up the fire-hose."

"Ah, catheter?"

"Wish I'd had a say in that."

"Okay, buddy," Eric said, "so I just broke three traffic laws, and perhaps something on the underside of the car, but I'm turned around and will be there before you can say—"

"Betty Bangle barely bounced her booty. But Barbra Billings belched barley beer between her buxom—"

"No, sir!" Brigitte snapped. "And you, Mister Dubroc. Why do you teach our son such things?"

"Bosom," Eric said, laughing. He switched off his link. The soft glow of his face fell sideways into the surface of Brigitte's Nish.

Wynn's wide grin worked magic on his mother's irritated frown. With a happy squeal, she fell over onto him again to start a tearful wet spot on the other shoulder.

*****

The next morning, Wynn awoke early, well before sun-up. He reached down to check, relieved the catheter had indeed been removed by the night nurse. Pushing back the covers, he slid out of bed to use the toilet in the small room adjoining his. He smirked at the floor tile cold against his bare feet. Even alone in the dark, teenage modesty reached back to close the hospital gown behind his underwear.

He flicked the light switch up. A translucent ring on the ceiling brought the lumens up slowly. With an auto-dimmer, it set a comfortable level for eyes accustomed to the night. His urine stream broke the surface of the water in the bowl with loud gurgles. A moment later, the light in the room dimmed, though not from a change in the fixture overhead.

Turning toward the open door of the restroom, all light stopped at the doorway. Out in his room, no light at all. Not the red glow of the call button on the bed, nor any of the lights of the parking lot which framed the window throughout the evening. A thick black curtain spanned the opening.

"What are you doing?" asked a voice in his head.

No familiar voice—not the night nurse, or anyone else out in the room. Yet it found a home in his mind.

Going pee, he thought. *And I hope whatever it is I'm seeing, or not seeing, goes away after I wash my hands.*

He shook off and tucked himself back into the flap of the underwear, turned and rinsed off his hands in the sink. Wynn dried them with the rough paper towel from the wall dispenser. He started to look, but restrained himself.

Just my imagination.

Walking out with his eyes closed, he took two steps before passing through the strange lightless presence separating the rooms at the doorway. His skin tingled, like from the heat of a campfire on a cold forest night. A moment later he sensed the cool air of his room. Wynn found himself at the side of his bed. He turned, eyes open this time. Blackness filled the bathroom doorway.

Did I switch off the light? Can't remember.

Back in bed he sat up. He rubbed the seam at the knuckle of his finger, where the new one had miraculously grown from a bloody stump.

"Going pee," he heard in his head.

"Is somebody there?" Wynn asked aloud.

"I am here."

Did that come from outside my head, or from the inside?

"Are you the one—the person—who carried me home from the boat?"

"Person. Boat. Home," Ahnim said.

"Yes, are you the same—?" he asked.

"I am not a person. What is going pee?"

"How are you not a person? You're speaking to me," Wynn said.

"I am not speaking to you."

"Yes, you are," Wynn said, "and your voice is a girl's."

"Girl. What is going pee?" Ahnim asked. "Do that again."

"No! Will you please stop with the pee thing already? Are you a girl or not?" Wynn asked.

"Define girl," she said.

"A girl is a person—a young person who—"

"I am not a person," Ahnim said.

"Okay," Wynn said, "not a person, but a girl. Unless I'm imagining this or dreaming. But I can see you, sort of. I don't know, you're like…smoke."

"You are a person," Ahnim said.

"We agree on that."

"Do you believe because you hear the words of your world in my thoughts to you, I must be a person also?" Ahnim asked.

"Generally how it works, yeah."

"What if there were someone, not a person, but they could...speak...to you, would you believe they were a person?"

"I guess so," Wynn said. "Is that—are you someone who's not a person—but something else?"

"Yes," she said. "I am something else."

Up until that moment, Wynn enjoyed the odd conversation. He could be dreaming, or experiencing some hallucination. Staring at the impossible blackness before him, and the clarity of her voice, it could not be more real.

In the room is a being eight feet tall, five feet wide, and so dense it blocks all light, or maybe absorbs it. And it communicates.

"Are you an angel?" he asked.

"What does the word angel describe?" she asked. "Perhaps I am, and the meaning of that word is what I am to you."

"An angel is a person—forget that. Angels live in heaven. They sometimes come to Earth. But they know what they're doing. That leaves you out."

The blackness moved out of the bathroom door frame, towards the foot of the bed. Light from behind poured around, bent where it tried to escape the presence. The mirage shimmered, like heat waves over the hot hood of a car.

"Are you—oh, this is crazy. Are you an alien?" he asked.

"Define alien."

"An alien is something...or someone, I guess, from another planet, you know, not from Earth."

"Earth is the name of your water world?" Ahnim asked.

"Yes."

Wow, Wynn thought, *that's just the kind of question an alien would ask. Sure as stink, she's gonna tell me she's an—*

"I am not an alien," she said.

"Not an alien."

"No, I am not. I do not come from another world."

"If you're not an angel, and you're not from another planet —"

"I was born inside a collapsed supernova. Each of us in the Joining were. We live between the stars and the worlds, where it's open and free. We move about as we wish. I am not from a planet."

The pillow hit Wynn in the back of the head, an odd sensation. Then the realization caught up to the rest of his senses —he'd fallen onto the bed.

"No, I do not come from a world like yours," Ahnim said. "But the more I understand the words, images and thoughts in your mind, it seems I might be a person after all."

Chapter Five

"You're going to be late for school," Brigitte called up, "if you don't get out of bed!"

"All right, mom!" Wynn yelled at the closed door of his upstairs bedroom. "I'm up."

Still on his back, he rubbed his eyes, stared at the ceiling above. It struck him as strange, foreign.

The new house, Wynn thought.

Not new as in never lived in before, this dwelling showed its age.

It smells like someone's lived here for a hundred years. Maybe even died here.

"I wish we were home," he said. Wynn remembered their previous house, and the summer day they were forced to leave after the kidnapping.

"Isn't this your home now?" asked the blackness. It sat in the chair by the window.

Wynn pivoted on his butt. His legs swung around to drop his feet over the side and down to the floor. Groggy, he turned his head to the right. Through squinted eyes he focused on the odd shape. It sucked up any sunlight streaming in through the dusty pane and faded curtains.

"What's this, Ahnim?" he asked. "You trying to do the arms and legs thing again?"

"Why did you lie to your mother?" Ahnim asked.

"It's kind of early to start with that. And I didn't lie. I *was* getting up."

"We're going to be late for school, Edwynn," Ahnim said.

"*We*—aren't going to be anything, Ahnim-*goyothalia*," he replied. A sneer punctuated the sarcasm. "*I* am going to school. You are not. You are—I know! Why don't you help mom with the laundry? It would take you, what, about a tenth of a second? Then you two could go spend some girl time at the mall."

"Your mother is unsure of my existence."

"Sometimes I wonder that myself," Wynn said.

"Are you angry with me?" Ahnim asked.

He stood and crossed to the door. His feet tangled in the mess of clothes, a backpack, and a bicycle rim with a flat tire. Off balance, noisy thumps announced his egress from the bedroom.

"Are you getting in the shower?" Brigitte called up the stairwell.

"Yes," Wynn shouted down. Then whispered, "and 'no' to you, Ahnim."

*****

His hair full of lather, Wynn pulled the plastic shower curtain aside to peer into the small space. The faded glow of green metallic paint glistened and sparkled on the walls. The dated style of the upstairs bathroom meant to emulate the interior of a classic automobile from the mid twentieth century. A steering wheel became the wash basin. Tuck and roll upholstery covered the vanity. Two rolls of spare wipes surrounded the chromed four-speed shifter rising from the loop-pile carpet.

"Thank you for not following me into the bathroom this time," he said.

"I understand privacy now," Ahnim said in his mind. "It bothers you to know I can see you when you have removed all your garments."

"It's just—yeah, kind of does, I guess."

Foam from the soap made a flop in the tub as he rinsed off his hair.

Ahnim would admit she could see him anyway, through the door, the walls, and the curtain. But he embarrassed easily. Her vision reached beyond the location of her coalesced thought. Her presence absorbed all light. She tasted the lively photons bouncing off his flesh. Many strayed under the gap at the bottom of the door. Like a child's puzzle, she began to realign them into the image from the steamy shower.

"I'll just not look this time," she told herself. She held up her rendition of a human arm in front of a head, all perfectly black. The crude shape presented an elbow joint and a wrist. With focus, Ahnim stretched forth fingers. Five of them projected out from the edge of a flat hand. Knuckles, wrinkles and claws. Frustrated with the difficulty, she allowed her mass of anti-photons to slump down in the chair. She'd seen Wynn do it when bored, or tired, or exasperated with her.

"Oh, c'mon, Ahnim!" Wynn hissed. The bedroom door slammed shut with a hurry behind him. "What now? Please don't tell me you've been watching another werewolf movie. Have you? Aw, that's just—fix that!"

Ahnim's hand morphed back into an ovoid blob, then into another attempt at a basic hand, still with five fingers.

"Look," Wynn said. He bent down in front of the chair. "This right here—opposable thumb." He held up his own hand, articulating the joint. "You gotta do this. See? See how it folds over to the inside?"

"Wynn?" Brigitte yelled up the stairs. "Who are you—are you on the Nish? Come down for breakfast."

*****

Brigitte guessed who he spoke to—the imaginary girl— the one who followed him home from the hospital. She hated this family joke, their curse, the leftover fears and mental scars from the kidnapping and Wynn's coma. His therapist explained the common coping mechanism would run its course.

Brigitte leaned against the kitchen counter, remembering yesterday. Wynn complained then of a lost shoe. His sister suggested he check with his invisible friend. A short time later and late for school, Brigitte heard him ask, alone in his room. He said 'thanks'. Then bounded down the staircase with a huge grin. He hefted one end of the living room couch to find the sneaker well underneath.

She researched the behavior that night in bed, the laptop on her knees. She flinched at the potential diagnosis: schizophrenia. Her stomach twisted.

A loud metallic pop from the toaster yanked her

consciousness back from its dark, worrisome place. The smell of breakfast triggered her stomach to growl. She bore a mild envy there was only enough for the two kids.

"Come down, Wynn! I've got some waffles ready for you, and blueberry syrup."

Nev sat in the corner of the small eat-in kitchen, her second waffle half eaten. A glass of watery orange juice stood at the ready. It washed down the soggy bites dripping purple onto the edge of the dinnerware.

"I thought his name was Gordon," Nev said. Her blank stare out into the yard matched the monotone delivery. Strands of hair draped onto the breakfast.

"Yeah," Brigitte said, "I'd so like to strangle the idiot who came up with that one. You fared better with 'Saralee', don't you think?"

"Sure, mom—I mean, Mrs. Matalon. Lucky me. Renamed after fifty-year-old pound cake. This whole mess is dad's fault. And he's not even here to deal with it. We're stuck in this stupid town and a skid-mark school with zero friends. He gets to spend a month in protective custody at the old President David retreat. How's that fair?"

"It's not President David," Wynn said, just arriving. He took the plate from Brigitte's hand and sat across from his sister. "It was Camp David, before the United States became GC- Four. They've changed it back to the original name - Catoctin Mountain Park. Get your story straight, girlie."

"I don't give a dog lick up your—"

"Hey! Watch that!" Brigitte snapped.

Nev rolled her eyes at the feeble attempt to stifle teenage

vulgarity.

"—crack," Nev finished. "I just want *my* name back. The government can keep their Witness Reboot whatever. Tell me those guys who took you couldn't find us if they wanted to."

"Those guys are all dead," Wynn said around a mouthful.

"You know what I'm saying. Not the *same* guys," Nev said. "Those thugs were hired by someone. I mean the ones who used them to get at us because of what dad was doing. They're still out there, right? Has anyone at the Bureau even told us who they indicted for that?"

"They're not going to tell us anything, Nev," Brigitte said.

Movement in the stairwell caught Wynn's attention as he started to speak. The two women noticed his momentary distraction, now frequent.

"She's got a point, mom," he said. "I don't care what it says on my new birth certificate, or the registration application for school. I'm not changing my name."

In a reflex, Brigitte turned her gaze toward the stairwell, half expecting to see someone. Wynn's undeniable stare spooked her. Embarrassed for not maintaining control, she closed her eyes to whoever inhabited Wynn's delusion. She refused to look for someone who did not exist, to let the urge to believe her son overpower her need for him to just be healthy.

"Don't forget," she said, "today's your appointment with Doctor Fonteno. You'll need to ride from school to the rail station and take the tram into town."

"We don't have trams for the 'lectrascooters anymore," Wynn said. "Remember? That was in Lafayette. This is Lochiel."

"Ugh," Nev growled. "We're lucky to have electricity in

this hole. We actually have to connect our scoots to the house, *ourselves*, with an induction beam. How humped is that? What's next, internal combustion?"

"All right! I'm sorry," Brigitte said. "Lochiel. I do know where we live. And, yes, you'll have to ride to her office without a tram. I forwarded the turn-by-turn to your Nish. You should be fine."

*****

Wynn imagined himself a salmon swimming in a river of humanity. Up the steps and through an entrance to the school building, he marveled at the crowd of students. He perceived them as moving at random.

"That's what you get when you register for school three weeks late," he said to himself, a little too loud.

"Excuse me?" A new voice said from behind.

Wynn pushed his way through the students going the opposite direction as him. He struggled to make it to his locker at the worst end of the busy main hallway.

"Just keep moving, Boy Wonder," a soft but sarcastic voice said. "We're almost there."

"Almost where?" Wynn asked over his shoulder.

"And poof goes the brain! To our lockers, duh!"

Wynn detected the warmth and firmness of a hand pressed into the small of his back, prodding him forward. He wished to turn his head around enough, but couldn't while they wormed their way through the other students. At last, they reached the last row of steel cabinets nearest the entrance to the crowded intersection. He glimpsed an opening between two obvious freshmen, and muscled his way past the wary young men. His shirt stretched across his chest as the girl tugged along behind him. She scurried to keep up as they fast-stepped the remaining few yards to their destination.

"Watch out. Comin' around!" she said.

Platinum blonde hair flew behind. She dashed under his shoulder and around to the front. Once in plain view, he found her angelic, hypnotic. What he perceived as natural beauty left him wide-eyed. In truth, the girl spent an inordinate amount of time to apply makeup with meticulous and painstaking effort. She refused to leave her vanity table until she'd dealt with the least imperfection.

Wynn stared long enough for Michelle Jean-Terese to lift one eyebrow in curiosity. She used an app in her NowSeeHear to unlock the small green door of her locker. In one swift motion, the girl dropped her Nish into a shirt pocket and caught falling items as the overstuffed container popped open.

"Are you going to open your locker, Boy Wonder?" she asked. Then placed a pink plastic stylus between her teeth.

He broke free of the dreamlike prison she'd bound him in. "Yeah," he said.

"You'll need your Nish, y'know," Michelle said. "That's how it works."

"Yeah." Wynn fumbled for his own device. It hid deep in the pants pocket on the side where he carried an armload of class-specific compulettes.

"Yeah," she intoned. "Aren't you the chatterbox?"

I'm a complete idiot, Wynn thought, *allowing a girl to get into my head like this.* He recalled an incident in eighth grade. The most popular girl set him up to fail in front of her jealous boyfriend. Then came insult upon injury after he sulked home. Brigitte complained about the blood stain on a "previously perfectly white dress shirt."

Nothing about the nose!

"Blood," he said to himself today.

Your blood is in the wrong head, as Dad would say. At least he understands. Though when he's home, he does whatever mom wants. Human females are dangerous.

The gorgeous blonde left him standing alone in front of the lockers.

Why would she bother to pay any attention to me, the new guy, the goofy outsider?

Reaching into the back slot of his compulette bag, he pulled out the one for the class he had managed to drop. Housekeeping – For the New Stay-at-Home Dad.

"You gotta be joking," he said. "Why did I let the registration bot talk me into *that*?"

He rammed it into the back of his locker, and slammed the door for a nice one-two. Momentary satisfaction drew out a pleased grimace. He jogged to the trailing end of the last dozen students rushing to beat the bell to their classes.

"Now left," said the digital voice of his NowSeeHear. "Now thirty feet forward. Now left. The door to your next class is on your right. There are six seconds to the bell."

Wynn ducked through the door to the alternate class for the fourth period of the day. The room glowed with the bioluminescent paint on the ceiling.

"Hello, everyone. Please take your assigned seats," the teacher said. "If you're new and cannot locate a desk pinging your Nish, find an empty."

Wynn's Nish crackled and sputtered, with no data received about where he should go in the classroom. The school's daily data corrections hadn't uploaded to the TerraNet yet.

"I am Mistez Rease Plantain, your Instructor for Advanced SocioSpeak, otherwise known as Interglobo- Glosology Two."

Wynn's teacher used the proper title for a gender-dynamic person. After he located an empty desk near the back, he leaned out and around the boy directly ahead. Attractive and statuesque, Mistez Plantain's dark skin set off the teal wrap. She caught him looking.

"Well, there," Plantain asked, "Make ashoppin' skin oh finna you myplace abutt?"

SocioSpeak, Wynn thought, *that's why I'm here*.

He struggled for the correct response.

"Hissa Boy Wunner los' way," said a now familiar voice. "But hissa shoppin' skin alladay, Mistez."

"Aha! Thassa likely scene, eh?" Plantain held forward a large, muscled arm, pointing to an empty desk. "That's a good spot for you, Mister Boy Wonder. Make it fit."

Chuckles around the classroom brought a wave of redness up Wynn's neck. He clenched his jaw around a growl. Knuckles gripped white around the edge of the desk.

He searched his memory for one of the focus axioms he'd been taught during martial arts training. Each instructor encouraged some catchy phrase to calm the mind in stressful situations.

C'mon, brain. Blow out the stupid. Find what's real. "Slow is smooth, and smooth is fast," he mumbled. *That's not the right one.*

He took another stab at mental clarity, but detected the breathy inhale of a female voice readying a close whisper.

"What's smoo-smoo?" Michelle asked from close behind. The pulse of her words flooded between the tiny hairs on the back of his neck. Goosebumps crawled across the back of his arms to meet at the spine.

With utmost care, Wynn rotated around in the smallish desk. His elbow pushed his SocioSpeak compulette perilously close to a fall from the surface.

"Nothing," he whispered.

"It's not nothing," she said, frowning. "I bet smoo-smoo is secret code used by covert agents. You're a spy sent here to plot the downfall of the public school system."

"Gordon?" Plantain asked.

That word...that's a name. That's my new name. Crap.

Wynn's mind stuck in the weird place Michelle's sarcasm led him to.

"Gordon Matalon?" Plantain asked again.

"Boy Wonder," the girl whispered, "that's you. The correct response is 'Present'."

"Present!" Wynn blurted out, his gaze fixed on Michelle Jean-Terese. He found himself chained by her impossibly golden hair, immaculate complexion, and gloss-red lips.

"I'm here," he said, turning to face the front. Plantain exaggerated her doubtful expression.

"Mmm-hmm," she said. "Think a-not, I'm-ah."

*****

Wynn sighed with relief for the end of the day at the new school. He made it to his locker to drop off the overstuffed bag, and got to his 'lectrascooter without another loss of focus. Then began the thirty-five minute ride to his appointment five miles away. His mother showed him the office building once the week before. He remembered the odd tubular block construction. The windows framed cheap blue tinted hemispheres. The aged structure would be hard to miss.

Downtown Lochiel rose from the surrounding suburban area. At the intersection of Market and Rodham, Wynn lifted his gaze. Ahead of him crested the high rise office buildings. After a long minute, the traffic signal changed in his favor. But two more vehicles crowded across in front of him at the beginning of their stop indicator.

"Thanks for not killing me!"

With an angry twist of the right-hand grip, the 'lectrascooter hummed beneath his weight. The small motor overheated from the long ride. It protested the demands put upon it to take the half mile hill at full power. With another nineteen hundred feet to go, the thermal circuit breaker snapped open, saving the windings and capacitors from certain death.

Wynn planted his feet on either side of the rear wheel to keep from rolling backward down the steep incline.

"No. Way."

I'll have to push it uphill, all the way to the doctor's office.

"Please continue forward progress," his Nish urged.

"Velocity is insufficient to achieve appropriate arrival time."

"No, no, no, you stupid—ugh!"

*****

His shirt damp with sweat, Wynn goaded the small motorcycle into the lobby elevator. A middle-aged woman wearing the uniform of a Rite2U delivery service followed in behind him.

"Are you supposed to bring those things inside the building?" she asked.

"Didn't see a sign otherwise," he said.

"That one stinks. Smells like burnt waffles, anyway."

With a tired groan, the elevator announced its pending arrival at the floor Wynn needed.

"I had burnt waffles for breakfast this morning," he said. Wynn backed the scooter out of the elevator car. "They didn't smell anything like this."

He leaned the scooter against the wall to the side of the therapist's office door. A black concave niche cut into the wall ahead of him. Bioluminescent lettering floated in the holographic space of the half dome. A cursive font spelled out in bright green phosphor-gel: Dr. Serene Fonteno, Psychometric Evaluations and Childhood Mental Disorders.

Wynn readied a sarcastic comment, but it stuck in his throat. A heavy sigh sufficed before his hand wrapped around the door handle. It rotated twenty degrees and released its hold on the doorframe.

The scent of sweet oils and incense wrinkled his nose. He

hoped his reaction went unnoticed. With relief, he found the office waiting room empty.

"Hello?" Wynn called out. He pictured himself as some lost second-grader.

"Come in, Mister Matalon," Doctor Fonteno said.

The female voice carried a twinge of irritation in the delivery. He rotated around to find an open door to a somewhat larger room. The faux antique lighting gave a warm incandescent glow.

He moved through the doorway, paused to take in the neoclassic reinterpreted style of the furnishings. Dark and gloomy, it met with an odd appreciation deep within his male psyche.

"Let's not waste any more of your parent's money, Gordon," Doctor Fonteno said. "It's already nine minutes after three. Please sit down."

Seated in the brown and cream basketweave chair, Serene Fonteno appeared stiff, her face tense.

"I'm sorry for being late, ma'am," Wynn said. "I—my 'lectrascooter hot-popped coming up that long hill. It was slow going to push it."

"That's certainly inconvenient," Fonteno said.

Wynn hoped for a sympathetic ear, but didn't get it. He crossed the room to an uncomfortable chaise lounge. The far end of it swept up into an ornate shield. Imitation hardwood carved down and across where someone might want to rest their arm. Its knurled surface poised to frighten any elbow.

Wynn stole a glance at Doctor Fonteno. She stared off at no place in particular with her mouth pursed flat. Dark rims of eyeglasses hid the exact direction of her gaze. She might have been reviewing a mental list of what to ask him, or perhaps something less important, like groceries, or the need to charge her car.

"Do you know why you're here, Wynn?" she asked, still with the blank stare.

"Because I—because my mom is worried about me."

"If you tell me what you think I want to hear, this isn't going to do any good. What *were* you going to say?" Fonteno asked. He expected her to work toward some doctor-patient bond. She did just the opposite.

"Wynn," she said, "don't try to figure out what I'm doing. Just say the thing that you can't say to anyone else. Say the thing that makes you afraid they'll believe you're hallucinating."

"Okay, I'll try to put this so you can—"

"Again, this isn't about me, Wynn, right? This is about you and what's in your life."

"In that case," Wynn took a deep breath. "Ever since the kidnapping, there's this...person...who won't leave me alone. No matter where I am, she's there."

"You're seeing a person...a girl," Fonteno said.

"Girl...I wouldn't call her that, exactly. And I'm not just seeing her. She's actually there."

"All right, Wynn. Has your mother or anyone else in your family seen this person?"

"Not like, 'hello, how're you doing' kind of thing," he said. "But when she's there, they can sort of tell...sometimes."

"But she's visible to you?" she asked.

"Most of the time—if she wants to be seen that is—I can see her."

Fonteno let Wynn's emotions catch up to his words. He stared off into nothing. Wynn did his best to put the experience of being near Ahnim into plain English.

"She's not—you're not *seeing her*," he said. "You're seeing the place where nothing else is right then."

"Help me understand that," Fonteno said.

"She's...black."

"You mean like you, of African descent?" she asked.

Fonteno's question landed far off. Wynn took a moment to consider it, in light of the discussion. He cracked a smile, then stifled it.

Wynn got his first clear view of the middle-aged woman. Shoulder-length hair showed dirty blonde with unabashed gray roots. Her square facial structure and strong jaw presented an eastern Euro-United shape. But her smallish nose struck Wynn as too perfect, an obvious rework.

"No, ma'am," he said, "not that kind of black."

Fonteno gave no expression or reply. Like a statue, she waited for Wynn to get to the truth.

"She's like...if I wasn't seeing it with my own eyes, I wouldn't believe it. I mean, she shouldn't be there, shouldn't be real, but she is. I'm not stupid. I know why I'm here. My mom thinks I'm crazy. That the whole ordeal has messed me up somehow. And I've considered that. The problem is...it *is* real. I'd almost rather it wasn't."

"How do you know what's real?" she asked.

"Huh? I mean, excuse me?"

"How can you be sure what you're seeing is real? Sometimes, when we've been victimized by some tragic event, our subconscious minds try to protect our conscious selves from the pain. The instinctive part protects the injured reasoning part by creating a believable answer for the question."

"What question?" Wynn asked.

"Why the hell did this have to happen to me?" she replied. *She might actually understand.*

"Do you think that's what this is?" he asked. "My head just making this up so I'll feel better?"

"Do you think that's what this is?" Fonteno asked.

"I just—pardon me ma'am, but I just told you it *is* real."

"Let's go back to the beginning," Fonteno said.

"I don't think we've ever actually—"

"Tell me about the boat," she said.

Although he'd never told Fonteno the whole story, his mother already met with her and laid out the events. *That sucks. She only knows what mom wants to be true.*

"The boat," he said.

"Yes, Wynn. What do you remember from that?"

"So, not the beginning."

"Isn't that when you first saw this person?" Fonteno asked.

"I guess so."

What about the part where they abducted me, drove me blindfolded for hours, and murdered someone right in front of me?

Wynn needed to vent his rage. He wanted to scream at the men who beat him, drove him to another state, took him out to sea, and mutilated his finger. His mother wasn't equipped to deal with the anger, or his temper. She always scolded him with, 'get a handle on that teenage testosterone'.

This is so jacked. Even newborn babies are said to suffer from PTSD, but not me. Guess I just had a rough weekend, what with a violent kidnapping and all.

"Wynn? You're drifting off," Fonteno said. "Don't hide in the memories. Let them out."

For the first time, the doctor's face relayed empathy.

"Right."

"So, tell me," Fonteno said, "about when you first met this person, the black one, when you were on the boat."

"Ahnim would say she's not a person," Wynn said.

"Is that her name? What was it?" she asked.

"Her name...there's a mouthful."

"Did you say—?"

"Ahnimgoyothalia," Wynn said. Each syllable accompanied a nod of the head.

"Okay, can you spell that for me?" Fonteno asked. She struggled to find her notepad.

"I don't think so. I asked her once, but she said letters are irrelevant."

"She said? So, she speaks to you? Sorry—wait, let's go back. Did you say that she's not a person?"

"She would say she's not a person like us...like how humans are defined."

"Let me get caught up," Fonteno said. "Ahnim—I think that's what you called her—is completely black, not a person, because she's not a human like we are. Is that right?"

Wynn nodded. *Sounds like crazy to me.*

"And," she continued, "she doesn't use letters? Doesn't spell?"

"Okay, yeah, that's about it so far," he said.

"Perhaps she's illiterate?" Fonteno asked.

This time, Wynn sputtered out a laugh.

"Illiterate? Ahnim? When she speaks, I just understand everything she says."

"Wow," Fonteno said. "Would you consider that to be a form of telepathy?"

Wynn gathered the words he'd wanted to share for so long. He considered Fonteno as someone capable of understanding. It occurred to him he'd pretty much spouted enough to give her reason to have him sedated and hospitalized.

I need to not come off like some psycho.

"No," he said, "No, I wouldn't say that."

"What would you say, then?" Fonteno asked.

"I would say," Wynn stuttered, "that it can be hard to know. Since all that happened and I woke up in the hospital— things are a lot more complicated."

"What are you afraid of, Wynn?" Fonteno asked.

Good question—I'm afraid I'm just going insane. And I'm afraid I'm not insane, and there's an alien from another dimension living in my bedroom.

"I'm afraid we've used up all our time, because I was late."

Fonteno glanced at the clock. Facial tension multiplied her wrinkles enough to double her age in an instant.

"Yes, that is about right, Wynn. However, we've made considerable progress today. Will I see you again a week from today?"

"Sure thing," he said. He stood, blood returning to his numb legs and buttocks.

"Three o'clock next time, right?" she asked.

"Three o'clock."

*****

Out in the hallway, Wynn noticed his 'lectrascooter, now spotless. Even the tires appeared fresh. The bike's control system recognized the proximity message from Wynn's Nish. It came to life without any error messages. The battery's charge indicator read full, and the thermal overload had been reset.

"Wow, okay. That's—wait a sec—Ahnim?"

He looked sideways down the hallway. Deep blackness filled the end of the hall where the fire exit door should be.

"Did you follow me here?" Wynn asked.

"Follow you," she said. "No, that would imply that I was at your school prior to being here. I was not."

"So, you just happened to be in the neighborhood," he said.

"You possess and intelligent and functional mind, Wynn. Why do I have to explain this to you repeatedly?"

Her darkness emerged from the wall near the emergency stairwell door. This afternoon's shape included arms and legs in correct proportions, with well styled hands, fingers, feet and toes. Still of the deepest black, she strode towards him amidst an aura. A cloud, like coal dust, hovered around her form. It stole the light from the space. The optical illusion shrouded her true dimensions.

Ahnim emulated a youthful, female physique.

"I'll agree with the 'intelligent' part," he said, "but the brain bender in there isn't so convinced about the 'functional'. You've been busy."

"Your transportation mechanism required a molecular realignment," she said. "The capacitive energy store was depleted."

"You fixed the burned out breaker and charged the battery."

"And you have neglected the surfaces which—"

"You cleaned it, too," Wynn said. "Thanks mom." Ahnim tilted her head as she'd seen inquisitive people do.

A black mop of thick curly hair swung out and around from her shoulder, to rest on what would be an elbow.

"What is the brain bender?" Ahnim asked.

Fonteno's footsteps moved from her patient area into the front office. Wynn worried his doctor might open the door and find him in conversation with thin air. Or worse, a naked teenage girl made from pure black powder.

He pushed the 'lectrascooter to the elevator and called the car up to their floor.

"The brain bender is the psychoanalyst my mother has me seeing," he said.

Ahnim absorbed the reflection from everything in Fonteno's office, including the notes made about Wynn.

"Her primary function," she said, "is to determine whether or not there is a malfunction of your cerebral cortex, or if you are engaged in self-destructive mental processes."

"Brain bender," he said.

The now mirrored finish of the scooter's tires squealed against the smooth tile floor of the elevator.

"Sarcasm," Ahnim replied. "She is tasked with finding the cause and a resolution to your errant behaviors. That is an honorable pursuit."

"She's supposed to dig out of me why a seventeen year old has an imaginary friend."

"You have an imaginary friend?"

"Are you kidding me?" Wynn asked.

The elevator shuddered its way down the short span to the ground level. Ahnim stood close to Wynn. The left handlebar of the scooter disappeared into her shoulder blade, and poked out somewhere on her other side.

"Hey, um," he said, "a good next step in the whole physical manifestation thing would be some...clothing?"

"This method of vertical motion is inefficient," Ahnim said. "Does your family believe because of our interactions, and my use of photo-reflective thought to manifest myself here, that I am the imaginary friend?"

"You're catching on," Wynn said.

After a brief pause, the double sliding doors pulled back into the wall. Bright sunlight intruded in from the windowed lobby. Her thigh and knee were bathed in the bluish rays that beamed in from the odd bubbles of glass. The particles of her surface scurried and danced as they gobbled up the light. With a hand she reached out to play her fingers in the streaming shaft that cut between her and Wynn. She studied the light where she caressed it.

He rolled the scooter forward a few feet out the doorway, then moved himself around so his face aimed directly at hers. "Two things—practice turning this part," he said, his index finger making a circle around her nose, "toward whatever you are looking at, and...?"

"Clothes," Ahnim said.

"Clothes, Ahnim. This is very distracting."

"The temperature of your ears has increased. What causes that?" Ahnim asked.

Perhaps, Wynn thought, *my problem is hormones after all.*

*****

The metallic red 2022 Barron Electrascooter hummed along faster than it ever did new. If it emanated burnt waffles, only the vehicles far behind noticed. But the minimal suspension struggled with the demands put upon it. Shocks hissed, and coil-mag springs bottomed out in an attempt to defeat the irregularities in the road.

"At one-hundred feet," Wynn's NowSeeHear blurted out, "turn south on Harmony Lane."

The digital voice carried a feminine tone. Not smooth or soothing in the least, more like a scolding from his mom.

"And why would I want to ride off into the farmland?" he asked. "*Go Home*, Nish."

The Nish increased volume and intensity of tone, typical for the device when the human argued against factual data.

"The intersection of Hackett and Country Club is closed due to a ruptured pipeline. Authorities are rerouting—"

"That's for cars, Nish," Wynn replied. "Reset naviguide to wheels equals two, plus sidewalks."

"Authorities are rerouting all traffic and pedestrians due to hazardous environmental conditions," the Nish voice stated. Wynn leaned the bike over hard and skidded onto the shoulder of the main road he followed.

"Harmony Lane, it is," he said.

The smells of plowed earth and pastures carpeted with prairie aster surprised Wynn. Like a game, he skirted potholes in the frontage road. He enjoyed the ride along the southern border of the farms. A large HuMeal chicken-flesh warehouse caught his attention.

He'd always before just merged into the city traffic, or hitched a ride aboard a scooter tram, ignoring the countryside. The worst of the fumes and pollution from the age of the gasoline engines dissipated. But every vehicle still required oil, and even electricity had an odor of its own. Out here Wynn discovered nature, and a comforting quietness not found in a lonely room.

His gazed locked sideways at an actual living horse standing near the fence, he missed the chance to swerve around another deep rut in the country lane. His back tire bounced hard to the right, which aimed him squarely into the second row of apple trees bordering the grassy field.

The solid tree trunk would win the battle against the boy on a bike. Wynn's fingers pinched hard between the grip and the brake lever as he made a last-second duck under the limbs. The front wheel spun to the left. Tossed down to the other side, his butt landed in a muddy clump of dichondra which grew in the deep shade.

Rolled onto his back in the wet tree well, he wrapped the fingers of his right hand around the painful pinky and ring finger of his other hand. The pressure under the nail beds started to rise, accompanied by the requisite throbs and heat.

He peeked at the tree through squinted eyes for a brief

moment. The towering adversary glared back from behind the coppery bark.

A strong hum filled his ears. He presumed it came from the 'lectrascooter's power controller. He reached up to click off the motor-stop switch. A press of the sealed thumbprint sensor only made the hum louder. It occurred to him the scooter's safety circuit shut down at the moment of impact.

So, if the bike was already off, what's making that noise? Bees.

The entire tree, now in full bloom, whirred with hundreds of honeybees, each one making the rounds through the five-petaled flowers. They'd been jostled out of their single-minded quest for nectar. Curiosity drew a handful down to where something bright chrome and red wrapped halfway around the tree trunk.

His instincts driven by fear, Wynn crawled head first on his back, elbows and heels digging for traction in the soft soil.

A somersault cleared him from the tree well. A quick sprint back to the road left behind all but the most aggressive fuzzy fliers.

The evening sun set as he paced, his transportation held hostage by a miniature air force. He spent an hour evading attacks, while he sought an opening to run in and locate his Nish. His bright red shirt gave off the scent of apple blossoms, not helping his cause.

"I can't believe I'm going to do this." Wynn covered his face with his hands. He winced at the possibilities. "Ahnim? Are you out there?"

A brief moment passed. The entire area around him became silent.

"I can be." Her voice in his ear, she connected with him from afar.

"I could really use—"

A thunderclap, a mild earthquake, and a girl lifted from the page of a glamour magazine stood at the edge of the dirt road.

"—your help," he said.

Ahnim's anti-photonic self slammed down from sixty-seven thousand miles above. She stepped up out of the impressions her feet had hammered into the road. Although she wore clothes, and recent fashions at that, the textures gave the appearance the surface had been applied, like thick paint, or paper mâché.

Knocked sideways by the shockwave, Wynn did his best to take it all in. Ahnim strode up to where he now knelt at the edge of the apple orchard, the perimeter of the bees' territory.

Dark-blonde hair, coiled and curly, fell down and around to cover her shoulders and frame the heart-shaped face. Tortoise-shell sunglasses would've been perfect for the beach. The jacket, in glossy red leather to match the ankle-high boots, pulled tight over a black and white striped sweater. Cuffs spilled down to the knuckles of freckled hands, green painted fingernails. A wide belt buckled around the midriff, fully apart from the painted-on, faded jeans.

"I take it you've been shopping at the mall?" Wynn asked, standing up.

"I still am," she said.

"And only with you, Ahnim, would that make sense. What are you doing there right now? And thanks for coming— uh— being here, too, by the way."

"I am attempting to convince the store manager I require this

'Outfit of the Day' from their display window," she said. "He exhibits impatience and a lack of willingness to understand my needs."

"Perhaps," Wynn said, "he'd like you to pay for it."

"Pay—yes, that is a word he is using frequently. That and 'shoplifting'?"

"You're pretty much done up now, with something like clothes. But there's something weird about it."

"Please explain. I don't want to be weird," she said.

"Oh, no, can't have that! Girl from outer space—no weirdness for you. Your skin and hair seem pretty right—wait. Please take off those silly glasses. You're like a summertime advertisement four months late. Thanks."

Wynn reached out to take the over-sized sunglasses from her hand. He expected hard plastic, not solid electricity. With a mild zap, the glasses vanished in a starry flash the moment her fingers let go of them.

"Wow! Are you okay?" Wynn asked.

"Yes, are you okay? I didn't mean for that to happen. To be truthful, I've never attempted to separate part of myself in that way."

"You mean, those weren't real glasses?" Wynn asked.

Ahnim stared at Wynn with beautiful, sea-green eyes. He held his breath, transfixed by his own reflection in the gleaming surface.

"Are you pleased with my revised facial structure?" she asked.

"Structure. Yeah, this is an improvement. Gorgeous—I mean, nice eyes."

"I practiced them in the mirror while zipping up the pants. Are you pleased with the color?"

"They're fine. Good choice."

"Wynn, what is 'Loss Prevention'?" she asked. "The store manager has left to communicate with that."

"*Now* would be a good time for you to leave the mall," Wynn said.

"If I convert the material to energy first, I can keep the outfit of the day?"

"Conversion of matter to energy is—"

"Atomic fission," Ahnim said.

"Yeah, no, better not. That's everyone's favorite part of the city. Let's not incinerate everything in the retail district. How about you just take one of those hi-res engrams or whatever it is you do. Use that as the template for what you're wearing—what you look like now. Does that make sense?"

Ahnim closed her eyelids, swayed a little to one side. Her stance became unsteady. Wynn reached out a hand to her arm to prevent her from falling sideways. The molecules of the slick leather squirmed under his hand. They scurried up and around, and through his fingerprints.

With her darling face right there, lit pink in the sunset, and her precious full lips so close, a rush of natural attraction pushed down through the heels of Wynn's feet. He found himself leaning into her. His brain put on the brakes, pressing down equally hard with his toes.

No way, he thought. *I did not just almost do that—did not just try to kiss her!*

"Is this better?" she asked. Her delicate eyelashes parted.

The clothing morphed to an exact copy of the store's outfit, atom by atom, right down to the creased leather and a single loose thread along the collar.

"You're perfect," he said, the words ahead of his ability to think clearly.

A tickle from six tiny feet roaming across the back of his neck amplified the creepiness of the moment. The soft underside of the honeybee under his collar sent a natural jolt, worse than the electric sunglasses.

Wynn spun around. His elbow missed Ahnim's nose by half an inch. In a wild fury, he hooked a thumb into the elastic of the collar and peeled his shirt up and off from behind. He tossed it into the air ahead of him. Ahnim stared in wonder as he flailed, dancing around. Wynn sidestepped across the road with yelps and wordless vocalizations, swatting at the back of his own head.

"The insect is still in your shirt," she said. "It is not on you."

"Are you sure? I can't get stung! I'm allergic!"

"I am sure," she said. "I can see the creature through the fabric. You nearly damaged it. You should be more careful around such small invertebrates. They're fragile."

"Fragile? The thing could've killed me!" Wynn yelled.

Ahnim laughed, the first time in human form. Imitation endorphins formed within her, hunting for receptors of happiness. Knowledge of physiology caught up with her ability to simulate a pretty girl. Ahnim evolved, with internal structure to her being.

"That was close, Wynn," she said with a wry grin. "Those little guys would decapitate you, if you get between them and a flower."

"No, seriously, Ahnim. Do you—you don't know what anaphylaxis is."

Forty milliseconds later, she did.

"It could have actually caused your death," she said. Her face turned fearsome. She stepped to the shirt where it lay in the dust and weeds. She picked it up and removed the bee from a wrinkled sleeve.

"It is trying to kill me now," she said. "I detect the stinger and venom with which it has pierced my surface. That is... astounding. On a planet of minuscule life-forms like whales, elephants and humans, there exists one even yet smaller. And it is deadly."

"Ahnim," Wynn called.

She turned her gaze toward him, though Wynn guessed she continued to peer intently at the bee from the side of her head.

At least she's learning to be polite about it.

"It's getting late. I should've been home almost two hours ago. I need to get to my 'lectrascooter. It's under the tree. My Nish is in there, somewhere. I landed on it. Squished it into the mud."

Ahnim flicked the dying bee from between her thumb and index finger. She stalked into the deep shade under the apple tree. A minute later, she emerged with the scooter, now completely free of any trace of dirt. His dusty shirt back on, he took the handlebars from her and swung a leg over the seat.

"Thanks a bunch," he said. She reached up and pulled the breast pocket of his t-shirt open. Dropped his Nish down into it.

"Don't forget this," she said.

"So," Wynn said, "do you want a ride back to... someplace? You can—you're welcome to come home—with me. You know, if you want to that is."

"Later, perhaps. I need to take care of something."

"I can't believe you just walked right into that swarm of bees," he said, peering past her into the darkness of the orchard. "That's just too dangerous for people."

Chapter Six

"Mister Zask," the sales woman called. "Are you out here?" Strong glare from a hasty arrangement of emergency lamps cast deep shadows throughout the store. The staff in the mall shop held flashlights, working one handed with difficulty. "Mister Zask," she called again. "There's a policeman here to see you."

"Who's here, Phyllis?" the manager yelled. As if the dark made his employees deaf, and shouting increased the likelihood of being heard twenty feet away.

"The police," Phyllis said. "He's here about that thing with the girl."

"That thing? Police? It's a little late now."

"Shall I send him back to the office?" she asked. "Well, I'm afraid," Zask said, "the only light in the office is the tiny green indicator showing the secondary lighting system is in working order."

She turned to aim a whisper at the plain-clothes officer. He stood in the darkness just to her right.

"I told him six months ago that thing never worked," Phyllis said. "Now it's *my* fault?"

"It's a frustrating situation," the visiting policeman said. "I don't think he meant—"

With a loud click, eleven thousand calories of bio-phosphorescence flooded across the ceiling. It slid down into the display walls halfway to the floor. Each of the four humans present pressed a hand to the face, shielding their eyes from the unrestrained glow.

Zask wasted no time. He went right back to morning prep of the store, ignoring the visitor.

"Sayed! Phyllis!" he yelled. "Let's get the inventory system back on line, and let the security guard know he's no longer needed at the entrance."

Detective Charles Lacour turned himself to face a whirring up and to his left. A fist-sized drone hovered a few feet away. Its four contra-rotating blades held it aloft while the projected laser grid measured the client. Having uploaded the officer's manly size to the women's clothing database, it flew off to find a lady smaller than an out-of-stock 26W.

"Excuse me," Lacour said, stepping closer to Zask. "Are you the one who called about the shoplifter who vandalized your store yesterday evening?"

Lacour found the man a bit short of stature. A goatee bristled with an obvious Medium Chestnut Brown to match the sweeping combover. The gray herringbone suit came right off the rack from the shop next door.

"Yes, give me a minute—Sayed! In my Nish there's a delivery at the back door. Go see to that." The slim man in pink sequins darted off to do his manager's bidding.

"Mister Zisk, is it?" Detective Lacour asked. "I have a busy schedule. Can we please—?"

"Zask. Yes, fine, let's. The corporation doesn't want to press charges but the mall's insurance agency insists upon it because of the widespread electrical damage. So, here you are."

"Can you give me a description of this person?" Lacour asked.

"Naked," Zask said.

"Naked, as in, she entered the establishment without any clothes on?" Lacour asked.

"She might've worn some sort of body stocking or something," Zask said. "Why pretend to be nude by wearing a 'nude suit'? Perhaps she had on a retro body mural. Those things were so terribly itchy. Thank the heavens we're past 2019!"

"So, she was either not clothed or maybe in a bodysuit or something to that effect, correct?" asked Lacour.

Zask nodded while the detective spoke, then picked up the conversation.

"She walks right into the display window and pulls the entire ensemble right off the glowplexi mannequin. Sayed asks if she wants a dressing room. She says, 'No, just the fabrics', the little tart. By then, she's got them mostly on and next is picking out sunglasses at the counter."

"What color was her hair, then?" Lacour asked.

"Blonde, natural, the lucky thing. People would kill for that head of hair she has."

"Long? Straight? Parted?" After twenty-three years of interrogations, Lacour tired of dragging the details from each victim.

"Long, halfway down the back," Zask said. "And curly, like

in spirals. She must've spent all morning on it."

"Did you notice her eye color? Skin tones?" Lacour asked.

Zask yelled across the top of the racks of clothes. "Phyllis! What would you say her eye color was? I didn't notice."

"Yes," Phyllis said. "It was jade green or maybe a blue—aquamarine maybe. She should've been a model instead of a brazen thief, if you ask me."

"All right, then," Lacour said. "Long blonde, curly, with green-blue eyes. How about ink or mods, or piercing, or the like. She must've had some sort of add-on."

"Nothing really," Zask said.

Phyllis edged her way up to the two men, to add her two cents and sate her curiosity.

"Quite odd, really," she said. "If she had anything at all—add-on's I mean—then it was everything. Her entire little body could've been one big painting."

"A painting of what?" Lacour asked.

"Of a young girl's body."

Zask nodded at Phyllis' description. He flicked his fingers her way to dismiss her back to the assigned tasks.

"Do you have a list of the items stolen?" Lacour asked.

"Of course," Zask said, "the system logged them as loss the moment the tags left the premises without going through the proper scanner exit."

"Which inventory system are you using?" Lacour asked.

"AccounTrement – the standard for clothiers. Nothing fancy, but a reliable way to get their minbies without having to irritate the clients by asking for them."

"I'm familiar with the system," the detective said. "And since she came into the store without her credit wire, or anything else, then AccounTrement didn't detect her as she walked out."

"She most certainly *did not* walk out," Zask said.

"Can you be more specific?" Lacour asked.

"That's why you're here! She stood right there." Zask gave a curt nod aimed a foot to Lacour's left. "I asked if she had her wire. She appeared puzzled. Then she says, 'atomic fission' of all things, flutters her eyelids, and looks as if she's about to faint."

"Go on," Lacour said. He made a note to check the employee handbook for the Tops N Botmz franchise. He'd need to know which hallucinogens the staff were permitted to use during breaks, and in what quantities. The Stress Free Workplace Act of 2021 had become a root cause for many reported instances involving zombies, alien abductions, and interminable rodents.

"That's when she jumped up through the ceiling," Zask said. "If we did manage to get the poor outfit back—"

"Excuse me, she jumped?" Lacour asked. "Where?"

"Where? Up, that's where," Zask said. He pointed an index finger up, though the intended sarcastic face remained level for the disbelieving policeman.

Lacour arched back to get a better view of the damage to the mosaic of foam tiles. They hung in a circular design at a height of twelve feet. A small area four feet wide ripped through from the underside to the space above. An environmental duct had been crushed sideways. Several electrical conduits once spanning the gap, now seemed to be missing a few feet in the middle. The ends appeared melted, though not blackened from any heat.

"Are you telling me the shoplifter," Lacour asked, "the

girl...went up there?"

"You still don't get it," Zask said. "Yes, she went up there, into the ceiling. But that's not how it looked before, you know? She did that."

"This massive gouge through the tile? The air conditioning equipment crushed?"

"That's what I'm trying to tell you," Zask said. "She fainted. But she didn't fall over to the floor, as anyone else does. She fainted up. And the little tramp took our perfectly good ceiling with her, along with an expensive pair of Waist-Not hiphuggers."

"Did mall security check up there?" Lacour asked. "Can't they access that through other means?"

"You need to go talk to them. They've already been through all that," Zask said.

"She could still be hiding."

"Oh, no, she's not!" Zask held his face in his hands. "She did the same thing to the roof about ten feet over. You can't see it from here. There's a hole just like this where she popped out on the top of the mall."

Lacour doubted the so-called evidence, and that a young woman fell up through a commercial roof made of steel and fibrous concrete.

"You're joking," Lacour said. "This is some sort of prank? Did Myles Harris put you up to this rubbish?"

"Go see for yourself, detective," Zask said. "Yes, it sounds like a ridiculous news-or-pay story that clogs your Nish. But I'm putting my sanity on the line. Phyllis too. That girl dressed herself from the window stock and then went straight up and out of the mall."

Charles Lacour prided his ability to spot a liar. Decades on the force gave him the experience to smell a rat, if there was a rat. These two people, three including the olive-skinned fellow in drag, believed they were telling the truth. To Lacour, it made sense now. This case involved facts beyond belief, so the Chief picked him to take the lead.

"Very well, then," Lacour said. "I'll forward my contact information to your Nish. If you remember anything that might help in the investigation, please do chime through, day or night."

"Will you have a case number?" Zask asked. "For the insurance company report."

"It'll be in with the data. Look for the purple 'C'."

Zask turned away, the conversation done as far as he was concerned. He focused on the image projected from his Nish. A hand's breadth out from his nose, a few trillion photons gathered themselves into a fourteen digit alpha-numeric spiral. Forwarded on to the corporate office, he'd get back to the details of running the store.

*****

Lacour waited nearly half an hour for a facilities technician. The man escorted him up into the plenum, the space above the ceiling of the various shops and kiosks. Lacour's undergarments grew damp with perspiration. He and the tech worked their way through the hot maze of pipes, cables, ductwork and support frames. They moved toward the section above Tops N Botmz.

"You said your name is Fagan?" Lacour asked.
"Kirk Fagan."

The tall man plodded along with no enthusiasm, bouncing the narrow catwalk. It rattled the metal mesh of the pathway twenty feet above the mall shoppers who bustled below. Each time the man's boot landed, Lacour feared he might be bounced right off the springy platform.

"How long have you worked here at the Lochiel Mall?" Lacour asked.

"Nine years in April," Kirk said. His whiskery beard bobbed and wiggled as he spoke. It matched the enormous pile of red hair on his head. Wild eyes belied a friendly smile.

"Were you part of the original crew?" Lacour asked. "I believe it opened in 2015?"

"I came on right after it opened," Kirk said. "Know this place as good as any. Ain't nothin' happened here I don't know about."

"I take it then you're familiar with the incident over at the Tops N Botmz store?"

"I know what everyone else knows," Kirk said.

"What's that?" Lacour asked.

"Lightning," Kirk said. He'd stopped and turned around to face Lacour when he said it.

"Lightning, you say? What brings you to that conclusion?" Lacour asked. He urged Kirk to keep moving along, not wanting to sweat through his only clean suit.

"I've seen many lightning strikes hit a large building like this," Kirk said. "I could show you a dozen just on the roof of this mall. It makes a hole in the roof, and tears up anything below. Circuits pop. Lamps blow out. Batteries fry. Minbie systems go up in smoke. You can't stop a force like that." Kirk stopped again to point ahead of them where light beamed into the space from above and below.

"That's the spot right up there," Kirk said.

The walkway didn't cross at the gash in the ceiling. It went by about a half-dozen feet to the right. The two men each swung a leg over the railing, to step lightly onto the suspension grid supporting the bio-lum lighting panels.

Lacour adjusted his Nish to project a bright beam forward to light the area ahead. The material had burst upwards from inside the plenum, out into the sky beyond. He expected blackening, or streaks of charred material, as when lightning arcs and spatters on its way in or out.

"That's a fancy trick you done with your Nish," Kirk said. "Never seen that one."

"Standard police issue," Lacour said. "The download costs less than the flashlights we used to hang from the belt." The detective leaned out a bit more, but a creak from the aluminum grid gave notice the weight limit had been exceeded. He pulled himself back to the catwalk. "You know, Kirk, I cannot smell anything burnt—strange. Lightning strikes always leave at least a faint odor from the charred substance."

Kirk stayed quiet as Lacour transferred his weight out to where the ceiling had been blown away from inside the store.

"May I borrow your knife," Lacour asked. "The big one."

"Big knifes are illegal. Can't have anything over three inches."

"Yes, I know that. But I need yours to slice off a piece of this acoustic tile." Kirk avoided the direct stare of the policeman. "Kirk, I don't care you have a knife that exceeds the legal limit. I can tell you have one strapped to your ankle. If you would, please?"

Kirk obliged, though he kept a wary eye on the cop.

Lacour stretched out with the chromed blade to where a larger section of the white ceiling tile warped. It had smeared out of the way when something flew past. Now curled and thickened on the corner, it left a solid piece, nearly the size of a man's shoe. It hung right where the detective could get to it without falling through to the floor of the shop. With some effort, Lacour managed to stand on his feet, without dropping either the knife or the remnant of the ceiling tile he cut away.

Lacour thanked Kirk for the use of the knife. He returned it without another word about its non-compliance to the restrictive local ordinance.

"This material," Lacour said, "was not damaged by the heat of lightning." The detective followed up with a reassuring smile. He pulled a black poly evidence bag from his suit pocket to drop the tile into. "But we can see that it was melted somehow. We'll let the good folks in the lab discover the cause."

The two walked back to the square entry port at the far end of the plenum space.

"Kirk, might I ask you one last question? It's the typical one, I'm afraid, which we always have to ask the witnesses. Where were you when the incident occurred?" Lacour asked.

"Oh, me and Frank were waiting in the parking lot," Kirk said.

"Frank?"

"Martin," Kirk said. "Frank Martin, my manager."

"What were you and Frank Martin waiting for?" Lacour asked.

"Well," he replied, embarrassed, "there was mention a pretty girl walked butt naked into the main entrance. We were hoping she was gonna come back out."

Chapter Seven

"You want another, Mike?" Trisha asked the last patron in the bar. Quite attractive once, the bartender's many years of morning regret weighed upon her like an extra dose of gravity. Her eyelids and cheeks sagged in contrast to the lifted and enhanced bosom.

Eric Dubroc wished for someone to use his real name. More than that, he needed to *be real* with someone. His family housed a thousand miles away, Eric stayed clear for their safety. Living alone in Ohio, he continued the depressing game of Witness Reboot life.

"Sure," he said, staring down into the empty glass. The last drop of vodka stared back. In the mirrored wall behind the bar, his dejected face sat atop a stack of upside-down tumblers. Brigitte always teased that she married him for his brains and his engaging smile—neither present today. The once graying sideburns earned by raising two teenagers, were now tinted with a lie. Hair grown shaggy failed to pass for youth. He turned away from the image, unimpressed.

"It'll have to be the last one," Trisha said. "Closing in fifteen minutes."

His conscience usually protected him from making a stupid

mistake with a woman not his wife. But during the hard days, like today, he found himself imagining the warmth of the stranger.

"You done with the vid-stream?" Trisha asked. "Nothing left on but the early global news."

She reached up to tap the small button hidden along the bottom edge of the wide screen. Bright images scrolled across and around. The massive band of frosted white plastic ran the entire circumference of the room. He paid little attention to it tonight, though he usually kept up on global events.

Something in the vanishing headline caught his eye.

"Wait a sec, Trish," Eric said. "Click that back on... please."

The announcer continued his 'exclusive' spin, just as they would spout on each of the other fifty-nine news channels. The voice dramatic, it rang with an exaggerated flair.

"It's been just seven months," the announcer said, "since the expiration of New-START, and the Russian Federation has changed their mind yet again. They've declared the Strategic Arms Reduction Treaty no longer has any bearing on how many WMDs they possess, where they place them, or how many vehicles are permitted to carry or launch the genocidal devices."

Trisha shrugged her shoulders, and resumed the tear-down and cleaning of the soda dispensers. Her world consisted of jealous ex-lovers, and a TerraNet bill three months past due. World dominance through nuclear intimidation sat pretty low on her radar.

The news anchor turned sideways, pretending to look at a floating screen.

"Our chief foreign correspondent in Moscow, Leonard Peterson, caught up with the Minister of Defense, Valentin

Matyenko, as he returned from an emergency meeting at the Kremlin."

Eric caught Trisha's eye for a moment. She smiled at his sudden interest in this roiling debate and inflammatory rhetoric. As his gaze reverted to the wide curve of the video arch, she took a moment to pop a button loose on her blouse. His full lips and dark skin enticed her. The Creole accent flavored a cozy baritone. It brought to mind slow jazz and dim lights.

"Minister Matyenko," Peterson said into his reporter's microphone. "I have a couple questions." Back in the bar, the plastic video screen shuddered from the winter wind whipping past a microphone on the far side of the planet. "Will Russia bring back the Cold War? Do you have plans to fortify nuclear emplacements that target North America?"

The Defense Minister wanted out of the bitter chill, angry at himself for having left his ushanka in the limousine. His ears burned from the zero degree air and the bothersome journalist.

"Privet, Mister Peterson," Matyenko said. "Shall I inform you of every classified military strategy, or only the ones specifically designated to your mother-in-law's residence in Maine?"

Eric let out an abrupt and derisive laugh. It startled Trisha. A wet glass slipped from her grasp into the small sink with a clank.

"Amusing as always, Valentin," Peterson said. "What are you willing to go on record with today, about the sudden change in Russia's friendship toward the West?"

"I will go on record with this," Matyenko said. "The Russian Federation is a sovereign nation. We will not be blackmailed by a handful of criminals who bought themselves political appointments in Western governments. And don't interrupt me with rubbish about democratic elections. There was an end date to the treaty for a reason. Things change, and they have. Compliance to these lopsided agreements has only served to pacify the Europeans. It provided a smokescreen for your military to devise even more lethal devices than the antique missiles we were forced to dismantle and bury. But don't lose heart, Leonard. That treaty was worthless when we signed it over ten years ago. What has been lost is merely your hope the NFL playoff coverage won't be pre-empted by anything less profitable."

The studio's anchor took the queue to end the coverage of Leonard Peterson's humiliation. He pasted on a proud face and squared his shoulders to the camera.

"That was Leonard Peterson reporting from Moscow. Now a word from our sponsors."

The last flicker of the anchorman highlighted his impossibly white smile.

Why would you smile after that? Eric thought.

The anchorman didn't exist, likely a 3D hologram. No matter how capable technology had become, it still made errors in tact.

Trisha walked up. An advertisement for the latest Toyota MegaCross threw digital dirt in a wild skid around the circular video screen. Several bottles rattled on the shelf as enhanced audio kept pace with the wave of rocks and gravel.

"Have you had any dinner, Mike?" She leaned in from her side of the bar.

"Just this can of cashews you save for my Fridays," he said. His eyes lifted up from the black bowl, intending to meet her gaze. He never made it higher than deep cleavage pressed up with her crossed forearms.

"I've got some leftover spaghetti and meatballs in the fridge, from Carluto's," Trisha said. "Way more than I can eat by myself."

Her voice, a soft and dangerous battering ram, cracked his wall of fidelity. His instincts told him to run.

"I didn't know you had a refrigerator."

"I wouldn't be much of a woman if I didn't have a kitchen at home to heat things up."

Heat. That doesn't fit with fridge. She's not talking about the refrigerator. She wants to...I can't...I should never.

"Come to think of it, Trisha," Eric said, "I could use a home cooked meal."

"It would be my pleasure, Mike."

"So, Trish. Did I ever tell you Michael is my middle name? I actually prefer to go by Eric."

Chapter Eight

Why am I creeping up my own staircase? Brigitte asked herself. *I don't want to wake Wynn. I'm just being quiet.*

She lifted her bare foot, slid it atop the next carpeted step.

Liar. You're on the way to get him up for school. It shouldn't matter. You're sneaking up quietly so, what? So you can catch the imaginary friend, that's what. You want to know if what he sees is real, not merely a symptom of post-traumatic stress disorder, or worse.

The door to Wynn's bedroom rose straight ahead at the top of the stairs. Sunlight beamed in past his curtains to flood across the floor. It glowed in the gap between the bottom of the door and the worn out carpet.

Just go take care of your son.

Her weight pressed down on the next step. The dry wood creaked. Behind his door, something or someone moved from the window. Brigitte recognized the slight shadow as from the feet of a person turning around. The darkness twisted and moved to the right beyond the door.

Every hair on Brigitte's body stood up. Her jaw clamped tight. She came up on the balls of her feet in an instinctual fight or flight mode.

"This is insanity," she said.

In a rush, she forced a smile and bolted up the remaining four steps and across the hallway. The cold metal of the doorknob caused her to flinch hard, as the tension in her body found an external trigger.

"Dang it!"

Not quite a cheerful 'Good morning!'

She couldn't will herself to turn away from the window.

Of course there's nothing there, idiot.

"Good morning," she said. The words stuck in her throat.

"Um...good morning?" Wynn mumbled from under the sheet. He reached down to grab a handful of blanket to pull it up over his shoulders. Brigitte stared at the spot on the floor by the window. Wynn raised his eyebrows, and spoke toward the headboard.

"Since when do—never mind."

"It's just after your ordeal yesterday," Brigitte stuttered, "with the crash, and the bees and all. I missed waking you up, like when you were little."

Wynn whipped the covers back and turned around.

His gaze held steady on the empty chair in the corner. She put on a warm smile, long enough for him to see.

There is no one in the chair, and I'm not going to look at it.

"Can I give you a ride to school this morning?" she asked.

"There's nothing wrong with my 'lectrascooter," Wynn said.

"Yeah, I went out to see. I'd just like to spend the morning with you."

"It landed in mud, mom. That's why there's no real damage."

We've had the bike more than a year, Brigitte thought, *with at least a couple of wrecks. The night's wind left the patio covered in dust. But not Wynn's bike. It's spotless. The paint sparkles like new. Maybe I'm the one going nuts.*

"Please let me drive you," she said. "We can stop for breakfast."

"You don't have any way to pay for breakfast," Wynn replied.

"Lucky Wishbone takes the state's Affordability wire. I've still got nearly a hundred on this month's minbies." She clucked her tongue and winked. "Apple pie, baby."

Wynn dragged himself out of bed. He hobbled across the room with the blanket wrapped around his waist. A full bladder gave him a bad case of morning wood.

"You're making it impossible to say no," he groaned.

An unforced smile crossed her face. Brigitte rotated to survey the incredible mess of Wynn's room. The empty chair in the corner by the window drew her in.

Not a mess. Not a single thing on it. Spotless, not so much as a speck of lint. Just like the 'lectrascooter.

Brigitte listened as Wynn locked himself in the bathroom, the shower running, and the infamous drip behind the wallboard next to the closet. Her pragmatic side considered it ludicrous to exercise parental intimidation over a ghost. Yet she stood, arms crossed in defiance. A fierce glare panned the emptiness for the enemy.

She armed herself with a whisper to sheer steel plate. "You just leave him alone," she said to the chair. Words spoken in defense of her child brought a measure of therapy.

Now, get a grip woman.

*****

A glance over at Wynn in the sedan's passenger seat revealed a war zone of crumbs, sugar, and apple filling strewn down the front of his shirt. Her hand moved the slightest fraction from the steering wheel. But he got to it first, brushing the mess down into his lap.

"Are you going to make me park a quarter mile down the street from the school, too?"

"Two blocks is good," he said.

"Awesome."

Don't try to fill the silence, she told herself. *Just enjoy the time together.*

"So," she asked, "were you able to get that class changed, from—what was it you called it? Happy Homemaking for Girly-Men? Seriously—"

"Yeah, no problem," Wynn said. "Got it changed."

"What to?" Brigitte asked.

"SocioSpeak."

"Oh, geez," Brigitte snorted and said, "my friend Dana Prower uses that on the Nish. Drives me nuts."

Her hopes at a chummy mother-son morning came to a halt as the car did, two blocks from his school's main entrance. She tensed as Wynn deactivated the car's restraint for his seat, and unlocked the door. He stepped out, pulling his backpack up out of the footwell.

What could I have said to make him just walk away?

Wynn bent over to slip the pack onto his shoulders. He made a motion for her to open the window while the car's gull-wing door motored down and latched into the sill.

"Thanks for breakfast. I enjoyed it," he said.

No kidding. Seemed more like torture.

"Me too." She wanted to ask if they could make it a regular thing, but she feared he might resist further motherings. "Hey, careful with the alt-life slang. Nobody says that anymore, remember? It's just Masc and Fem, now. Let's be respectful."

"Always—I'll let you know if I need a ride, okay?"

"Okay. Have a nice day, *Gordon*," she said. A wide grin smoothed the delivery of the reminder to stay in Witness Reboot character.

"You too, *Jacqueline*," he said, the first time he'd used her assigned alias. A silent salute wrapped up the conversation.

*****

Wynn climbed the steps to Lochiel's District Seven High School, and found himself up in his head again. The clamor of the other students pressing through the same four doors began to fade, strangely insulated by an odd surrealism.

She's here, he thought. *Ahnim is here, at my school, where I've told her it's off limits. Not that she'd actually listen. Anti-photon girl is stubborn. Perhaps they all were. What if there're more out there, more of her! One's enough. One psycho chick from another planet is definitely enough. Did she say planet? No, space, she said. Ahnim said human physicality didn't possess the senses to detect the realm in which her family exists. She converted her thoughts into energy, then matter.*

And there she stood, just inside, right in front of him. Other students moved around and past her as she blocked the center of the main hall.

She's gotten the hang of converting energy into girl.

He stood transfixed at her radiant beauty—the same person from the apple orchard. But far more than an image of thought.

"You're here," he said past a parched throat. "And they—everyone—can see you. That's new."

She cracked a smile, glancing a bit to her left and right at the dozens of teens.

"Four hundred three to seven hundred thirty-two does the trick," Ahnim said. "Is this better?"

"Four hundred to what?" Wynn asked.

"If I limit my spectrum to between four hundred and seven hundred nanometers, I can attain optimal resolution as a point five micrometer-per-second solid."

"Yeah, cuz, I was just going to say that," Wynn said.

"No, you weren't," Ahnim said. "And there's something else."

"Of course there is. What's up?" Wynn asked.

"I've missed you," she said out loud.

"Sh-hhh! What?"

Wynn reached out and took hold of her hand. It was warm, like flesh, no longer tingly and artificial. He led her sideways through the intermittent throng into a recessed doorway. Leaned in close, he spoke quietly, almost a whisper. Her hair smelled like Christmas and sugar cookies.

"You can't just say stuff like that for everyone to hear," Wynn said.

"What would happen if everyone heard that?" she asked.

"It's not so much what. I mean, this kind of conversation should be private. Why did you come to my school?"

The crush of people in the hallway thinned out. Ahnim rose onto her tiptoes so her warm face came within an inch of his.

"Is this private enough?" she asked.

"To tell me why you're here, yeah."

"This morning, we didn't get to talk. Your mother came in and interrupted our usual morning conversation. Like I said, I missed being with you. I had to come."

"It's only been since yesterday," Wynn said. "Like maybe twelve hours."

"Hours. Time. The Immini are not bound by the temporal plane. I know time is important to you, Wynn, so I try to be considerate of that. But for me there is only the present."

Wynn found himself listening to the color of her eyes.

"Good morning, Boy Wonder," Mistez Plantain said. "You-na girl gotchabrain bein' last askiddin-in fuss bell, eh? Trouble catchin' la-slow butt, see?"

Ahnim smiled big. It ruined Wynn's ability to focus. "She's right," Ahnim said.

"You understood that?" Wynn asked.

"It certainly makes more sense than this modern English you keep misusing. Maybe you should learn that language instead."

"That's a good one," he said. "Now you're giving me advice on how to speak correctly, on my own planet."

The digital interpretation for the clang of a cast-iron bell warbled and clacked. Only the eldest in the building remembered the real thing.

"So, Ahnim," Wynn asked, "what are you doing here at my school?"

"If I'm correct, the appropriate action would be for me to register for classes." Speechless, Wynn's jaw dropped open. "It would be best if I follow the rules," Ahnim said, "so that I fit in."

She's serious. She actually expects to become a student at my school.

Ahnim spun on a toe and headed towards the administration offices. The bottom hem of her red leather jacket rose several inches above the ultra-low waisted jeans. Wynn caught himself leering at the exposed skin, the sway of the curves below it.

"One of her finer x-chromosome specimens, to be sure," said a voice at Wynn's ear.

Barry Doter rested a friendly hand on Wynn's shoulder. His own eyes followed after Ahnim. One of the few Wynn trusted, Barry offered companionship when the two Dubroc's arrived at D7 High, as Gordon and Saralee Matalon.

"One of who's what?" Wynn asked.

"Mother Nature," Barry said. "She's got a good eye. You just gotta know *that* DNA didn't happen by accident."

Wynn shook his head in disbelief of his new reality.

"Unreal," Barry added. Ahnim stepped through an open door and into a dark hallway.

"You have no idea," Wynn said.

"You know her? What's her name? Does she have a boyfriend? Can you—"

"No, I can't get you her Nish link."

"Smart man, savin' it for yourself. I would," Barry said.

"Shouldn't you be in GenCal?"

*****

To Wynn, the four class periods before lunch dragged on forever. He imagined the trouble Ahnim might cause on a campus full of unsuspecting humans. The announcement for lunch blared through the intercom.

"Today's menu brought to you by Footsie Chicken," the voice said, "Try it with the new root-beer, or a mixed-fruit additive!"

"Why do they call it a menu?" Barry asked. He hustled to keep up with Wynn's stride. They made a bee-line for the dispensing machines in the school's cafeteria.

"What are you talking about?"

"They can call it whatever they want," Barry said. "But chicken flavored goo is the only thing they serve, no matter how many colored squirt nozzles we get to choose from. To say 'menu' is—"

"You eat three feet of the crap every single day," Wynn said. "Now suddenly it's a problem?"

"Hey! There's the new girl. Please at least tell me her name." Barry pointed her out across the room without being too obvious about it. At least one other person in the noisy room caught on.

Michelle Jean-Terese kept a close eye on the competition.

Wynn observed Ahnim, believing she'd picked up on human traits and mannerisms while on campus.

"Is it me," Barry asked, "or was she wearing red this morning?"

She's pretending. Ahnim's pretending to search the room for me, like any human might have to. I know for a fact she can see me from fifty miles up. Thank heaven she hasn't freaked anyone out. Of course, the day's not over yet.

"Hello, gentlemen," Ahnim said. She approached them as they were halfway along in a line. Nearly fifty students awaited their turn at the chicken-goo spouts.

"No cuts," said a round boy with no friends.

Ahnim responded with a pouty lip, swiveled hips and batted lashes. Six guys in line told the boy to shut up or get a beat down. A handful of nearby girls hummed sarcastic appreciation for the one getting attention.

"Hi, I'm Barry." He wiped off a sweaty palm on his pant leg first.

"Anna," she said. She sensed his pulse accelerate during the brief handshake.

"Anna," Barry said. "It's good to finally meet you."

"Hi," Wynn said, hand out. "Anna, is it?"

Barry stepped up in line. His head sideways, he nearly fell into the person ahead of him.

"What's your family name?" Barry asked.

This I gotta hear, Wynn thought. He contained a mix of amusement and fear during the awkward moment.

"Anna Marie Lumiere." She held a flat smile for Wynn. He countered with a sincere expression of doubt, his arms crossed for effect.

"Loo-me-air?" Wynn asked. "Is that...Hungarian?"

"Great-granddad got off the boat in New Orleans, same as yours, M'sieur Dubroc," she said. Ahnim caught her error before

Wynn did.

"So you two know each other?" Barry asked. The lunch dispenser pinged his Nish to place the order. "Three, ketchup, smoked, extra-hot."

"Oh sure," Ahnim said. "Me and Gordon Matalon go way back."

"You want a plate of chicken goo, Anna?" Wynn asked.

Ahnim smiled and shook her head. Her mane of blonde coils made up one-fourth her petite stature. Wynn kept one eye on her, and the other on the dull brown paste spiraling onto his kelp-fibre plate. The green platter doubled as a tortilla if you had strong teeth and gums.

"Hey," Barry called, "I found three seats together that haven't been puked on yet!"

"Always a plus," Wynn said. He and Ahnim caught up. They elbowed their way into position along the crowded bench. "So, Anna, did you get registered for classes? How'd that go?"

"I did," Ahnim replied. "The aide was helpful and got me logged into the scheduling kiosk. We experienced a slight delay, since I don't—didn't bring my Nish with me today. However, I convinced the machine I did indeed exist, and qualified for any of the ninth grade curriculum."

"No doubt," Wynn said. "And which classes did you register for?"

"Um, let's see. My schedule is GenCal, Dialogics, Culturemo for Immigrants, SocioSpeak, lunch, Boys' P. E., Modern Government, and Welding."

"Welding certainly suits you," Wynn said. "Manipulating the atomic structure of metallic objects is right up your alley. Tell me about the whole Boys' P. E. thing, though."

"I hoped we'd exercise together and stuff," she said.

A large glob of smoked chicken goo went sideways in Barry's throat. He excused himself to the restroom to cough it out the rest of the way, and wipe the tears from his eyes.

"Is he going to be all right?" she asked.

"Absolutely! Now, Ahnim, what's with the French last name? And what exactly are you doing?"

"Lumiere means 'made of light'. Don't you think it's a good choice? Wynn, I know my being here, and visible, causes you to be nervous. It's because I wasn't adapted to your environment. But I'm trying to improve on that. Do you like my new body?"

"Your body is fine, Ahnim—"

"That's what several of the other males in the hallway stated," she said. "Fine."

"Terrific—we should sort out what this is going to be like, you being here."

"With you," she said.

"I'm having a hard time figuring out how this is going to work, you know? I mean, at home—"

"Your mother wants me to leave you alone," Ahnim said, her sadness genuine.

"Does she even know you're there?" Wynn asked.

"Where you're concerned, Brigitte's intuition is acute."

"Her what? Her intuition?"

"Most humans ignore their intuitive perceptions. Since I've been on your world, there've been several who acknowledged my presence, though I tuned my reflectivity beyond the visible. Two children waved at me, and a newborn in a stroller at the park reached out and grabbed my nose."

"Babies in strollers. How do you know my mother wants you to leave me alone?"

"She told me," she said.

"She told you. How'd that go down?" Wynn asked.

"Brigitte could tell I'd been in your room. She spoke to the emptiness. I got the message."

"So," Wynn asked, "what are you going to do?" He feared Ahnim might expect to remain as a human, to follow him everywhere.

"What does it look like I'm doing, *Gordon*?" she asked. Barry had returned and stood directly behind Wynn. Ahnim winked. "Somebody needs a wet willy."

"What," asked both boys together, "is a wet willy?"

"Saliva on the fingertip. It goes in the ear canal of the unsuspecting—"

"Ugh! Who *does* that?" Wynn asked, incredulous.

"There's the bell," Barry said. He rolled up the last of the paste into the edible plate and crammed it into his mouth. "See you in P. E., Anna?"

Wynn cocked his head to the side a bit. He gave Ahnim his best 'Well?' face.

"I didn't bring any shorts," she said, her shoulders shrugged.

"C'mon," Wynn said, "I'll introduce you to the boys' coach. He can help get you unregistered and switched over to the girl's side. Be sure to explain it wasn't your idea. Tell him the school's registration bot made an error in the class assignment."

"You want me to lie to him?" Ahnim asked.

"In this case, telling him the truth would be worse. Trust me."

*****

Wynn dressed out and trotted onto the soccer field when he noticed Ahnim leaving the coach's office. She headed in the direction of the school administrative wing. His mind swirled with the idea of her as a human, or posing as a human, and the plain fact she might not exist at all, at least not in the way he did. But she participated in conversation, and interacted well with students and faculty.

People can see her. She's real. This is not a dream. I am not insane.

Bright color flashed a moment before the soccer ball bounced off Wynn's groin. The first wave of testicular agony bent him over at the waist. The second wave dropped him to his knees. Prompt nausea turned his guts to hate.

"Oh, no! I'm so sorry!"

Derrick Curran ran up to offer condolences in the loss of any children Wynn might've wanted. A silent gesture all males know to give one another.

Wynn opened one eye, but it refused to focus.

"It's their fault, you know." Derrick said. "Girls like that one —the one you were locked up on—they screw us up."

"First, I'm gonna beat your ass," Wynn said between gasps. "Second, I have no idea what you're talking about."

"I already apologized, Matalon," Derrick said. "And I can outrun you by a mile. What I don't understand is, if you've got that new girl interested in you, why are you risking your life with Michelle Jean-Terese?"

Wynn got up onto his feet, and slapped the soccer ball down out of Derrick's hands. He meant to throw it squarely into his classmate's forehead. Derrick dodged easily and kept talking like nothing happened.

"I mean," Derrick asked," you know her boyfriend's out for blood, right?"

"Whose boyfriend?"

"Michelle's been with Lorenzo Flores since freshman year, off and on, anyway. Regardless of what she thinks, Lorenzo counts her as his all the time. He heard you're chattin' her up and asked to sit with her in Plantain's class. He's watching for you."

"I didn't ask for anything, and people should mind their own business, including you," Wynn said. "Yes, I'm still pissed about the ball to the nuts."

"Well, anyway," Derrick said. "You're on his kill list over her. Speak of the devil. Gotta go."

Wynn whirled around to face whatever or whoever this Lorenzo was. The adrenaline hadn't cleared from his system yet. His neck and arms flexed, fists clenched. Michelle leaned against the other side of the fence between the boy's and girl's section of the exercise field.

"Aren't you happy to see me, Boy Wonder. Why the ugly scowl?"

With effort, Wynn forced himself to relax and assume a pleasant smile. The closer he got to her, the easier that became. Every gesture she made and word spoken hooked his brain. Michelle drew him in. The previous conversation with Derrick drained from his head.

"You can call me by my name, you know," Wynn said.

"Gordon," she replied. Not his name, the word stabbed into his chest. "You don't care for being my Boy Wonder?"

"Depends on what that means, I guess."

"Well, Gordon, you're the boy I wonder about a lot lately." Michelle turned her womanly charms to full power.

"Do you want to go out?" Wynn asked.

The question fell out of his mouth without reason behind it.

"Okay," she replied. "Where are you taking me?"

She toyed with Wynn, as she did most boys, knowing they were clueless about having to plan a date in advance. Michelle enjoyed watching him stew. An aspiring actress, she used the pretense of friendship with girls, or the teasing of ready young males as practice for manipulating the camera lens.

"Matalon!" The coach for the boys P. E. class already made the entry of truant. "Matalon! Get your sorry butt back to the showers. You're marked absent."

Wynn turned towards the man in the dark green polyester. Pointing to the soccer game underway, he messaged he would catch up with the rest of his team.

"No sir!" The coach yelled. "Tomorrow you can try thinking with the other head."

Wynn closed his eyes in embarrassment. When he opened them, Michelle bit her lower lip. She glanced down at his shorts and back up into his eyes.

"How about," Michelle said, "you decide what you want to do with me if we go out, and let me know."

"Can I 'Net you?" he asked.

"MJT-a-la-mode on Groupies," she said.

"I'll save that into my Nish."

"Naturally."

Wynn watched her as she made her way back to the volleyball courts, where the rest of the girls stood around in cliques and pockets of gossip. During the slow walk back to the locker room, his mind went in three directions at once.

Thinking with the other head. Well, thanks Dad. At least your fatherly advice is widely accepted. Wherever you are. Good of you to care. Mom believes she's a failure. Who said she's supposed to do all this by herself? 'My family will be safer with me out of the picture for a while,' you said. Safer from what? Some homicidal foreign government spies? Second rate thugs for hire? I could use some useful advice now.

"Hey, Dad!" Wynn spoke aloud to himself. "See, I've got this fantastic girl at school who likes me. Now what? Or maybe, Hey Dad, I've got an alien being from outer space who's stalking our family. However, she's somehow adorable now, and she likes me too. And mom thinks I'm schizoid, cuz you know, aliens aren't real."

Motion caught Wynn's attention. He flinched, but didn't duck. Instinctive reaction to the white towel did not factor in the weight of the balled fist hidden behind it. His upper teeth made an odd creak as they snapped up and behind his lower incisors. Starry twinkles flooded from his nose and up into his eye sockets. Ghostly birds followed him down to the unforgiving cement path.

For a moment, his mind went back to the dark hiding place, the wooden bench in the yacht. Pain and dizziness mixed with fearful memories. A metallic flavor triggered a rush from within. His arms flailed and feet kicked. Expending every ounce of fight in the first moments, he would not be taken so easily again.

Today however, there were five of them. The attackers dragged him helplessly across the ground, each limb clamped tight in the grip of someone as strong as he. Gaps between the concrete slabs grabbed at his shorts. Two hands held him by the hair, pushing, pounding, angry. Down a flight of steps, his tailbone cracked on the third bounce.

Searing pain struck out through the hip bones and into the knees and ankles. Flipped forward with a harsh shove from behind, Wynn caught a glimpse of the word McDonalds. The crown of his head slammed into the bottom of a garbage can. He tasted ketchup, maybe mustard. The two flavors helped chase away the sickening taste of his own blood.

"Pull his butt outta there!" Lorenzo Flores shouted.

Wynn's shirt tore away. Hands wrapped around his throat. They yanked hard.

"I've seen you before, Matalon," Lorenzo said. "You looked smart enough. Turns out you're just crust on a dog's hole."

"Ugh!" One of the younger attackers reeled at the evidence of brutality and intimidation. "So much blood!"

"What did you expect, cherry-boy?" Lorenzo asked. "You shouldn't have come if you ain't got the 'nads to deal with it. Now get him on his feet!"

Wynn refused to stand up. Halfway through an internalized kung-fu chant, he held breath constriction. He paused a few more seconds to get the energy down from his adrenal glands and into his good leg. A third boy joined in, taking Wynn by the elbow.

Perfect—the power of three plus my own. Just need to land the toe. Too much blood in my eyes. Can't get my hands to my face to wipe them out. Here goes nothing.

With no clear line of sight to accurately target the point of his shoe, Wynn opted for the heel as the best defensive weapon for the moment. As the three boys swung him up, he pulled hard against their arms. He struck out with his right foot at chest height. It landed square in Lorenzo's sternum. The blow sent Lorenzo careening backward against the far wall, the air knocked out of his lungs. The others stood stunned, unaware they should expect more from the determined victim. A quick twist of Wynn's body wound up a second boy's wrist further than designed. A high-pitched squeal urged Wynn on to the next available bone, joint, or unguarded nerve channel.

Reaching out blindly, he scooped up a leg at the knee. With a sharp dive of his shoulder, Wynn poised himself under the person's center of gravity. His legs straightened to stand up, and the other's head landed with a clunk.

Three down, two to go. Maybe I should run for it before Lorenzo Flores gets his wind back.

The better plan worked, though with significant discomfort. Each time his foot pounded against the ground, his cracked tailbone brought searing pain.

*****

"Geez, Matalon!" Barry yelled. "What happened to you?"

"I went dumpster diving and...then the...garbage truck showed up at the worst possible time."

"I wouldn't believe you, except for the Hunt's package stuck to your head. Is that blood?"

"No, ketchup or barbecue." He ran a finger across his teeth for any missing or out of place. They all hurt. Some teeth touched where they hadn't before.

"That's a load of crap, Gordon," Barry said. "Who did this to you? Lorenzo? Your nose is still running with bloody boogers. You gotta go to the paramed."

"Yeah? Okay. Can you point me in that direction?" Wynn asked.

"Point you? I'd be some friend if I didn't take you there. C'mon."

*****

Ahnim changed the images on her bare toenails six times while waiting for the guidance counsellor to get a break in her schedule. She went with the faces of the starting lineup for the 2023 LA Lakers and their coach. A little busy, but a popular choice.

"Anna Lumiere?"

"That's me," Ahnim said. She copied a bouncy stride of the other freshman girls.

"Hi, I'm Izzie Holden. How can I help you? Have a seat."

"I signed up for a class I don't think will work out for me," Ahnim said.

"Typically, we require new students to try out a class for at least a week before we approve any transfers. I see you're assigned to Boys' P. E. Didn't you request that?"

"I did, yes, but—"

"We can set up whichever gender choice you request,"

Holden said, "but prefer only one flip per quarter. And it requires an approval comm from your TransPath support coach."

"It's not that," Ahnim said. "I mistook the option as meaning that girls could be with the boys, during the exercise sessions and games."

"Why on Earth would you want to do that?" Holden asked. "Setting yourself up for peer ridicule if you ask me. High school is challenging enough without—well, my opinion. What is it you want to do?"

"I want to replace that with something more appropriate. Maybe something that would offer—"

"Nearly every class is to the forty-eight student max. Choices are limited this far into the school year. There's an opening for a student aide in the Paramed clinic. Do you have a fear of bodily fluids, or foul odors?"

"Not especially," Ahnim said.

"Do you have any experience with minor medical procedures?" Holden asked. "You won't have to reattach any fingers or anything, just help with bandages, upset stomachs, and displaced visual implants."

"I'm pretty good with amputated fingers," Ahnim said. "The rest I'm sure to figure out."

"You're in luck, then. The training class for the Paramed assistant postponed for a week. It starts tomorrow. I can take you down and get you introduced to Tina Evans now."

"Thanks, I can't wait to start."

Chapter Nine

Obvious to Nurse Tina Evans, Wynn's injuries stemmed from a brutal assault.

"I can't treat you unless you tell me the truth, Gordon," Evans said.

"I fell into a garbage can," he repeated. "When I tried to get out of it, I tripped and fell out...of it. Then—do you have to call my parents?"

"The administrative office is calling them now. Graphicons of your bloodied and swollen face have already been forwarded to the Badgies."

"You're awfully quick on the Nish," Wynn said.

"It's pretty much automated," Holden said. "So don't give me too much credit. All right, Barry, is it? You tell me what happened."

"On the way back to the showers," Barry said, "I happened to glance between the buildings. Saw my friend."

"That's it, huh?" Tina asked.

"He didn't see anything, miss," Wynn said. "He wasn't there."

"In that cooler you'll find some cold packs," Evans said.

"Barry? Are you listening? Get a cold pack and help him hold it over the nose and mouth. On the wall is a tampon dispenser. Grab a couple. If the nose keeps bleeding, stick them up there. Pop them out of the seal first, right? You don't know."

"I'm not supposed to touch those. My mom—"

"Okay, they aren't tampons. They're boy's proboscis anti-coagulators. Use 'em or don't."

Wynn turned to Barry and nodded, rolling his eyes. He pointed to his butt without being obvious about it.

"Can I," Wynn stuttered, "have another cold pack for my...um...?"

"Turn around, Gordon," Tina said. She stuck a couple fingers into the waistband at the back of his shorts, yanking them down about halfway. His lower back and upper buttocks were raw. A contusion formed right at the tailbone.

"I'm guessing that hurts more than the nose," she said. "You'll need to see a doctor for that. But that's what you're choosing anyway. Let's go. I'll sign you out at the school lobby."

*****

"Lorenzo! My arm's broken!" Terence said.

"Shut up! It would've cracked."

Of the four who agreed to help Lorenzo, one ran off. The others wouldn't finish the job.

"Spec this, Lo," said Sid, the only one not injured. "James busted his head in back. He's all white, zombie or something. He puked, and now he's all quiet. Could be a concussion."

"Yeah, and I don't see nothin' wrong with you," Lorenzo

said. "You managed to get out of the way plenty when Matalon went nutso on us."

"I'm taking them to the Paramed office," Sid said. "You can do what you want with Gordon."

"You better not turn, Sid."

"Did I say that? But if you're not going to help James, I guess it's on me."

Sid pulled hard to lift James onto his feet, and got him moving toward the administrative wing of the school. It took a whole class period, but he managed to get the three of them to the Paramed's door. He found it closed and locked.

"She should be here," Terrance said. "She's always here."

"Yeah? You come here a lot?" Sid asked.

"No, maybe a few times."

Footsteps and a loud voice echoed from the other end of the hall.

"You need to see Miss Evans?"

"Mrs. Holden!" Sid called. "We need some help. James Turner hit his head."

Izzie Holden quickened her pace. Ahnim kept up beside her, but with much shorter legs, she broke into a run. Her thick hair bounced right and left, swishing over the leather.

Arriving to the three boys, Holden felt through the matted blood to the flat spot on the back of James' skull. As he slid down the wall to land butt first on the polished floor, Holden moved to pound her fist on the door.

"Mrs. Holden," Ahnim said. "Your medical office doesn't stock the necessary equipment to repair his injury."

The counsellor turned towards the young face. Ten minutes

ago, Ahnim blushed at the mention of transexuality. In the presence of injured children, her voice and demeanor matured.

"My arm hurts like it's broken," Terence said.

"Okay," Holden said, "we'll get you inside and find the instafoam cast."

"Door's locked," Sid said.

Ahnim knelt beside James. Her eyes closed, she inspected every cell, every molecule of his damaged cranium, and the small artery which leaked through its perforated layers. She stood and stepped to the door, grabbing the stainless steel lever handle.

"It's locked," Sid said louder. With a squeak, hardened metal lost the battle with interstellar will. Ahnim left the door handle down in its new, droopy position, then held the door open for them.

"Bring them in," Ahnim said. "The cast is in the white drawer, second one up from the bottom." They laid James on a cot that pulled out from the wall at the end. "I'll watch him while you help with Terence's arm."

James bore a slight resemblance to Wynn, with a generous mouth and strong chin. His hair cropped in a semi-military style. It surprised Ahnim how the durable human body could be brought to finality by a single torn membrane no wider than a millimeter. This particular body would become non-functional —he would die—if she did not intervene immediately.

With a look over her shoulder, she made sure no one was watching. She grinned at how she spontaneously acted human, even when she didn't need to. Standing up against the raised platform that supported the thin mattress, a black spike extended from her left thigh. It lengthened forward, then curved up and into the flat underside of the metal trundle. Up through his neck and into his head, she searched for the injury. Ahnim found it in a small artery, its delicate tip mashed sideways. A pulsing pool of blood pressed against the two halves of the visual cortex. If he didn't die, he'd be blind.

"How's he doing?" asked Holden, pointing from the other end of the room. "We should keep him awake. There's a bright orange pen in that tray. It has an ammonia inhalant. Click the button a time or two under his nose."

Ahnim rotated her head towards the countertop. With no one looking her way, she stretched her arm over the six feet to snatch up the pen. The anti-photon needle she guided inside of James' brain never wavered from its task. With her ability to manipulate elements, she replicated the needed cells along the outer rim of the damaged artery.

A few snaps in and out of the ammonia inhalant did nothing yet, as she buried the diffusor into the heavy fabric of his shirt.

Another thirty seconds should do it, Ahnim thought. *Such fine detail, one molecule at a time. And this section of the brain isn't getting the blood it needs.*

"Hey," Tina Evans said, entering the clinic, "what the heck is this?"

"Glad you're here," Holden said. "This is one potential fracture of the right tibia." Facing away from Terence, she mouthed, "I don't think so." Rolled eyes told the rest. "Over there, we may have something more serious. Felt like a good crack on the back of his head. I'm nobody to say how bad. Anna there has some pretty good bedside manners."

A warm hand squeezed Ahnim's shoulder. Tina Evans stood

only a few inches taller than her, whereas Holden towered a good head and shoulders above. The Paramed scooted close to the patient. James had ceased voluntary movement for almost two minutes.

"Hi there," Tina said. "He doesn't look so good. Perhaps I should take over."

"I'm Anna. I just transferred to your class?"

"My class? Not sure what you mean."

Tina reached across Ahnim's forearms to feel for a pulse in James' neck.

"Paramed Assistant—I'll be your new assistant." Ahnim needed ten more seconds to complete the microscopic reconstruction of James' artery. Inside Tina's mind, the woman readied a stern directive for 'Anna' to get out of the way. Rising muscle tension in the Paramed's left arm signaled the precursor to a gentle shove. Ahnim counted eight point seven seconds to go.

This isn't going to work. I'm going to need to take this to the next level of interference if I want to save this life. I have to save this life. Eight point six.

From the top of Ahnim's shoulder, a black bulge swelled from a single point of nothingness. Flat spears of anti-photons thrust outward, one for each of the five humans in the room. At near the speed of light, the daggers impaled their brains. Neurons stalled. Synapses backed upon themselves. The two main areas of the human brain to measure or comprehend time came to a screeching halt. Like a streaming video stopped to buffer, all time in the small clinic ceased to move forward. To the human occupants, the remaining eight point five seconds never happened. They would never remember their heartbeats, or even the thoughts that raced nowhere. Within James, the blood ceased to spill, pressure rose in the capillaries, tissue regenerated and flared with life.

Snap.

Atomized ammonia from the tip of the orange pen found the correct receptors in James' nose. He took in a great breath of air. Ahnim put the pen into Tina's hand.

"There he is!" Ahnim said, a happy glow on her face. "It's okay. You're going to be okay. You bumped your head a bit."

"I knew she'd be right for the clinic, Tina," Holden said. "Spec that!"

Tina caught herself before tipping into the petite blonde at the patient's bedside. Steadying her own balance, a pouty scowl crossed her face. The boy on the cot didn't have anything wrong with him.

But dried blood speckled his shirt.

"What I need to know is," she said, "where did all *this* come from?"

Tina turned out of the way. Holden stretched to see where she pointed. Dark splotches spread all over the front of James' shirt and pants.

"Yeah," Holden said. "Terrance here has the same thing all down his front. And it's all over his hands, too."

"Tell 'em, Sid," Terrance said.

"Shut up! That's all from James' busted head, anyway."

"Tell us what?" Tina pressed. "Oh, I get it now. This," she said, twirling a fingertip around at all the little dried drops on James' shirt, "is not from these three. It's from the poor guy I just escorted to the Badgies. He's the one who got beaten and dragged down the stairs."

"This is the other side of the story," Holden said. "I bet you're right."

"Yep! I had a hunch," Holden said. "He didn't strike me as one who would take it and not give it back some."

The two adults spoke about someone else, a third injured person. Ahnim scanned all the blood spatter on the three boys. *It's all from the same person, but not from them. Who? I've seen this exact genome series before. This half of it in Brigitte Dubroc. But all of it's in—*

"Wynn!" Ahnim shouted. A pane of glass in the cabinet directly ahead shook in its place.

"His name was Gordon," Tina said.

Ahnim whirled on the toe of her boot. Her face contorted with rage, fists clenched at her sides. Veins swelled on her forehead and neck, like a real human ready for a fight.

"Who hurt him? You?" she screamed. "Was it you?" She took two steps toward Terrance. Half his size, Ahnim intended to cut him down to hers. Holden moved quick.

"Now wait a minute!" She might as well have pushed against a tractor trailer.

"It was Lorenzo!" Terrance said. "Lorenzo Flores—he had us do it! But he's the one who hurt Gordon so bad. I didn't know it was going to be like that."

Tina caught motion past the door as Sid made a hasty exit. His heavy boots stomped and echoed in the hollow concrete hallway. Ahnim stood fuming at the back end of the narrow office.

"Move out of my way," she said. "I'm leaving."

"You need to just calm down," Holden said. From a dozen

places on Ahnim's body, thin black spikes protruded out through small gashes in her surface. To Holden, the sight was something out of a horror film. "Anna, you really, *really* need to calm down."

Ahnim inhaled a great, hissing breath. Her neck and throat flushed and swelled. A fierce roar shook the walls. What humanity she did possess transformed back to energy. Like before, anything of Earth in her way fared poorly as she made exit of the school grounds.

James lifted his head from the cot. Several loose papers fell to the floor. Three people hunched over their knees, their faces covered. He propped himself up on his elbows, surveyed the shattered mess. He faintly remembered a beautiful young girl standing over him.

"What'd I miss?" he asked.

*****

The hard plastic chair for visitors in the school's security office didn't help the broken tailbone.

"Seriously," Wynn said, "I'd prefer to stand."

The Badgie, rotund and perspiring, hooked his thumbs through his duty belt. It disappeared under the massive roll of fat at the front. The three bottom buttons of the uniform shirt strained at the fabric.

Corporal Bruce Dogsby kept Wynn seated. A quick, sideways glance preceded a searing threat.

"You do as I say, and things'll go better for you," Dogsby said.

Sirens wailed in the distance.

Corporal Dogsby stepped out of the doorway to peer out into the parking lot. A car pulled up in a bit of a rush. He squinted from the windshield's glare. The driver got out and made straight for him. He pushed his chest out to nearly the same diameter as the spare tire underneath.

"Can I help you, ma'am?" he asked.

"My name is Brigitte—Mrs. Matalon. I'm here to get my son."

"He's being processed right now," Dogsby said. "Do you have any firm-copy identification?"

"Identification?" Brigitte asked. "Yes, I'm his mother. What does that mean, 'being processed'? Processed for what exactly?" She reached down into her purse to locate her Witness Reboot issued driver's license.

"Mom!" Wynn called from inside the office. "Is that you?"

"You shut it!" Dogsby barked. He aimed a pudgy index finger at Wynn's nose.

Wynn scooted around and behind the Badgie, the barest of light streaming between the guard and door frame. Mother and son failed to make eye contact. Brigitte's fingernails dug into the skin of her palms, her jaw rigid.

"Are you—" she muttered, with a quick glance at his name tag, "Corporal Dogsby, did you just refer to my open blouse?"

"Excuse me?"

"Are you looking at my breasts?" she asked. "There, you just did it again!"

"No way!" Dogsby stuttered. Back on his heels, he almost stepped on Wynn's feet behind him. "I swear—wait—you have to comply with—"

"Rocktower Security has strict rules in their employment guidelines," she said. Her voice raised in volume enough for the few bystanders to catch a few words here and there. "They have a zero tolerance policy for any sexual harassment. Once they catch wind one of their officers has a problem with leering at women's breasts, I'd bet they'd have to confiscate his personal Nish. They'll check if there's any copies of inappropriate video or images. Maybe even some leechware to download personal photos from some school-girl's Nish to yours?"

Dogsby blanched. He held out his hands in surrender, as if staring down the barrel of a gun.

"Okay! Okay!"

"Okay, what...Bruce?" Brigitte asked.

"I'm not lookin' at nothin'!" Dogsby said. "It was all just a misunderstanding, right?"

"I understood you to say that my son's done being processed, and free to come home with me," Brigitte said.

The Badgie caught on. He took a step out of the doorway, and another off to the side. All the while being careful to avoid the crazy woman's shirt. Wynn wasted no time making exit of the security office and straight to Brigitte's outstretched arms. Then he pictured himself hugging mom in front of his high-school.

"Hi," he said, "I know you're into safety and all, but instead of me sitting up front in the seatbelt, may I lie down in the back seat?" She nodded with a mom's agreeable concern.

"Thanks," Wynn said, "My butt's killing me."

Brigitte held Wynn up with one arm, carried her purse and his backpack, and managed to sneak her middle finger up behind her as they hobbled away from Corporal Dogsby.

The thin gas springs failed to hold the car's wing door up. She propped it up with the top of her head, and remembered a day when only the hatchbacks fell down on you. A moment before Wynn lowered himself onto the bench seat, Brigitte caught him panning the horizon. His eyes narrowed.

Driving into traffic, Brigitte pondered how life used to be so much easier. If not easy, at least planned. Eric received his master's degree in micro-tech. His astounding dissertation on bio-circuits for macro-molecular motors launched their livelihood and lifestyle. He dodged the military's constant encouragement to bring his work to them, 'for the betterment of mankind'. Eric and Brigitte lived in whichever city they pleased. A magnificent home, the best cars, private education for the kids. All so well planned. A controlled ease, for her at least. Free to be the ever-ready mom with a bottomless wire.

Then Eric's employer announced the major shareholders sold their stock to a department of defense contractor. Details hidden under layers of shadow businesses and corporate dark corners. Within a few weeks, the media figured it out. Darmin-Stoyl Medical Devices had become the puppet of the GC-Four military. They came to be known for their quest to develop new and improved ways to cause death for the buyer's enemy.

Late one night, after a failed attempt at intimacy, Eric confided he'd been ordered to relocate to a new facility on a weapons development base. He was to guide them in the use of his cloned nano-tubes to create a deferred effect poison. It could be ingested, or inhaled by the unwitting target, and later activated by a signal from a pocket transmitter, or an orbiting satellite. Death might be delayed for days, years, or decades. It would forever lay dormant in the bones.

Brigitte encouraged Eric to refuse. But the GC-Four would move forward with the project one way or the other. Loose ends would be taken care of along the way. He could do the most good with the technology by remaining involved, even if it meant getting a little dirty. Along with the dirt came bodyguards, secret surveillance, safe rooms, and few friends.

Today, speeding along in a filthy Daimler Dart to Saint Lucia's Affordable Care Center, the weary mother came to another decision—enough was enough. She wanted her life back.

"Comfortable?" Brigitte asked. In the rearview mirror, Wynn's shoes stuck up on the passenger side. Lying face down, he bent at the knees to fit his lanky frame across the narrow vehicle.

"As in, my butt hurts half as much like this as it does sitting? Yeah."

"Okay, then. Spill it," Brigitte said. "What in the heck happened to you?"

"There's...this girl," Wynn confessed.

Brigitte rolled her eyes, allowed the bouncing of the car to bobble her head for her.

"And, there's an ex-sort-of-ex-boyfriend," he continued, "that took exception to my being with her."

"By being with, you mean—"

"No mom. Being with means talking, with clothes on, in public, conversation."

"Okay, sorry. Go ahead," she said.

"Anyway, she keeps starting it. And I like her well enough. I understood this guy and her were history."

"Maybe *he* doesn't think so," she said.

"I'm guessing. He and four other guys ambushed me while I was on the way to the locker room. Wish I would've ducked a little better than I did. Took me a minute to get my head back on straight. By then they'd dragged me down into the basement. That Lorenzo is one pissed-off motherf—whoops— sorry. He tried to break my neck or something. Lucky for me he wasn't very good at it. He finally gave up and just shoved me down into a garbage can. Glad it was full. Gave me something to land on."

"Oh, geez, baby. I am so sorry."

"Remember those classes dad made us take?" Wynn asked. "The ones with weird Mister Soichiro?"

"The guy with the white whiskers and ponytail—all the humming?" she asked.

"Yeah, so, I was doing that stuff, upside down in the garbage can. There I am humming that stupid Chinese song, and trying to breathe in through my bellybutton like he told us."

"How'd that work for you?" Brigitte asked. She noticed the big orange and yellow sign for the urgent care clinic ahead, clicked the turn signal on. Straining her chin up, she searched for her son's face in the mirror.

"Surprisingly well, as it turned out!" Wynn said.

"Yeah? Tell me."

"I did the thing where you use the opponent's energy, and sure enough they pulled me up like a slingshot right into Lorenzo's face. I breathed out and down through my butt— don't laugh!—and just like that, three moves and three of 'em went down or ran home to mommy."

"Seriously," Brigitte said.

"We should send a thank-you card to weird Mister Siochiro. That silly crap actually worked this time!"

Brigitte wished it worked before.

"Okay, we're here," she said. "Let me go in and get you registered. No sense you going in right now and having to sit, right?"

"Appreciate that," Wynn said.

*****

Nev headed out of the school building, her day over. The indicator on her Nish showed a call coming in from her mother.

That's strange, she thought. *Mom should be at work.*

"Everything okay?" Nev asked.

"Your brother got jumped at school, took a couple pretty good shots. Not, you know, like before. We're on the way home from Saint Lucia's on Kensing. Should be home in half an hour I'd guess."

"Is that what all the fuss was about today? You'd think there was a bomb scare or something with all the police, and fire trucks, and the 'anti-school-freakout-mobile-something' that took over."

"The Academic Terrorism Mobile Command Unit?" Brigitte asked.

"Mmm-hmm, that one," Nev said.

"At your school today?"

"Still is," Nev said. "The Badgies closed off the entire west wing. Lots of commotion around the Paramed office, or the rooms on either side of that."

"Wild. Are you on the way home?" Brigitte asked.

"I'm going to the library to study quantum physics."

"You and your brother have the same sarcasm. I have your father to thank for that."

"Does he know about Wynn?" Nev asked.

"Oh, no, I haven't even—maybe you should call him?"

More strangeness. Why doesn't she call dad herself? Maybe she doesn't want to talk to him. Maybe they're fighting again.

"Sure, mom," Nev said, "I'll call him."

"Okay," Brigitte said. "Please do that. Bye."

Nev conjured an image of her father. Her Nish needed one to recognize, to initiate the auto-link to his. But his face faded.

What kind of daughter are you, she thought. *Can't remember your own father?*

She visually tapped the 'contact search' icon floating up and to the right.

"Dad," she directed.

"Contact not found," the Nish replied.

"Michael Matalon." She hadn't reached out to him since being issued the new Nish by the Witness Reboot staff.

Yeah, what kind of daughter are you?

"Link established," the Nish said, "Awaiting response."

To Nev, Eric must have fumbled his Nish when he went to get it.

"Who's Genie?" asked a woman's voice over the Nish.

"Give me that." Her dad's voice.

He used to call me Genie, when I was small enough for him to carry on his shoulders.

Several seconds of silence ensued. Then the link

disconnected, as indicated by a solitary beep on Nev's end. She considered giving the command for a relink. Angry fantasy collided with what she wanted to be true. Breaking through her emotions, the image of her father coalesced in the space between her and the gate ahead. Eric had called her back.

"Hi, daddy," she said. "It's Nev."

"I know, silly. I called you. How's school?"

How's school? He never asks that. Dad always asks how my day went.

"Math sucked," Nev said. "The glop dispensers went offline for whatever reason toward the middle of the second lunch period. They brought in actual food from another school. Tuna sandwiches and carrot sticks."

"You know there aren't any more tuna, right? That's probably just—"

"Okay!" she said. "I don't want to know. Thanks for ruining what I believed was lunch."

"You're kind of cranky," Eric said. "What's up?"

"I don't know. What's up with you?"

"What do you mean by that?" Eric asked. "Is something wrong?"

"Actually, there is. Wynn got beat up at school today. Mom took him to the wanna-be-docs, you know, since we can't afford real medical care. She asked me to tell you. So...I'm telling you."

"How's he look? Is he okay? Did she call the Witness Reboot hotline to let them know?"

"I haven't seen him. No, not really, and I don't know who she called. Who answered your Nish when I called a few minutes ago?"

"Did you call me a few minutes ago?" he asked.

Guess we're done worrying about his son. Back to being evasive. We all know what that means. Lovely family life this turns out to be.

"A woman answered," Nev said.

"I don't think so."

I don't think so? Please, God, do not let this be true. Make me an idiot, but don't let it mean my dad's having an affair.

"Really, dad? 'Who's Genie?' What's that? Who is she?"

"You're being pretty disrespectful," he said. "As your father, I deserve better. Nobody answered my phone. If you called before, you linked to another person's Nish, not mine."

"Fine."

"Not fine—you owe me an apology," Eric said.

"Sorry," Nev said. A long, awkward silence did nothing to wash away the tension of the moment, the hurt and mistrust. "Are you coming home?" she asked.

"I hadn't planned on being home until after next week."

"Okay, please allow me to rephrase that," Nev said. Covering irritation in her tone, she stuck to polite words and grammar. "Wynn got beat up today. That doesn't happen, usually. I mean, he can handle himself pretty well with anyone his age. He needs you. Mom needs you...back here...*with us*."

"I'll see what I can do, Nev. There aren't a lot of options for me right now."

I am not an option. Your family is not an option.

"Yeah, well, we don't have any." It occurred to Nev those might be the last words she'd ever speak to her father. "Dad..."

"Yeah?"

"I miss you," she said. "We need you home. Everything you need is right here, or wherever we are."

"Wish I could be there," Eric said.

Chapter Ten

"Nev!" Brigitte called from the dining room. "Would you please get the door? Either someone's there or the mat sensor is sending falsies to my Nish again."

Nev laid on the floor with her feet up on the couch, reading a new sci-fi romance novel, Love at FTL. "Can't?—ugh!" Nev said. "Why is everyone else's time worth more than mine!"

She slapped the e-reader down onto the matted rug. Then flipped over backwards to land on her hands and knees. A couple of stumbling steps got her to the door. Blurred motion through the stained glass portal window gave proof of a visitor.

"Hi, I'm Michelle. Is Gordon home?"

Nev recognized the girl as one of the more popular faces of the Juniors. Immaculate clothes and makeup, perfect hair and teeth. Nev considered Michelle's family as being a few big steps up the ladder from the Matalons.

Why would she want to date my brother?

"Hello," Nev answered. "C'mon in. Have a seat. Don't mind the mess."

"Thank you," Michelle said. "I'll wait here for Gordon."

"That's just it. He doesn't do stairs unless there's a fire or bacon. Broken butt." She pointed behind herself, then thumbed up the stairs.

"Excuse me? Can you let him know I'm here, please?" Michelle pressed.

"Sure thing," Nev said. She flicked the rim of her Nish with a yellow fingernail. "Wakey, wakey, sib. Gotta visitor." She feigned disinterest, but no other girl from Lochiel had wanted to ship with her brother. "Downstairs! Where else?"

Wynn ducked his head down into the stairwell, expecting Barry Doter. But Wynn daydreamed about Michelle Jean-Terese since first meeting her.

"Wow, hi!" Wynn said. "I mean, welcome to our home. This is a pleasant surprise."

"Hi, Gordon. I hope I'm not interrupting. I'd heard what happened, and I wanted to come by to apologize and see how you're doing."

"There's nothing you need to apologize for," he said. Wynn craned his neck around. No mom visible, he waved Michelle to join him upstairs.

As she headed up, Wynn bulldozed a clear spot in the middle of his room.

Yeah, cuz that's not obvious, Nev thought. *Where in Lochiel did she find those baby-blue denims? And didn't they have any in size four? She had to get them in size two just to prove a point?*

*****

Michelle found the only place to sit in Gordon's room, a simple black captain's chair. She settled herself down, wary of his strange facial expression.

"Okay if I sit here?" she asked. "Oh, of course. No problem."

"I enjoyed our visit yesterday," she said. "But after what happened, I felt awful."

"Why's that, Michelle? You didn't have anything to do with that."

"I kind of do, I guess." Michelle chewed on her lip for dramatic effect. "You see, Lorenzo and I used to be, you know, a couple."

"I know that. But you aren't now." Wynn appeared confident and relaxed, but severe pain in his tailbone strained the control of his voice.

"Not right now, no. We're kind of off, I guess. So, are you all right? I mean, your poor face! Your upper lip is swelled out to the tip of your nose. Does it hurt?"

"Yeah, a bit. What did you hear?" he asked.

"It was all over school today. Lorenzo challenged you to fight over me, and you beat each other up."

Wynn laughed. The split in his lip stretched apart enough to dim the humor of the moment. He watched Michelle for a minute, imagining a future together. But something held him back, an apprehension deep within.

"I did fight over you. Didn't plan to though. Your ex got a head start on me."

"He tends to do that," Michelle said.

"Has he been this way before, with other guys? Does he make a habit of ambushing anybody that talks to you?"

"I wouldn't call it a habit," she said. "But he's pretty possessive. I guess you'd say he knows a good thing when he sees it. Doesn't want to let it go."

"So where does that leave you and me?" Wynn asked. "Do you consider yourself free to go out with someone, with me, I mean?"

"Are you asking me out?"

"I don't want—yes, I'm asking you out,"Wynn said.

"What don't you want?" she asked.

Wynn laughed again, then fell over onto the bed, moaning. He held pressure against his face to keep it from breaking open again.

"I don't want to get my face beaten, that's what. I'd prefer we just went to eat someplace simple—The Wishbone maybe. You know, then go check out the Tumblr gallery at Mall Town."

"The Wishbone?" she asked.

"Yeah, and definitely no volunteering me for amateur MMA, or Simuboxing. I'd like to save my lips for something better than target practice."

"I've never been to the Wishbone," Michelle said.

"The Lucky Wishbone," he said. "You gotta try the chicken livers and the spicy shrimp-sauce. And it's not ground goo either. Real chicken from a real...chicken."

"Is it greasy?" Michelle asked. "I don't do greasy."

"Are you kidding? The only thing *not* deep fried are the milk shakes!" It took Wynn time to understand she had no interest in dinner on the cheap side of town. "It's okay. We'll find something that doesn't cause a zit breakout the next morning."

"Um," she said, not smiling, "I don't get zits."

"No, of course you don't. Your skin is perfect."

His mother coming up the stairs broke the brief awkward

silence. Both teens put on their best innocent face.

"Wynn?" Brigitte called. "Are you talking to someone? How are you, baby?"

Moments before his mom appeared in the doorway, Michelle mouthed, 'baby'. Wynn closed his eyes and nodded.

"Oh, hello," Brigitte said. "Wynn, I didn't know you had anyone over—up here."

"Mom, this is Michelle. Michelle, my mom." Michelle stood and offered a polite hand to the mother.

"Oh, okay," Brigitte said. "Do you go to Mamanou, too?"

"You mean D-7, mom, right?" Wynn eyed his mother carefully.

"Yes, of course I did, actually," Brigitte stuttered, "mean District—D-7."

"Yes," Michelle said, "Gordon and I are in a few classes together. He coaches me on chromosomal manipulation. I whisper SocioSpeak to his back, when Mistez Plantain calls on him."

"I see," Brigitte said. "So, you help him cheat?"

Wynn flushed under his shirt and up his neck. Michelle sat, unfazed by the pointed question.

"Precisely," Michelle replied. "I brought his grade up two points. If he gets a clue, maybe he won't have to take it again next semester."

"And I owe you for that!" Wynn said, bounding out of bed and escorting his mom to the door. She leaned into him a little. He smelled the liquor on her breath. Brigitte's ritual late-evening glass of wine started early, and she'd gone through half the bottle.

"Okay, mom—*Jackie!* How about you and *Saralee* go watch

that vid you've been going on about. You know, the one about the family that goes into hiding from the mob?"

Brigitte gave up and let Wynn lead her to the top of the stairs. Once there, he held her elbow so she wouldn't try to make it down herself. He aimed a hiss at his sister to get her attention. Nev glared between a furrowed brow and the upper edge of the e-reader. Wynn gestured behind his mother's head. Thumb and pinkie stretched out from a fist, like someone tipping a brew. Nev didn't want to know if her only attending parent was drunk by the middle of the afternoon.

Brigitte's bare heel slipped off the carpeted edge of the first step. She bounced down a couple more. Wynn had a tight hold on the back of her tank top. That gave her a chance to get her other leg under, to hold her own weight. In her inebriation, reality took on that delayed misunderstanding of events.

"Let the hell go of my bra, Wynn!" she snapped. "Frick! You just about screwed me up going down the stairs!"

Wynn checked the living room floor, no Nev. He started to call for her when two warm hands wrapped around under his arms where he held Brigitte.

"Got her," Nev said. "Hey, mom, let's do that—go watch that vid—in your room."

"I don't wanna watch any—"

"Oh, yeah! You've been after me for a week about that sappy old movie. Who's that actor you've been gushing over?" Between the two of them, the siblings managed to get their mother to the bottom of the stairs without a tumble or any more foul language in front of the guest.

"McDermot?" Brigitte asked. "Oh, heck yeah. Have you seen

that guy in his underpants? No, I guess maybe it'd be better if you said no. No, mom I don't—didn't—haven't."

"No, mom, you're right," Nev said. "I have not seen that. Wow!"

"Got her?" Wynn asked. "I'd like to—"

"I said I got her," Nev said.

Wynn hobbled back up the stairs. He nearly ran headlong into Michelle at the top, as she headed down.

"I should go," she said. "Maybe you should help with your mom."

"She'll be fine. You don't have to leave," Wynn said.

"I'm free next Friday evening, if you still—"

"I do still want to go out. We can skip the Wishbone. I was just joking, really. I'll pick you up and..." With no idea what to plan for, his mind reeled from having to corral his drunk mother.

"We have all week to plan it," Michelle said. "No rush. I'll see you Monday at school?"

"Oh, yeah. I'll be back Monday. Hopefully not looking like this." He pointed at his face and crossed his eyes to add a humorous effect.

At the open door, Michelle turned and curled her fingers up and over Wynn's strong shoulders. A wave of heat and tingles flooded up into his head. Smart enough to know when to kiss the girl, Wynn pulled her to him.

The moment he moved closer, she pressed a hand firmly against his chest. She smiled a 'wouldn't you like to have this' smile. Michelle turned to walk out to the street, leaving him bewildered, as intended.

*****

"Lacour!" The officer on duty at the station desk yelled through the door to the men's lavatory. "Detective, are you in here?"

The polished flat surfaces at right angles only intensified the contralto.

I can't even take a crap, he thought.

"No, I am most certainly *not* in here," he said. "I've left for the day, actually."

"When you return tomorrow, be sure to apologize to Chief Tolleson for not seeing him before you left."

Lacour waited for the slam of the heavy oak into the painted frame.

"Sure thing," he said to the empty restroom. At the end of a tiring shift, Lacour just wanted to make a quick stop for take-out. Then head home to his rented two room loft downtown.

"Excuse me, sir," he said, leaning into the glass-walled office as little as possible. "Is there something?"

"There is, Charles," the Chief said. "Please come in and sit down. This won't take but a minute, I'm sure. After all, you've already left for the day." A patronizing grin broke across Tolleson's five-o'clock shadow.

"There was an incident at one of the District schools yesterday. I believe D-7 High."

"I heard. Don't know any details," Lacour said.

"I'd appreciate it if you'd head out there first thing, before you come into the station. Save you over an hour driving."

"May I ask, why would we be getting involved in an internal

dispute at a school?" Lacour asked. "Wouldn't the District Superintendent's staff assign someone to investigate the matter?"

"Initially, they reported a brawl with minor injuries," the Chief said. "That's not what we're interested in. There's something else in the report. This flagged our link to the CrimeData network server. It's why I've asked for you personally."

Lacour leaned his head to the side, curious. He listened to his supervisor present the details.

"Shortly after the schoolyard disturbance," the Chief said, "a visitor maybe, or someone posing as a new student to the school, became irate and caused a scene upon her departure from the premises."

"Is there a description of this visitor?" Lacour asked.

Chief Tolleson leaned over his desk's glass top. It doubled as a secondary display for his office computer. He tapped the file icon along the center row of the day's work, and held a second to copy it. Along the upper right was the station roster. He tapped open the detectives' group which spiraled out to show each of the twenty-two names. With Lacour's wedge highlighted, he held another second for it to paste.

Immediately, the notification of the incoming file blinked in Charles' Nish. 'Female. Fifteen to twenty years. Long blonde. Long curly. Long extra. Blue. Blue-aqua. Anglo. Sixty to sixty-three inches. Tattoos none. Mods none. English with no accent.'

"You have my attention," Lacour said. "However, there's nothing here that leads me to believe it's the same girl from the mall. Could be any one of a thousand girls in Lochiel. Perhaps fifty in that one school."

"Read the section about the structural damage, the damage to the ceiling of the clinic."

'Possible use of explosives to destroy the gypsum ceiling, supporting framework and the roofing structure directly above the clinic office space. The reinforced flat roof was penetrated from the inside out. An ovoid rupture in the roofing material extends down to the office. Floor tile immediately below the ruptured ceiling are burned and/or pulverized. No obvious damage from heat or open flame. No smoke damage.'

"I can be there by zero seven hundred," Lacour said.

*****

Brigitte daydreamed of her husband home. She'd pretend they were together when she'd go out. The wife carried on a one-sided conversation with her imaginary spouse, her defense against the loneliness.

"Flight 917 now arriving from Cleveland at Gate F," the intercom blared.

Now that he was here, to walk through the airport door in the next fifteen minutes, her stomach burned.

This is going to be tough, she thought. *But if I'm—we're — going to hold our family together, this conversation has to happen. It's going to get worse before it gets better. But it will get better. The two hour car ride back to Lochiel will be the best time to do it. We'll do this before we get home and the kids start something, to vent their own frustrations his first day home.*

"Daddy! Daddy!"

A boisterous toddler shoved past Brigitte's knee. He ran headlong toward a goofy guy who emerged from the ramp onto the concourse. She turned around to find the mom. Arms crossed and face stoney, the woman chose baggy sweat pants, oversized sweatshirt, and plastic slippers over socks.

When the travel-weary husband moved in for a welcome home kiss, he got a cheek. The poor man's face said it all. "Welcome home, loser."

Lovely.

Brigitte caught her own reflection in a wall of polished glass tiles. Baggy clothes. Hair barely combed through. No make-up, nor anything remotely inviting about her.

Well, there you go, Brigitte. Hypocrite. Not Brigitte. Not anymore. Not me anymore. Not Mrs. Eric Dubroc, proud wife of the dashing and genius bio-med graduate. I've been reduced...to Jackie Matalon, pretend significant other to the make-believe Michael Matalon, the...the...I don't even know what my husband does anymore.

"I'm not even sure if I could find him if I tried," she said out loud. He'd never given her his current address in Cuyahoga Heights. Though he once sent a photo of a featureless apartment, rented furniture.

Over a hundred passengers disembarked from the plane. She searched through the crowd entering the terminal.

Maybe he changed his mind. He changed his mind. He doesn't want to come home. My own husband doesn't want to come home to me.

Another fifty passengers filed through the gate. Brigitte failed to recognize her mate of twenty years.

She moved sideways twice between the others waiting for their friends and kin, to keep a clear view of the emerging passengers. Brigitte's eyes flitted among the faces, desperate to make contact. Just as she didn't notice the man, aged and worn, he too searched the crowd for the young girl he'd left behind— the one he envisioned.

The woman waiting for him today, unable to catch his eye, measured so much less than she'd ever been. Like two strangers on a blind date, each one scanned the multitude of faces for a connection, be it even the shared hope of the lonely and lost.

When the last of Flight 917's human cargo sauntered across the threshold, the door closed. A gasp rose from deep within Brigitte's body, where disbelief and sadness hide together.

The idea of him not being where she needed him, when she needed him, hit her like the hot blast from an oven. She teetered back, rigid and ready to burst. Already off balance, she turned to leave, and bounced right into the back of a man.

"Oh, wow," she said. "I'm so sorry. Please excuse me."

"Hey, no problem—"

They stared at each other. The strong love, once tangible over any distance, now failed to span a few feet. Without a word spoken, Brigitte and Eric raised hands to interlace fingers as they had done since the first date. Foreheads pressed together, the connection sparked again, though dangerous feelings dived deep. Just to find each other in the same room proved difficult. Neither of them dared to start the dialogue, to hammer the wedge between them.

*****

Earlier that morning, Wynn begged, and even pleaded. He'd promised to pay her back. His mother finally relented. Brigitte loaned him her credit wire for the evening. Wynn's date with 'the most fantastic girl at school' would not be limited to a seventeen-year-old's meager budget.

As directed through his Nish, he found the Take-it-or-Leave-it vehicle he'd leased for the day. His mom being gone to pick up his dad at the airport, he walked the half mile to the maroon Peugeot four door swivel-back. The online agent app offered the choice of nearest vehicle to his location, or a preferred model further away.

"Looks like my grandmother's car," he said to his reflection in the driver's window. Wynn withdrew the credit wire from his wallet. Then dipped it into the receptacle attached to the meter module embedded into the driver's window frame.

"Welcome, Jacqueline Matalon," the car's interface said. "This vehicle is now linked to your account. Drive safely."

"Let's hope that doesn't happen all night." Wynn pressed four fingertips under the door sensor. With a sticky squeak, the driver's panel came out and up, to pivot up and over the front fender. A dark stain glistened where the previous client spilled soda on the threshold. Cloth upholstery on the rear bench seat shimmered with white dog or cat hair.

"You morons! I told you—*specifically* told you—no *animals!*"

The car started up without issues, and Wynn found it easy to pilot. Designed for rental fleets, the comfortable and slow machine used program code written to keep users out of trouble.

Sporting the latest revision to the urban-auto application, the Brazilian manufactured French import communicated directly with the traffic signal system. The Peugeot wouldn't run a red light if your life depended on it. A governor on the powerful electric motor reduced its output by fifty percent. The brakes activated themselves at the yellow traffic light, coming down hard after.

Halfway to Michelle's parents' home, the interface caused a warning icon to flash on the instrument panel. The audio accessory came on, but not with any song.

"Jacqueline Matalon," the digital voice said, "please activate your NowSeeHear or other registered TerraNet device." It blasted like a trombone with a French accent.

Wynn tapped his own to force a link up with the car's cpu. As a precaution against auto theft, the vehicle interface ignored any input other than that of the payee.

"Jacqueline Matalon, please activate your NowSeeHear or other registered TerraNet interactive device," the car warned. "You have thirty seconds to comply. Without driver authentication, the vehicle will cease function. Egress mechanisms will be disabled and the local authorities will be notified of a stolen vehicle."

"Mom!" Wynn snapped. With the holographic projection of his mother's face floating on the dashboard, he found it challenging to focus on the road ahead. "It's me. Hey could you help me out? Are you crying?"

"I'm fine, Wynn," Brigitte said over Wynn's Nish. "What's up?"

"The car is trying to contact you—the driver—you, to

authorize something. It can't detect your Nish in the car. This may not work. It's gonna shut down the car."

"Oh, okay," she said. "Hold on a sec." Eric and Brigitte mumbled back and forth about hacking a 2017 Hemi 'Cuda and "the last day of our no-kids trip to Hawaii."

"All right, Wynn," Brigitte said. "I'm sending you an email with an attachment."

"An email? What? Nobody gets those on—whoa—wait. Okay, I got it, something. Now what?"

"You do know how to open an email attachment, don't you?" she asked.

"Like I said, nobody—everybody uses iCloud Raindrops now."

"Just blink at the paperclip, Wynn," Brigitte said.

A few seconds later, the car's forward motion pulsed for a few seconds, then surged, like the engine experienced a miraculous doubling of horsepower.

"Jacqueline Matalon," the car's cpu said, "thank you for the insurance authentication. We apologize for any interruption in your Take-it-or-Leave-it vehicle rental service."

Whoa, that seriously worked, Wynn thought. *Every now and then mom or dad come up with some spectacular moves. Old people must learn something along the way.*

"Mom, that did it. Thanks for the insta-bail!" After a few long seconds of silence, the space before the windshield went clear. She'd already broken the link.

Except for the occasional stutter, the heaviness of the Peugeot disappeared, replaced with an eager and willing throttle. With only one major intersection to go before he reached

Michelle's neighborhood, Wynn stomped the pedal at the green light. Both front tires howled and sizzled. Putrid white smoke billowed out from under the front fender wells.

"No way!" he said. "Even Barry's uncle's Corvette won't do that."

At the edge of the driveway to her parent's home, Wynn pushed away all thoughts of squealing tires. He opted to roll in with a slow and careful manner, leaving far too much room between him and the family's retro hippie van. The odds were good Michelle's father would be watching at the window. He'd be waiting for the handsy little creep arriving to take his daughter out.

Walking to the front door, Wynn noticed the custom paint on the modern remake of the ancient German microbus. Giant purple and pink flowers. Make Love, Not War.

There's a good bet that does not apply to me and their daughter .

"Oh, Gordon!" Michelle said, overly dramatic. She burst from the front door and bounced out to land in his arms and bury her face in his neck. The protective father indeed watched her rehearsed scene. A rerun for him, only the boy was different.

"Hi, Michelle," Wynn said. "Are you ready to go?" With luck, he wouldn't have to actually meet the parents. Wynn tugged her towards the car, but she let go.

"Almost," she said. "Just need to put on some cologne. I can't decide between my two favorites. What would you like me to wear tonight, Gordon? Something elegant, or something sexy?"

Standing on the front porch, her parents within earshot, she swayed before him. Michelle's hands clasped behind her back with imitative innocence. The evening sun glinted orange and rose across her pouty smile.

This is why dad's best advice about women was for me to just become a castrated monk. Girls are mostly insane, beginning with insanely mesmerizing. He sucked in a deep breath.

"I would like you to wear...a coat. It's going to be a little chilly outside tonight."

Without so much as a blink of her lengthened and bleached eyelashes, Michelle grabbed his hand and pulled him through the entrance to the home.

"You must be Gordon Matalon." Wynn did not expect Michelle's father to be benign and mellow, dressed in a tie dyed t-shirt and cut-offs. Hairy legs ended at suntanned bare feet in hemp sandals. "I'm Tom Jean-Terese," the father said.

"Candy," the mother said, hands on hips except for a brief wave. "So, what are the plans for this evening? You know Missy has to be g-f—gluten free, right?"

Michelle tromped up the staircase, her complaint about the motherly advice muffled by the walls and corners.

"Um, well," Wynn said, "first we're going to the new exhibit at the Tumblr Vine Gallery in the mall."

"I hear that one's amazing," Candy said. "My Shao-Lin-Yoga club and I went to the grand opening. All the micro-indies were themed on the 2019 Saint Patrick's Day Massacre, and the subsequent KKK riots in Harrison."

"Okay...that's...far out..." Wynn said. Videos of blood in the streets and the tit-for-tat lynchings by evil men didn't appeal to him. "This one's about cars that still run on gasoline."

Michelle bounded down to the first floor, swinging a purse

and a sweater.

"Then dinner, I hope," she said. "I'll be starving by then. Of course all the vines have instream ads for the foodie-counters around the corner from the gallery. They pump the smell right into the mall."

"Olfactory advertising isn't anything new, Missy," Tom said. "When they still had theaters with seats, you know—like you'd actually go into it and sit for two hours—we'd use a paint brush to smear melted butter onto the air conditioning vents. Sold a lot of popcorn that way!"

Michelle shook her head at how her dad always wanted to be in on the conversation.

"The Vine Gallery and foodieness," Candy said. "Then what? It'll only be eight-thirty by then."

"Well," Wynn said, "that's where...I have a kind of a surprise."

The three of them stared at him, waiting. He'd hoped for some encouragement.

"I scored two tickets to see Haim," he said, "at the Houma Terrebonne Civic Center in Thibodaux."

Michelle screamed and jumped onto Wynn's shoulder.

"Isn't that down in Thibodaux?" Candy asked. She pretended to not know it was far away. Feigned uncertainty meant to dull the parental concern.

"That's what I was just saying," Wynn said.

"Haim is the bomb," Tom said. "Love, love, love those sisters...and Este's expressions!"

"Please tell me you're serious," Michelle said. "Say it again."

"We're going to the Haim concert. It's their 'Hands Off —

I'm Kidding' Tour."

"I'm thinking," Candy said, "since that's such a long drive, maybe we should—"

Tom interjected with a modest recommendation. The parents would use the Nish tracker app to keep tabs on their daughter. Tom explained this would be a first date in another city. His words drowned beneath Michelle's constant squeals of delight, and fawning over her date's excessive spending.

*****

The drive to the mall took only a few minutes. Wynn missed the entrance closest to the gallery, and had to take the long way back through the busy parking lot. Michelle talked non-stop the entire time. She never once asked a question, other than to finish her stated opinion with a 'you know?'

With a sigh of relief, Wynn spotted an empty parking space. He pressed on the accelerator, and the Peugeot leapt forward. Its battery controller allowed full flow of amperage into the high-torque motor. He missed the rear corner of the car to the left by mere inches.

"Be careful," Wynn heard in his ear.

"What? I'm sorry," Wynn said. "This isn't the car I'm used to."

"I didn't say anything," Michelle said.

Swinging a leg out, Wynn caught movement in the rearview mirror. Ahnim filled the reflection. Her face stolid, not a hair moved.

Is she really there, in the back seat? Did Michelle see her?

"Are you coming along, Boy Wonder?" Michelle asked.

Wynn stood next to the car, his eyes wide. He didn't dare look through the rear window.

"Lost you there for a sec," Michelle said.

They walked together across the parking lot and up onto the curb. He enjoyed the warmth and soft skin of her hand. Fingers tangled, they broke grins as they kept their gaze locked on the front door of the gallery. But Wynn's mind swam with thoughts of Ahnim.

Ahnim sat motionless in the rear seat of the Peugeot. Faced forward, she observed each motion, every touch of the two teens walking away. The photons bouncing off Wynn carried his scent, his vibration. They fell into her. Those from the other, the female, had a foul taste to them—a burning, like acid. Where the light from the young couple merged, there grew a dark seed in this child born of a singularity.

Ahnim's created heart flared with an emotion foreign to her sexless species. The Immini did possess personalities a human might describe as masculine and feminine, though not true gender. Individuals displayed varying degrees of polarity. Love did not occur with a pairing. In space, the Immini expressed oneness with the Joining. But Ahnim desired the forbidden long before she met Edwynn Dubroc. This human brought focus to her obsession.

The urgency—this longing of the star-child—stoked the fire within her. It swirled and struck deep, seeking a partner of her negative emotions. Through the eons of existence for the Immini, over the countless light years traveled across the galaxy, this one moment burned hot. A rented four door sedan rested on the surface of a mere spec amongst the stars. In the back seat, the first of the Immini experienced something mighty, something horrid.

Ahnim found jealousy to be a living hunger. And it fed on thoughts of revenge.

*****

Each of the two hundred 3D video displays in the mall's Tumblr gallery used the latest near-field technology. They focused the audio for a looping vine into an area for just four or five people to stand in. Techies labeled it as a Puff, or a local subset of the Cloud. The viewer must wear a Nish or similar TerraNet personal device. Strolling from video to video, the audio changed accordingly. Without your Nish tuned in, you'd only hear attendees laughing, their commentary, and occasional sniffles at a heartfelt micro-story.

Wynn and Michelle found themselves waiting their turn to press into a small crowd. The group didn't move on, but watched the same thirty seconds over again. Giggles turned to frowns, which turned to gasps of horror. People left shaking their heads, some in tears.

"Thissa got-see," Michelle said in SocioSpeak.

The two edged in until their Nish grabbed the signal from the Puff. On screen, the back and forth tempo of a game of ping pong. Capturing the action, a view from the steady camera angle at the outside corner of the net. A young lady with the ebony beauty of east Africa bent low, continuing to volley her opponent off screen. The girl wore the blue and green jersey of the Platinum Stars soccer club. A huge grin lit up her face.

The person holding the camera panned to the left. Careful rotation maintained point of view from the four inch tall net. To the amazement of the gallery crowd, the woman's cat perched on the opposite edge of the ping pong table. It batted the balls right back at her, wild eyes focused.

At about the halfway mark of the vine, a loud pounding at the front door of the woman's apartment startled everyone. Whoever stood outside demanded to be allowed in. Blurs and whispers followed. The three females in the room dashed to where their all-black burkas hung on hooks on the wall. Within three seconds, the girl holding the camera settled onto the couch between the other two. The old cellular phone recorded the scene. A door burst open, and three men with machine guns boldly entered the modest home.

"What were you doing?" one man screamed. English subtitles attended his arabic.

"Ping pong," said the tall woman, her voice calm and steady, emotionless.

The man turned violent, kicking the edge of the game table. It collapsed in a fragmented heap against the wall. The fearful cat struggled to drag itself out from under the broken particle board and aluminum tubing.

"You women should concern yourselves with your duties and your chores, not frivolous games. Or distractions that lead your weak minds to evil."

"Yes, sheik," she said. "Forgive me."

"And you certainly don't need the extravagance of a stupid pet!"

Gunfire.

Part of Wynn wanted to disbelieve the authenticity of such a brutal act caught on camera. It gave stage to hatred, and for a world that comforted itself with brave fantasies of actually doing something to stop it. Since the kidnapping, he understood the reality of how humans preyed upon one another. He wished to go back, to remain naive about such things.

"This series was supposed to be about old cars," he said.

"It's about oppression, Gordon," Michelle said. "You're talking about the advertisements for the gallery that highlighted just a couple of vines. They showed how the auto industry executives knew all along that carbon emissions poisoned the planet. Instead of making changes right away, they invested in companies that would later profit from the manufacture of emission-control devices. The worse the pollution got, the higher the demand for the anti-pollution products. So they waited, and worse, they colluded with the old Congress to delay the mandated restrictions. By the time the anti-pollution rules hit the car industry, they'd been purposely making cars with bigger engines even more hazardous to the environment."

Wynn did not expect to get lectured on the date, *from* his date. A long sigh accompanied his irritated facial expression.

"Hey," she said, turning him to her. "That last one was a real downer. You want the ones about cars? Let's go. The map shows the series starts on screen fourteen, right around the corner. Okay?"

Another crowd took their place, already to the part where the poor feline is decimated by the thug wielding a full-auto military weapon. Standing at the back of the gallery, Ahnim experienced each and every display simultaneously. In less than three minutes, she compiled the two hundred parallel streams of hate, suffering, slavery, abuse, and greed. Though she would never succeed in her registration as a high-school student, the past few days proved to bring all the painful education anyone would gladly forsake.

Wynn and Michelle continued to stroll about, taking in the various renditions of human oppression set to music, or theatrically portrayed. They made good use of the emotional filters that girded their young souls. Making an early escape from the harsh realities and amateur hype, they were off to find a good burger-to-go for the long drive down to Thibodaux.

The being from space, once so insulated there, became a girl of flesh, with human emotions. Ahnim stood frozen in the midst of thousands. Her new heart listened to the countless cries for help from the many tiny someones. Such widespread hate and violence could be managed, kept far from her beloved Wynn. Though it would require less restraint. None of this horror would ever reach him. She'd make sure of it.

*****

"I would've liked to have seen my children—our children," Eric said. The correction came too late to blunt the sarcasm. "They couldn't be here on my first day back?"

"Wynn has a date." Brigitte said. "Girl from school. Pretty."

"At least he's not running around with some girl who's going to get him beaten up."

"That's the one," Brigitte said.

"Are you kidding me? You let him—?"

"Let him? And who is this 'you' you're referring to?" Brigitte asked. "The *you* is supposed to be the two of us. It takes two parents, you know. That's the problem, Eric—he's going to be eighteen soon. When he *does* obey me, he's just being polite. It's not like he needs to be mothered much anymore."

"All right, sorry. I get it," Eric said.

Brigitte despised the quick back-stepping her husband often used. His words never made up for the previous stab. The hurts mounted, apologies faded.

"Do you?" she asked.

"He's growing into a man."

"So, you *don't* get it," Brigitte said. Eric cursed and spun on a heel. Only home for half an hour and already tired of losing the arguments. "Wynn is not a man, not yet. He's just a tall boy with big thoughts and blue balls. He needs an example—*your* example of what it means to be a man. You were there for him most of the time—I know! I'm not gonna beat you down for the job. You had a job to do, a career. You've always done your best to manage both ends of this. He's lost, Eric. Ever since—"

"Is he still—how's that going?"

"He sees the therapist once a week," Brigitte said.

"What does she have to say?" Eric asked.

"Nothing, of course," Brigitte said. "As if HIPAA wasn't bad enough, now we've got FOPP. I'm his parent, and I can barely get her to admit he does more than show up. Oh, but she sure as heck has something to say when he's late, which is pretty much every time."

"Okay, but, what about here at home? Still with the imaginary friend foolishness?"

"It's only foolishness to the rest of us who can't see her," she said.

"Oh, great!" Eric said. "Now he's got you believing it. Sure this isn't just some teenage undercover angel?"

"Please don't minimize this, Eric. I live with this every day. When he got beat up, I picked him up at school. We went to the clinic, right? They patch him up, and x-ray a few things. On the way home he pulls down the visor on his side and opens the mirror."

"How—what mirror?" Eric asked.

"The makeup mirror!" Brigitte snapped. "C'mon, you know the little one under the visor. Anyway, he's got it open, not so he can check for pimples, or his swollen lip, or anything normal. Oh heck no, he aims it to the back, so he can see the back seat."

"So?"

"So he *can see her* sitting in the frikkin' back seat, Eric! He smiled at her. And based on his expression, she either smiled back or flipped him the bird."

Eric sat speechless. He had plenty to say, but didn't like where the conversation headed. He envisioned himself as the typical dad, playing basketball, discussing motorcycles, food or something equally shallow.

But this pretend girlfriend nonsense, Eric thought. *And he has a real girlfriend. Why carry on with the imaginary thing?*

"I have to ask you about something else," Brigitte said. "I stumbled upon Nev's diary. She left it open on the bed while she showered. I hated myself for picking it up. You know how I am about that stuff. Anyway, I was...shocked...at what I read in there, for the last entry she'd made."

"Busted her, huh? She *experimenting*?"

"No, Eric. Her first—never mind. What I found was...she called you."

Eric sat down on the corner of their bed. To be seated was two steps from walking out. At least if he had to make both moves—standing and walking—he might stop himself from making another bad decision.

"So, who is she, Eric?" Brigitte asked.

"She's nobody," he said.

"Yeah, well, somebody's getting it, and it's not me."

"That's not how it's going down, honey."

"Steer clear of the whole 'honey' thing," she said. "That's not going to help right now."

Eric dropped his chin into his chest, rubbed at his temples. "Honestly, I—"

"Oh, yes, please do be honest," Brigitte said.

"I couldn't do it."

"Couldn't? Or wouldn't...what, Eric? What is it you aren't doing with this woman?"

"We're not doing anything! Here it is. I couldn't. When it all came together at her place—she invited me for dinner. I just stood there like an idiot, thinking about my wife and my family, and everything I have to lose. How I couldn't throw it all away, just to *feel* something."

"Yeah, cuz that's what idiots do, Eric. Stand butt naked with another woman, nothing on his mind but the wife and kids. Right!"

She wouldn't believe him, not at first. It wouldn't matter anyway. Brigitte wouldn't put up with this kind of mistake. She'd either leave him or she wouldn't. He had to take the chance that she'd believe the deeper truth of his actions.

*****

"I said," Michelle yelled into Wynn's ear, "I have to go to the bathroom."

The alt-rock band nearly halfway through their set, now was a good time for the two to head up to the mezzanine. He excused himself, moving to buy her a gift from one of the vendor stalls along the back wall. Wynn held their two lemonades and got in line, while Michelle blended into the darkness and bodies.

She assumed since they'd beaten the crowd to intermission, the line to the stalls wouldn't be long. As it was, four girls stood outside the entrance. Many more waited inside the restroom. Michelle's feet ached. The burger gurgled in defiance. Forty-five minutes of holding in the gas while next to her date wore out her patience.

Oh please, she thought. *Hurry up!* After a glance around, she walked off a quick toot out in the hallway. *Finally, and only a hundred other's to blame for the stink.*

Once she made it to the middle stall of the water closets, she found no paper on the last roll.

"Hey, psst," she said, bent over. "Can you pass me some wipe? I'm out."

The person in the stall next door ignored her. Reaching her arm under, Michelle felt up the inside wall of the partition to grab the loose tip of their roll. With a smooth pull she had all she needed to get the job done.

"Thanks for nothin' chicky-poo," she said. "Oh, by the way, nice boots!"

Michelle finished washing and drying her hands. She checked her makeup in the mirror over the sink, when she caught a glimpse of the red leather boots next to her. Her peripheral vision filled with a mountain of blonde curls over more red leather, waiting.

"Just wanted some off your roll, darlin'," Michelle said. "It wasn't a come-on."

Ahnim could calculate the gravitational stresses required to pull herself across the light-years. But she found herself wholly unprepared for a one-on-one confrontation in a girl's restroom. Borrowed humanity did provide for the clenched fists and ears burning red, like any fuming homosapien might display.

"Oh, now look at you," Michelle said. "You're the little freshman teasing Gordon and Barry in the cafeteria. What a coincidence. You just happened to be at the same concert as my boyfriend. You came a long way just to sulk in the corner, little one."

"Is he? Your boyfriend?" Ahnim asked.

"What, you gonna stalk him now? Can't hold his attention? Well, you can get all up in your furry little head, and make believe he's with you."

"I don't do make believe," Ahnim said, blushing at the lie.

"You know," Michelle said, "Little Orphan Annie, is it?"

"Ahnimgoyo—"

"You *are* pretty," Michelle said. She leaned closer, to attack in a whisper. So her adversary could feel the hot breath. "Almost pretty enough for him, but not quite."

Chapter Eleven

"Sid," Lorenzo said into his Nish. Seated at his home computer, his friend's head floating in front of the display screen irritated him. The icon pulsed ready. He blinked twice for off. Sid and his mouthful of after-school snack faded away. "You need to spec this. I sent you something about Matalon."

"Are you still all about that?" Sid asked. "You've got to quit freakin' out about him and Michelle. The badgies are finally off my back."

"You just get your Raindrop on line. I'm seein' this, but I need you to tell me I ain't crazy."

"I can tell you all about your crazy," Sid said. "There ain't no ain't about it!"

"You seein' it yet?" Lorenzo asked.

"Yeah, so what? What exactly is this? Some kid got yanked and holed by a couple of old pervs. How's that our problem?"

"That could be," Lorenzo said. "But look at the pic of the guy, Sid. Scroll down."

"Okay, so it sort of looks like Matalon. Hair's darker and a lot longer, though—"

"You're such a—ever heard of a cut and color? My mom gets

one every week."

"So again, why do I care?" Sid asked.

"Because Gordon Matalon is not who he says he is," Lorenzo said.

"How did you even come up with this?" Sid asked. "This is from almost a year ago."

"I ran Bloodhound on him. It doesn't even have a single detail about his life."

"Bloodhound," Sid said. "That's for digging up old pics of celebrities and babes, Lo. You ain't doublin' down on me, are you?"

"The app don't care what the name or gender is. It searches the newsfeed archives and any trash folders not emptied. Step A: scan a 2D image and a few seconds recorded from a Nish call projection. Step B: upload to the Cloud for the photometric algorithm to run. Step C: forward all the downloaded advertising crap to your parent's list of contacts. Step—"

"I know how it works, Lorenzo," Sid said. "So, you found pics of his face."

"Yeah, but then read the article around the pics. 'Lafayette Teen Missing For Week Found in Parent's Front Yard. Sixteen year old Edwynn Antoine Dubroc of Lafayette was discovered on the front lawn of his parent's posh home yesterday. Initially presumed dead, he later appeared to have only minor injuries. Taken by ambulance to Saint Ignace Medical Center in Baton Rouge shortly before noon. His parents, Brigitte Dubroc and Eric Dubroc stated he was in a coma...'"

"He gets out about two weeks later," Sid said. He'd skimmed ahead to the next page. "You're right, anyway, Lo. It's definitely him. And that's his mom. She showed up at the Badgie's office to pick him up after the beat down."

"I'm searching for the article about the investigation— can't find it," Lorenzo said. "I'll try one based on the journalist who wrote the first two articles. There's one where he goes missing, and the one when they find him. What's the reporter's name?"

"It's a fem, Lo," Sid said. "Hot one, too. But then aren't they all—Megan Li."

"Haven't seen the pic—whoa!"

"Now you did."

"Now I did," Lorenzo said. "Okay, so searching all articles...journalist Megan Li...plus Dubroc...nothing."

"Can't be nothing," Sid said. "They always do a follow-up story. It says in her first and second stories there's some kind of link to organized crime or espionage or some crap. They just don't let that kind of thing go."

"That's what I've been trying to tell you, Sid. I'm gonna call him."

"Call who—Matalon?" Sid asked.

"No, Sid," Lorenzo said. "I'm going to call Edwynn Dubroc."

"And what's that going to do that a beat down couldn't? You should just quit her. She's trouble, and you know it."

"Hold on," Lorenzo said. "His Nish just linked. He must be —"

*****

"Are you going to say something, Lorenzo?" Wynn asked. "Or are you going to just breathe heavy?" The audio system of the

Peugeot found the Nish signal, and amplified the conversation throughout the vehicle's ten speakers.

"Oh, I've got something to say this time, that's for sure. There's more to Gordon Matalon than what everyone sees."

"What are you talking about?" Wynn asked.

"When you were out with my girlfriend yesterday, did you tell her about your past?"

"The way I see it," Wynn said, "if I was out with Michelle, she isn't your girlfriend."

"We'll see about that. She may not be so willing to hang with you and the rest of the wipes at the stupid gallery if she knew who you *really* are."

Wynn tensed. Lorenzo's voice carried a confidence, cockiness. He pulled the rental car over to the side of the road and parked next to the curb. With four hours left on the contract, he'd use it up driving to his appointment with Doctor Fonteno.

Could he possibly know? No way. He's an idiot thug.

"I'm just the one who got the girl, Lorenzo," Wynn said.

"Seriously, Matalon? That the best you got? Or, should I say —Dubroc?"

During the Witness Reboot training, each family member practiced how to deal with this moment, should it ever come. Wynn remembered being told what to say, but he forgot the specific words.

Movement in the rear seat of the Peugeot startled him, exacerbated by the tension in Wynn's muscles and nervous jitters.

Ahnim reached a hand forward to rest on his shoulder. "You okay?" she asked.

Wynn shook his head. He blinked the Nish to mute. "No, I'm not okay. I'm on the Nish."

"I know, with Lorenzo Flores, from your school," Ahnim said. "He's the one who hurt you."

"Yeah, you know about that, huh?" Wynn asked.

"He's lucky I—never mind. It's been a challenge for me to not defend you."

"You still there, Edwynn, good buddy?" Lorenzo asked. "I know you are."

Ahnim huffed, like an angry person might. She climbed through the gap between the two front bucket seats to land with a bounce on the passenger side.

"He's mad about Michelle Jean-Terese," Ahnim said.

"Is there anything you don't already know?" Wynn asked. "Are you?"

"Am I what?" she asked.

"Are you mad…about...her?"

"Let's discuss that later," Ahnim said.

"What's his beef?"

"Beef?" Wynn asked.

"Your emotional stress is extremely elevated, Wynn. More so than would be if this was just an argument between jealous boys. Tell me what's wrong."

"Where are you learning your vocabulary?" Wynn asked.

"I watch reruns of Here's Lucy while you sleep. Now listen, you're going to be late for your appointment again. You need to get going."

Wynn checked the time. He rotated the Peugeot's motor actuator to Drive and pressed on the accelerator. Back on the road, he remembered what to do if his identity became compromised. With the Nish back off mute, he kept the conversation going. Then, he forwarded the link's metadata to the Witness Reboot Emergency Hotline. To do that and pilot the car through the busy downtown intersections proved risky.

"Lorenzo, I have a question for you," Wynn said.

"You haven't answered mine yet," Lorenzo replied. The car in the lane next to them honked and the driver shouted obscenities. The cars' side mirrors rubbed.

"I'll drive. You talk," Ahnim said. The servo for the driver's seat track ran fully backwards by itself. Ahnim pushed herself onto Wynn's lap. Even at a perfect size two, she barely fit between the steering wheel and Wynn's torso. She took the wheel and steered through the next few blocks without hitting anything, like she'd done it a hundred times.

"Maybe," Wynn said to Lorenzo, "some breath mints would help you with social interaction. It's got to be rough for you."

"You come here and suck one, you—"

"Don't change the subject, Flores. Did you know that Flores is Spanish for...what is it again? Oh, yeah, it's a word that means a dude even dudes won't date. What is that word, Flores? Oh, is it *pansy*?"

Car horns honked again. Ahnim's hair blocked any view of the traffic signals ahead.

"Oops," she said. "Okay, so that's *them* signaling *me*."

The sedan careened around a corner too fast. Wynn slid sideways onto the passenger seat. Ahnim held tight to the steering wheel and kept her foot down on the pedal. Wynn lost his place in the conversation. He meant to keep Lorenzo linked to his Nish while the authorities ran a trace. His head jammed against the passenger door's window, Wynn smiled with a wicked grin. She turned toward him, her own smile reaching to where her face curved into the shadows of the blonde mop. The car swerved a few more times, now far above the legal speed limit.

"You'd better watch where you're going!" Wynn said.

"You're the one who told me to look where I'm looking," she said. "Remember?"

"You and I know that, Ahnim, but the rest of the world is freaking out."

"So, Dubroc or Matalon," Lorenzo said, "or whoever you are —"

Wynn muted his Nish again. "I just heard the clicks from the fed's tracking system. They're listening in, likely tracking him now. He's screwed."

"Won't Michelle be interested," Lorenzo continued, "to know you're spending the day with your little freshman whore?"

"I heard that," Ahnim said. She turned her head around to the front, smile gone.

Wynn's Nish pulsed with a text message displayed across the top of the glowing projection.

"WR Failsafe activated. Team notified. Call tracked successfully. Cut link now."

"Are you mad?" Wynn asked her. The car slowed to a stop outside the psychotherapist's office. He swung the door up, got out and pulled it back down into place. He motioned to her through the window. With exaggerated worry, he asked again without words.

"I'll wait in the car," she replied.

*****

Ahnim watched Wynn go into the building, up the elevator and through the entrance to Fonteno's office. No matter how far away, his warmth reached to her. She laughed inwardly at her odd appreciation for the shape of his chest and abdomen.

There's no real sense to this, she thought—*not for an Immini. Humans are chemically motivated animals. It's not right for me to experience these bouts of loss every time he interacts with the other...the female.*

A tiny chirp brought her attention to the right. Wynn's Nish laid on the threshold between the passenger door panel and the side of the seat cushion. A couple of black spikes gently retrieved it, cradling the device as they retracted into the palm of her hand. Trying it on for the first time, she mused at Earth's affinity for technological accessories.

Their brains carry out all the same actions as this silly object. Why don't they just adapt themselves to what they want to do? Many of Earth's creatures have the bio-transceiver in their brains. Humans are capable of sending thoughts to each other should they choose. Horses and elephants do. Raptors use it to cause their prey to hold still for one second too long. But the humans—they wish for what they already possess.

Like a symphony conductor left alone with a toddler's xylophone, she piddled around with the rudimentary programming and links to the TerraNet Cloud. The metadata of the trace from Wynn's Nish to Lorenzo's lay buried just a few layers deep in the virtual mud. She dug it out.

*****

"Detective Lacour," the dispatcher said, "I'm going to link you to the net lab. One of the techs, Sharp—he says you'll be pleased."

"Thanks, Deb. I still owe you that frappé," Lacour said.

"Yes, you do," she said.

Lacour's Nish bleeped three times while the connection made.

"Lacour here. You have something for me?"

"It's me—Sharp. More hits on the trace for the little blonde. She just popped up on a private PC this time. She's standing right in front of the screen's camera now. The IP is showing as leased to Byte-Me Communications. Their account records list it as assigned to Flores, Myrna and Salvador. Street address is 9297 South Tempest Lane. That's in Fannett."

"I'm writing...Fannett..." Lacour mumbled.

"That's twenty minutes from your location, detective. Plenty of time for her to blast a hole through another roof. You should have Deb send—"

"—Deb send a car," Lacour said. He tensed with nervous excitement, their first live sighting of the darling terrorist. Caught on seven cameras at the mall gallery yesterday, two squad cars had arrived to search for her in vain.

"That's Jefferson County, right?" he asked. "Might they have a deputy in the neighborhood?"

"Deb would know," Sharp said. "Hey, someone else just walked into the room. High-school kid maybe. Whoa! Oh, no, detective! H-h-holy—!"

"What's going on? Sharp?" Lacour asked.

"Blondie just ran the kid through with a freakin' spear or something!"

"Spear? Are you sure you're seeing it right?" Lacour fumbled with the door handle of the car, frantic to get the cruiser started and rolling. "Sharp, are you still on line with the Flore's computer? Sharp!" The vehicle's electric motor whined as he mashed the pedal into the carpeted floorboard.

"Sorry, detective," Sharp said. "The last thing I saw was her taking the poor kid apart. My god, he was twice her size. She went right thru him—*literally* picked him up off his feet."

"What do you mean, 'the last thing'?" Lacour asked, bouncing. The chassis of the old police car strained to handle one hundred thirty miles per hour on the crappy road.

"She carried him—his pieces, anyway—out through the window. But the window wasn't open. The glass just melted. I don't know. Then she turned directly to the camera—*at me*. She used the spear, or whatever that was. Camera went black. Link to the IP was broken. I can't get it back."

"Okay. All right." Lacour said. "You did everything you could. Deb, are you on the line with us?"

"Right here, detective," she said.

"Where are we?" Lacour asked.

"Two Jefferson County units are en route—two minutes and six minutes. I'm trying to get the parents to answer now."

"Put me through when you do."

Chapter Twelve

Eight minutes after three, Wynn thought. *I certainly wouldn't want to disappoint dear Doctor Fonteno with my being on time. Like I've been on time for anything since…*

Oh you freaky, beautiful, nut-job alien…

"How did I get you as my guardian angel?" he asked into mid-air.

Fifty-eight. Fifty-nine. Nine minutes after three.

With a smug grin, Wynn tossed his bag on the chair and strolled to the couch. An exaggerated plop down elicited a groan from the few springs and decorated frame.

"Late as always, Mister Dubroc?" she asked.

"Consistent."

"And unnecessarily morose and sarcastic today," she said.

"All that brain-bending from a single word, doc? You *are* good."

Her eyelids lowered, Fonteno held on tight to the heavy sigh which billowed up from the frustration. She reached over to a small box on the end table. From inside she withdrew an electronic cigarette. After a brief moment to consider, she rolled her lip in resignation to the bad idea.

"I'd like to know, Wynn," she said, "just how messed up your life is that you'd bring this crap attitude to the session. Either you want me to call your parents and ask them to never send you back, or you've finally had enough of all the turds everyone's dumped on you, and you're ready to deal with it."

He sat up, his elbows on his knees. He stared directly into her eyes, his soul thick and solid.

I'm so sick of being Gordon Matalon.

"Fine," he said. "You want it? You can have it."

"Give it to me," she said. Fonteno blew a puff of steam from a long drag on the e-cig right into his face. "What makes you think you've got it rough, compared to the rest of humanity?"

"For starters, Gordon Matalon is the biggest loser in the universe. I can't even be me. I have to be him. He can't even talk to a girl without getting a beat down."

"But you're not Gordon Matalon," Fonteno said. "You're Edwynn Dub—" Wynn leapt to his feet. He reached behind him to his wallet. Yanked out his identification card. Surprising even himself, he hurled it at the wall over Fonteno's head. It left a slight nick in the paint before it bounced to the floor.

"Here! Then take the piece of—I don't want it anymore! I'd rather take my chances as a Dubroc. Stand up and fight those monsters. If they come again, I'll be ready. Me and Ahnim will tear them a new ass."

"You and Ahnim?" Fonteno asked.

Wynn stood in the center of the room, fuming, heart pounding. His breath whistled in and out of his nostrils as if he'd just ran a hundred yard dash.

"And..." he said, "I hate your stupid couch."

"I knew you would," Fonteno said. "I chose that one for your sessions."

"You—wait, what?" Wynn asked.

"I've got a whole room next-door full of stupid couches. Custom fit to piss off each and every one of my patients." She only had four to choose from, but the exaggerated statement emphasized her tactic. Often useful as motivation, she used it to break down difficult clients. "Now, tell me more about Ahnim."

Wynn's eyes burned holes in the gaudy fabric. He had permission to hate it. The fury expended, his mind turned back to Ahnim.

"That's the one," Wynn said.

"The one who's been by your side. The one who saved you in the boat. She gets it."

"Yes, she does," Wynn said.

"And as long as you have her, there's someone besides you who knows what you went through there. Someone who understands the pain and the fear."

"She was there," Wynn said. He turned slowly, put his foot against the edge of the chaise, and gave it a shove into the corner. "She gets it, all right. If it wasn't for her, I'd be dead, or worse."

"May I ask you a question?" Fonteno asked. She switched off the e-cig, dropped it into the box.

"Isn't that pretty much all you do, doc?" Wynn asked. "Is she here?"

"Ahnim?"

"Yes, is she with you?" Fonteno asked.

"Yeah, she's with me—probably more than I know. Even when I can't see her."

"Can I speak with her?" Fonteno asked.

"This should be good." Wynn smirked as Fonteno glanced around the room.

"Ahnim?" she called.

"Seriously?" Wynn said. "This ain't like rub a genie out of the bottle kind of thing."

"How do you do it then?" Fonteno asked.

"How about you wait till I go get her, assuming she'd be willing to have a chat with my brain bender."

"Where is she now?" Fonteno asked.

"She's waiting in the car. You don't have a waiting room up on this floor. And the main lobby of this building stinks like my grandmother's closet."

Fonteno smiled. It did. "So, would you go ask her if she'll come up?"

"I'll ask." Wynn walked out and took the elevator down.

I can't believe we're going to do this. Just so sick of pretending.

Ahnim sat behind the wheel, just as when he got out. He rapped on the glass, but no response. She stared straight ahead, almost in a trance. On her forehead hung a Nish just like his.

He patted his head and searched his pockets.

What'll she find in the Net? Nothing she can't find on her own, I'd imagine.

He rapped harder. This time he startled her. Ahnim smiled big and reached over to swing the door up.

"Done already?" Ahnim asked.

"She wants to meet you," Wynn said.

Ahnim nodded with a puzzled expression. Out of the car, she

met him on the sidewalk.

"You forgot to close your door," Wynn said.

The door lowered and retracted into the frame. "You've got some amazing powers, girl," he said.

"I got bored waiting," Ahnim said. "Read through the owner's manual. Did you know you can program any Peugeot to detect when you exit the vehicle, and then have it close it, lock it and run the windows up? The air-conditioning is now scheduled to start at 3:55 today."

"Okay, so you can read, big deal. I can make armpit farts. So what else did you do while I was gone?" he asked.

"Had to take a bed sheet filled with dead body parts to the landfill," Ahnim said.

And she's picked up some dry humor.

The two of them walked through the entrance to Fonteno's office. A half-dozen scenes played out in Wynn's head about how this might go, all of them bad.

Okay, this should be good practice for when she meets my folks. Wait, why would—? It's not like she's wife material. Can you marry an alien?

"Oh, hi!" Fonteno said. She expressed genuine surprise Wynn brought an actual person up to meet her. Jumping up out of her chair, they shook hands. "It's an honor to meet one of Wynn's friends. He's told me—Ahnim is it?—some things about you. I'd like to get to know you better."

"Hi," Ahnim said, "you can call me Anna."

The two teens stood together, hands in their pockets, embarrassed smiles.

"Wynn, my dear," Fonteno said, "why don't you retrieve the

stupid couch?" She made sure to lighten the directive with a wink and a nudge.

"So, Anna—or Ahnim—that's short for something, right?" Fonteno asked.

Ahnim looked sideways to Wynn for help. Like him, it excited her to get the truth out in the open.

"The name my family gave me is Ahnimgoyothalia."

"That's a—wow. And I complain about having to spell out Serene once a month. How did the two of you meet?"

"You're okay with her knowing?" Ahnim asked. Wynn nodded. His courage grew with Ahnim in the room. That, in itself, put his head and heart in conflict.

What could they do? Wynn thought. *Lock us both away in an insane asylum for what, collusion and alien abduction? I suppose the government might try to have Ahnim deported.*

"I hovered in a geostationary orbit over the Yucatan peninsula," Ahnim said. "Screams came from a tiny boat. I thought about going down to help, which for me is the same as doing it. Turns out I didn't fit inside the boat. By then it was too late, you know—for the boat. I encountered two evil minds there, in people—men. I'd never experienced anything so horrible before."

"What's that, Anna? What was so horrible?" Fonteno asked.

"Hate."

"From the two men?" Fonteno asked.

"Yes," Ahnim said. "They hated me, hated each other, hated Wynn—their whole lives, it seemed. Nothing about them, inside or out, was good. They cared about no one but themselves, and what they could take from anyone."

To the psychotherapist with decades of experience with children, this innocent and lovely young woman dictated the truth of her existence.

"Go on," Fonteno said. Her thumbnail dug into the skin on her other hand.

"It was my first time controlling the atmosphere of a planet, you know, and the seawater. Hindsight being what it is, I should've been a little more careful. I got enthusiastic about the opportunity to interact with...humans. The whole thing kind of got away from me."

"And that's when she found me," Wynn said.

"Were you in the boat? Sorry, dumb question." Fonteno said.

"There wasn't a lot left of the boat at that point," Wynn said. "I hid in the bench, in the mess."

"It was quite a mess?" Fonteno asked.

"No, yes, it was, but no," Wynn said. "I was in the kitchen — the mess. That's—"

"Understood," Fonteno said. "I don't go sailing often. Keep going. You found Wynn."

Ahnim sat with her hands clenched between her knees, staring at the rug. She appeared lost in thought, remembering the day. To his surprise, she lifted her hand to her nose to wipe away a tear. Her eyes full, she shook with nervous tension.

Fonteno reached over and popped a tissue from a nearby container, leaned forward and handed it to her. Ahnim stared at the object, frail and sheer fabric meant to carry away liquid evidence of sadness.

Immini did not shed tears. She shouldn't be crying.

"I lifted him—Wynn—lifted him from the box and the

wreckage of the craft. I held him for a while, not really sure what to do. I detected his damage, and I didn't want to make it worse. He was in a lot of pain from his finger."

"His finger," Fonteno inquired. "Was it broken?"

"Severed," Ahnim said. "The evil men cut it off with a knife. The pain and the fear inside of him—it was overwhelming for me."

Fonteno glanced at Wynn's hands. She'd heard from Brigitte Dubroc that Wynn insisted his finger had been injured during the kidnapping. No evidence of any trauma appeared in the medical report. The doctors examined him and found nothing.

"How was his pain and fear overwhelming to you, Anna?" Fonteno asked.

"I could, and I still can...feel everything he does." She met Fonteno's gaze. "We've made some kind of connection. It's something I can't explain."

"They call it love, my dear." Fonteno motioned for Wynn to approach her chair. She reached out and took Wynn's hand to inspect it. "Which one?"

Wynn pointed to the index finger.

"That one? Are you sure?" Fonteno asked.

"Yeah, I'm sure," he said. "It's hard to forget when somebody holds you down and removes your finger."

"But Wynn, the physicians have already done a full—"

"They didn't do *squat!*" he yelled. "Turn on some light and take a better look at it. The intern didn't care about anything but my nurse's boobs. He didn't even—look, doc—right there! This finger used to have a scar on the tip from when I was ten, whittling with my dad's pocket knife. The scar is gone because *it's a new finger*. Get it?"

Under the improved light of the table lamp set at full wattage, a hairline ring at the circumference of the middle joint became clear.

"It didn't occur to me," Ahnim said, "until we were on the way back to the coastline, that I should've retrieved it—the original. Where was it?" She stood and walked to Wynn's side, her hand caressed his shoulder as if to comfort him for the loss. "I made it three times before I got it right. It's a reversed copy of the one on the other hand, but new."

"Even the fingerprints are a mirror image of each other," Wynn said. "I downloaded an app that compares prints. It's an exact replica, just reversed. You can check it out if you want."

"You *made* this?" Fonteno asked. Ahnim nodded with enthusiasm, though melancholy.

"I don't...I'm sorry," Fonteno said.

"Of course you don't believe me—us," Wynn said. "Half of what happened those two days the cops labelled 'likely hallucinations caused by severe trauma', or some crap. You'd have a hard time coming to terms with reality, too. Try flying two-hundred miles an hour over the ocean in the arms of an interstellar, anti-matter sea urchin."

"Anti-photon," Ahnim corrected.

"Whatever," he said. His anger found a point of release, and Fonteno meant for that. But she struggled to come to terms with the information. "It was unreal, *and* it was real," he said. "It happened. You can either choose to accept it, or go get yourself some patient who sniffed too much glue. You can take *his* head apart. My point is, Doc...everyone assumes I've been just imagining...her."

Fonteno moved her gaze from Wynn to Ahnim. By all accounts, they experienced a shared delusion. She encountered this unique psychotic disorder once before. Twin brothers exhibited similar anti-social behavior. One certifiably insane, and the other unwilling to allow his sibling to endure a fractured life alone. He pretended to be schizophrenic.

"Anna," Fonteno asked, "where are you from?"

"Do you have a preferred frame of reference?" Ahnim asked.

"Okay, are you from Louisiana?"

Wynn turned and walked toward the wall, snickering. He ended up in front of a fake Andy Warhol print. He tried to appreciate the blaring colors and needless repetition.

"I'm not from this planet, if that's what you're getting at." Ahnim said.

"Right, then you're from where, outer space?" Fonteno asked.

"The human vocabulary is limited. To describe my natural environment using words like flying, or outer space, or hyper-something, isn't going to get you there. For instance, do you believe in ultraviolet light?"

"Of course," Fonteno admitted.

"Why do you? Can you see it?" Ahnim asked.

"It's a widely accepted fact there are wavelengths outside of the visible spectrum."

"Have you heard of dark matter and dark energy?" Ahnim asked her. She returned to her seat on the corner of the couch.

"Sure," Fonteno replied. "There's actually supposed to be more of that than the matter and energy we *can* interact with. But that's in between the galaxies, not near a planet. Our science can only detect the theoretical existence of those concentrations. The measurable effect of the visible matter doesn't account for all of the gravitational influence throughout the known universe."

Ahnim turned her head to speak to Wynn's back. "You said she was an idiot."

"So," Fonteno said, suppressing a smirk, "you're from where this dark matter is? It's not often I get to meet an extraterrestrial."

Ahnim reached her hand out toward the doctor. Her fingers became a black sheet of pure anti-photons. The liquid flowed across the space between them. It pierced right into Fonteno's chest and out the back of her chair.

"Can you feel that?" Ahnim asked. She stood and took two steps closer. The sheet morphed into a pillar the same diameter as her young girl's forearm.

"Yes, I can," Fonteno stuttered. "What are you doing to me?"

"I *am* dark matter," Ahnim said.

"Ahnim!" Wynn called. "This is getting freaky. Let her go."

"I'm not holding her. She's free to get up if she wants to."

"Oh, I knew this was a bad idea!" he said.

Ahnim withdrew the black probe from Fonteno, frozen in place.

"You," Ahnim said, whispering, less than a foot from the doctor's face. "You are a physician, a trained psychometric evaluation specialist. You seek the truth of what occurs in the minds of others."

Fonteno nodded from her place on the now soggy cushion. Pale fingers gripped the arms of the chair.

"I *am* telling you the truth," Ahnim continued. "No, ma'am,

I'm not from Louisiana. I'm not even from your precious 'outer space'. My first memories are of being spit out the south end of a black hole. After that, I'd guess my life is a lot like yours. Except that y'all make hashmarks on your calendars, like it matters how many times you've looped around the star, or pivoted on this lopsided—"

"Ahnim! We used up my half hour for today," Wynn said. "Let's let the lady off the hook for Earth's axis being off by twenty-three degrees, okay? It's kind of not her fault."

"Sorry," Ahnim said to Wynn. She turned back to see Fonteno ready to faint. "I'm sorry." She walked over to the window, pushed the heavy drape over to one side just enough to let some natural light in. "One thing I've learned about humans —you're all searching for the truth. But when you discover it, you're still not satisfied. What *is* right gets discarded and replaced with what you *want* to be right, or what you assumed before the search began."

Wynn headed out the door. He shot a psst at Ahnim to follow. She made it as far as the office doorway.

"Wait...wait..." Fonteno said. The lump in her throat choked back the words. "Please don't." Ahnim paused for her. "Please, Anna...leave Wynn alone. You can't do this. You should get out of his head."

"You know what?" Ahnim asked. "What you were just thinking right then? That's the best idea yet. We *should* just make our own truth."

Ahnim hurried to catch up to Wynn. He held the elevator door open for them.

"What was all that?" he asked. "I mean, did you have to stab her through with one of your arm things?"

Ahnim put Wynn off with a raised finger. Other noises captured her attention. She envisioned Wynn's near future, the next five or ten minutes.

"We're not getting out in the lobby," she said. The elevator car shuddered, then continued on to the garage in the building's basement. "There are men entering the building now. They have weapons, and in each of their Nish are images of me...some of you."

Her words stunned Wynn. Only a few minutes ago he stated how he'd be ready for a fight if someone came after him or his family again. His masculine side won the internal battle with any boy's natural cowardice.

"I'll protect you," he said. "Stay close." With an arm wrapped around her shoulders, he led her out into the garage. Their footsteps echoed off the concrete walls. A chill ran up the back of Wynn's neck. Ahnim sensed his tension. Though Ahnim could move the moon out of orbit should she choose, she developed an odd comfort, secure in the arms of this man.

"Just wait here," she said. "They'll follow us up the alley. Once they've all left, we can go to the car."

"Once who has left?" Wynn asked. "Can you tell who they are?"

"They're with the local police department," she said.

"Not—? Not—?"

"Not someone here to kidnap you. They're after me," Ahnim said. "They've chased us up into the next neighborhood —all except one. He's on the way to your brain bender."

"What do you mean 'they've chased us'?" Wynn asked.

"I've caused them to see us running away."

A quarter of a mile from the building, the image of the teenage couple running hand in hand showed only from behind. From any other angle, the hollow shell gleamed fluid and black.

"And *I'm* supposed to save *you*," he said.

Though the danger had passed, Wynn's strong arms encircled Ahnim, with her facing away from him. He enjoyed her warmth, softness. At that moment, she became human to Wynn. He lowered his face down into her hair.

I could hide in here.

"You did," Ahnim said. "You did save me."

She turned to face him. He wanted the embrace to not end, not yet. His hands ended up on the back of her neck, behind her shoulder. Her mouth a magnet, it drew him closer. Though Ahnim had no need for breath, she made some just for him, for that moment, and every moment after. He swam in knowing that. Her lips sparked a memory, bending to inhale the fragrance of a rose. The outer petals brushed him, alive, created for the sake of beauty alone.

"Now that I've got you," Wynn said, "I'm not quite sure what to do with you."

*****

On the fourth call attempt in twenty minutes, Serene Fonteno left Brigitte Dubroc a voicemail. If the wrong person intercepted the Nish-dot-vcl file, it might jeopardize her license to practice psychotherapy.

"Yes, Mrs. Dubroc, you've—darn! I mean, Mrs. Matalon.

Oh, I'm sorry, should I hang up? Can I cancel this? Brigitte, please call me as soon as you receive this. Edwynn is in serious danger. Oh, this is Doctor Serene Fonteno."

A pounding at the door to her reception office startled her.

She nervously swiped at her own Nish. She meant to prevent anyone from knowing she'd broken patient care protocols. In her mind loomed the haunting vision of the girl's arm turned black, a blade of dark electricity.

"Wait!" she screamed. "Brigitte, you've got to call me back right away."

"Open the door immediately," Lacour said. "This is the Lochiel Police Department."

"What do you want?" she said through the glass. "I'm in a session right now."

"I have a warrant to search the premises for a known terrorist."

"I can tell you there are no—"

"Her name is Anna Lumiere," Lacour said. "She may be using that name or similar alias."

The door opened. Fonteno stood aside, shaking.

"The person you're looking for," she said, "I believe she may have been here."

Lacour stepped into the room. He waved a hand at the doctor to cut her off. Without another word he stalked through the reception office and into the therapy lounges. He glanced up at the ceiling. No gaping holes.

With a blink command to his Nish, it projected a strong and life-size 3D holographic image. A petite female appeared in a lavender denim jacket, white jeans, bright yellow deck shoes and a waterfall of golden curls. The girl walked through a crowded area. Legs and feet fluttered in the periphery of the camera's cropped viewpoint. Lacour steadied himself, so the semi-transparent glow wouldn't bounce or sink into the hardwood floor.

"Do you recognize this person?" he asked.

"Yes," Fonteno said. "That's her, his girlfriend, Anna. They just left about five minutes ago."

"Whose girlfriend?" he asked.

"Edwynn—Gordon—wait. I'm bound by regulations governing doctor-patient confidentiality. I cannot divulge who my patient is."

"The girl is not your patient?" He didn't bother to wait for her to shake her head. "Then, you can tell me about her. Why was she here?"

"I didn't expect her to be a real person. I assumed she— that the name was just an illusion, a figment of someone's imagination. When they came up together, I was quite nearly at a loss for words. The last thing for her to be—wait. I'm sorry. I need to sort this out."

"She's a wanted criminal," Lacour said. He took one small but direct step toward her, closing the gap. Fonteno used the technique herself to intimidate clients on the verge of becoming violent. She crossed her arms under her chest, and circled around behind the detective. In being protective of Wynn, she found herself having to guard her words about Anna.

"I haven't seen any evidence she could be a terrorist." Fonteno recalled the black spike through her torso. She couldn't deny that act as violent, violating. But no pain, only touch. As if this person, this Ahnimgoyothalia, connected with another person to such a degree even their very molecules were something to caress. "She didn't hurt me. She was invited in."

"You were lucky. I'm relieved she didn't harm anyone here. Did she speak with you?"

"Yes," Fonteno said.

"Why was she here?" he asked.

"My patient needed to make some progress—is making progress. Introducing me to her was the next step."

"And now that you've met her? What is the next step— for you, of course. I realize you cannot discuss the patient."

Lacour perused the office. With an app in his Nish, he took snapshots of the notebook on her desk. Images sent to the police lab, technicians zoomed in to dissect the doctor's scribbling about one Edwynn Du—something.

"As far as she goes," Fonteno said, "I must determine whether or not she's a risk to my patient."

"It certainly sounded that way in the message you were leaving. What's so urgent that a Mrs. Matalon should know about a danger to...her son, maybe? You're refusing to divulge pertinent information about a criminally violent fugitive."

Fonteno unwittingly backed herself into the corner of the office, as well as her fears for Wynn.

"If I tell you about the girl," Fonteno said, "you must promise me you'll do everything you can to protect him— protect Wynn. He's been through so much already. I'm afraid this girl has preyed upon his vulnerabilities."

"I have no interest in making your patient's life more difficult," Lacour said. Fonteno considered whether to back down or pretend she hadn't notice the lie.

"How'd you know she was here?" Fonteno asked.

"We've been tracking her for the past few days. She's carried out destructive acts in locations to cause harm to larger groups of people, like school children. The traffic cameras detected a person matching her description. She caused a disruption and near collision about a half mile from here. Then she was captured by the lobby and elevator cameras of this office complex."

"Perhaps the best thing," Fonteno said, "the right thing to do for my patient...is to help you before she does something to harm him."

*****

The four uniformed officers ran together up the alley of the commercial district. They should have closed in on the fugitives. The farther they chased, the less they gained on them. At the crest of the hill ahead, the young couple paused to tempt the police. Neither showed any signs of tiring, let alone perspiration. Giddy expressions lit their faces. As they turned to dash around the corner of a building, the girl's radiant expression centered on full lips pressing outward.

*****

Hidden in the shadows, Ahnim and Wynn explored every possible way to kiss. His mouth grew sore and though he wouldn't admit it, she'd exhausted his tongue. He came up for air to the dark and musty reality of the parking garage.

"Um...wow!" he said.

"Wow is a good word for this." Her arms draped around his neck, she pulled herself up again to where they were face to face, her feet dangling a foot off the ground.

She's impossibly light, he thought, *yet so strong.*

*****

Winded and frustrated, the four pursuing cops paused to rethink the situation. One went back to get a cruiser. The two in the worst shape would turn right. They'd attempt to cut off the couple if they turned back toward their own vehicle. Officer Johnson, the athletic one, would resume the chase.

*****

Ahnim's legs wrapped around Wynn's waist. The rubber soles of her shoes squeaked on the smooth wall as she hooked them together behind his butt. That brought a huge grin to her face, and a good reason to dive in for another deep kiss.

*****

Officer Johnson slowed from a sprint to a jog. The kids, hand in hand, loped about fifty yards ahead. Around him, the tall grass and weeds crackled in flames. The couple took this path only a minute before. Bare earth burned hot beneath his shoes. A swath of overgrown foliage laid charred, as if a streak of lightning ran across the ground to where the couple now stood. And there they were, ignoring him. A mirage, shimmering, locked in a lovers' embrace. His view closer, the two bodies flowed together like melted wax.

*****

Wynn focused his complete attention on where their two bodies met. His hands touched more than skin, he tasted more than her flavor. At some level, his own cells merged with hers. Ahnim's surface inundated his own. Her particles washed through the fabric of his clothing. They mingled into his outermost layers of flesh. She met his body with her living light made fluid. He lost himself in the girl, with no desire to be found. They marveled at each other and the miracle of two made one.

*****

"Mom, it's me again," Nev said. "I'm sorry to bother you. I know you and—that Dad is home. You guys have stuff to discuss and all. Trying to give you your space for the day. Still need a ride though! Stuck here at the pharmacy. Scooter's dead at school. Maribeth drove off while I waited in line. Okay, I'll try Wynn. He may still have that rental car. Bye."

Nev walked back into the cool of the superstore. She figured one way or the other, it'd be an hour before someone gave her a ride home.

Home, she thought. *Not exactly where I want to be either. That should be fun, walking into that fat glob of tension between the alcoholic mom and cheating dad.*

"What does that mean, Daddy?" a toddler said. The child's tenor pierced Nev's clouded mind. It pulled her up from the depressed place she found herself.

Nev noticed a small crowd gathered in front of a wide video screen. It served the lounge area of a coffee house nestled along the inside front wall. At least fifteen people stood together, plus the baristas who'd given up trying to serve the distracted clients. Everyone glued their eyes to the newsfeed. A few discussed some recent development. Adults stood pale with fright as the news anchor repeated the terrible message.

"Farmers express grave concern over the situation," came the narrative. Images of groves and irrigated fields. Many contained the same odd, white boxes in the frame. "Here's our Natural Science Expert, Doctor Logan Forbes to tell us more."

"You're right, Janice," Forbes said on the screen, "the entire agricultural industry is reeling over this incomprehensible blow to mother nature. Investigative sources tell us the phenomenon has now been confirmed as more than just here in the GC-Four, but actually a global pandemic."

Nev sidled up next to a young woman her own age. The girl had shaved one side of her head. In place of hair, a high-quality tattoo of Edvard Munch's painting, The Scream. Deep reds and blues flowed down the nape of her neck. The girl smirked a bit as she sensed yet another person staring.

"Some pretty fragg licks, donya?" the girl said sideways to Nev. Her eyebrows flicked toward the videos. Dropped out of school as a freshman, the girl's SocioSpeak failed.

"N'up yet. Gives?" Nev asked.

"The bees," the girl said. "All gone. We're so screwed."

"Bees?" Nev watched the screen as it split into three separate feeds from around the globe. Everywhere, people panicked. It didn't make sense at first. Flashes of military intervention, riots, hazmat teams taking samples in an orchard. Box after box of dead bees, millions...billions...each and every bee colony opened bore the same microcosm of genocidal horror.

Not a single bee survived on the entire planet.

Chants and yells on one of the newsfeeds caught Nev's attention to the right. The reporter covering the scene directed the cameraman to zoom out and pan right. A couple dozen protestors picketed, hoping for their message to be carried on network media.

"So, Logan," the news journalist said on the screen. Sudden concern pushed the smile from her face. "What does this mean for us? Isn't pollination involved somehow?"

"Yes, of course, Janice," the reporter said. "Although several other species of insect pollinate the individual plants that give us produce, none come close to the efficiency of the honeybee. But this extends far beyond fruits and vegetables. For instance, ninety percent of alfalfa hay is used to feed the dairy cows, livestock for beef, sheep for wool, goats for milk, cheese and affordable leather. Its existence depends on the honeybee to germinate for the next season. Without them, it's only a matter of time before our agricultural ecosystem grinds to a halt."

"Consumers should expect an increase at the grocery store register, then?"

"Yes, that's true in the short term—" The view of Logan Forbes blurred as the camera knocked to the side. Within a minute, it became clear several members of the mob wrestled the equipment away from the news team. A bearded man wearing a ragged t-shirt with the peace symbol stood centered in the unsteady frame of the video recording device.

"People of Earth," he said, suppressing a grin, "today we bring to you the prophetic words of the universally revered man, Albert Einstein. 'If the bee disappeared off the surface of the globe, then man would have only four years of life left. No more bees, no more pollination, no more plants, no more animals, no more man.' So heed his warning," the bearded man continued. "The last harvests are upon us. Next year will be the last of the fruit. After that the wildflowers will shine in their glory no more. Then your farms and ranches will be themselves harvested by the banks demanding their repayment. In the final harvest, man will chase down his neighbor, as the only thing left to eat will be each other."

A few cheers and several jeers erupted off screen. The hairy man who co-opted the handheld microphone only memorized that much of his speech. His thirty seconds of fame came to an end as a cowboy boot flew in from behind the camera. The thick heel bounced off his forehead. Three county sheriff deputies rushed in to take him down.

As the camera laid on its side in the dirt, the excitement ended with a dusty view of feet trampling in the scuffle.

"Heck, don't arrest him," the tattooed girl's father said. "Give him a job as a decent news reporter!"

About half in the coffee shop crowd laughed in nervous agreement.

"Yeah," tattooed girl said, "but what if he's right? What then? You know what they say: 'cannibalism starts at home.'"

The dad shot a well-worn glare at the disappointing daughter.

Ain't that the truth, Nev thought.

"Are you gonna answer or not?" Wynn's voice yelled in Nev's Nish.

"Oh, sorry," she said. "Dunrong. Didn't hear your ring over the noise."

"Perhaps if your ringtone for me wasn't that loop you made of me snoring while hung over, you'd be able to—"

"And thank you for calling me back," she said. "I need a ride."

"Call mom," Wynn said.

"Did, of course. Ziff-I'ma Nish-u onna firsty?"

"Please," Wynn said, "just speak like a human. I'm so sick of —"

"If you ever want to become employable, you'll have to learn it," Nev said.

"What did mom say?" Wynn asked. "How long before she can be to you?"

"She didn't. I've left like a hundred—"

"—two."

"Four!—messages," Nev said. "I'm stuck here at Tar-jay's."

Wynn pictured her location. "Way up on Cosmo? Okay, we'll cut over on Little Bowl Road. Hopefully the 'on-homes' won't be bumper-to-bumper. We can make up time."

"Oh, nice try, brother. That one's from about sixth grade vocabulary list. Who're you trying to impress?"

And, who is this 'we'? Nev wondered.

Chapter Thirteen

The real Wynn and Ahnim giggled as they peered from behind a massive recycling truck in the alleyway.

Fonteno stood waiting by the passenger door of a blue four-door sedan, the unmarked police car. Lacour never did come around to open the door for her. He climbed in his side, preparing to drive away. Fonteno yanked up on the car door before lowering herself into the police cruiser.

"This could be bad," Wynn said.

"Then why are you laughing about it?" Ahnim asked.

"I was laughing because you were laughing. Why were you laughing?"

"I was laughing because I could easily make us both invisible," she said. "But hiding and peeking around corners together is way too much fun."

Lacour discovered the nearby rental car under the name of the patient's mother. A link to the manufacturer's remote control system should have allowed him to disable the vehicle where it sat. But the day before, Wynn unknowingly bypassed many safety protocols within the car's cpu with Brigitte's intrusive email virus.

With the police gone, the young couple emerged from their hiding place in the garage. Back in the Peugeot, the car moved out smartly as Wynn pressed down a fraction of an inch on the accelerator.

"Finally!" he said.

"Finally, what?" Ahnim asked. She rode in the rear seat to keep her arms wrapped around his neck. And he grew fond of the feel of her hands.

"Finally, I get to drive in the ride-share lane." With no traffic ahead of him on the bridges, Wynn sped up. The governor should've kept the velocity at one-hundred-four percent of the posted speed limit. A hum from the electric motor under the hood grew louder under the strain and wind resistance. The air outside tore at the side mirrors, and through the cooling intake along the smooth front facia. They arrived in the parking lot of Tar-jay's in half the time traffic laws would've allowed.

"There she is," Ahnim said. She pointed to the slim girl in a cream sweater. Nev stood alone between a red-brick column and a haphazard pile of faded red concrete spheres.

"Got it." He skidded the car to a stop directly in front of her, the anti-lock braking system apparently no longer operative.

Nev climbed into the passenger side of the front seat. She glanced over her shoulder. The girl in the car was not Michelle Jean-Terese.

"Are you going to introduce me to your new friend?" Nev asked.

"Nev, this is Anna. Anna—"

"Hi, Anna," Nev said. "You go to D-7? Don't remember seeing you there."

"No, I checked it out," Ahnim said. "Not so sure it's the best fit for me."

"Yeah, well, maybe *you* get a choice," Nev said.

They ran out of conversation shortly after pulling away from the superstore. Nev began to speak of an incidental topic. But one of Ahnim's hands slid down under the front of Wynn's shirt collar. Her fingers traced the hills and valleys of his neck muscles and clavicle.

"Bender day today?" Nev asked, her gaze avoiding the lovers.

"Yep," Wynn said.

"How'd that go? Usual twenty-four minutes of pretending everything's okay?"

"Actually, no. This time I introduced her to my imaginary friend."

Nev squared to her brother. She nodded toward the back seat passenger.

"Sure you want Anna to find out about things on the first date?" Nev asked. "The consequences extend beyond you, don't forget."

"Oh yeah," Wynn said, "she's known about that since the beginning." Nev rotated her head around to get a clear view of the face behind them. Ahnim pulled in close to whisper something into Wynn's ear. He nodded, then laughed more than he had in the past six months.

"Do I get to know what's—?" Nev asked.

"*I am* his imaginary friend," Ahnim said.

"Oh, I get it," Nev said. "You two set up the brain bender with the whole 'real-life-not-so-invisible-girl' thing. Bet *that* pissed her off."

"She had a hard time believing the whole extraterrestrial angle," Wynn said.

"So now we're not from planet Earth?" Nev asked.

"You are," Ahnim said.

"Have you figured that out yet?" Wynn asked Ahnim. "I mean, using our star charts, not your 'up that way' silliness. Which constellation?"

"Originally, Sagittarius, but now—hold on." Ahnim ran the window all the way open. She climbed halfway out to perch her butt on the sill. Roar of the wind at seventy miles an hour buffeted the car's interior. Her hair blew in all directions, but Ahnim's clothes didn't move in the wind. The jacket stayed steady as if she were indoors.

Nev leaned over close to Wynn. "Where did you find this nut, in a freakin' squirrel's nest?"

After staring up past the Sun, Ahnim came back inside the window, to squat on the seat.

"Definitely not Sagittarius, much further out, in Telescopium," she said. "But I did grab onto Antares for a better pull on the way here. That's one healthy star! Only been past a few like that since—"

Wynn turned back to look at Ahnim. Suddenly, a three-ton plumber's service truck pulled out in front, too late for Wynn to swerve or slow down. With the safety sensors deactivated, the rental couldn't deploy the auto-braking system. The Peugeot slammed first into the iron and plastic pipes sticking six feet out the back of the truck. Several penetrated the windshield, then curled off in different directions. Crackling and squealing, they burst across the car's interior in a fraction of a second.

One of the pipes went down across the top of the dashboard, into and through Nev's chest. It impaled her front to back, with the jagged end of the white pvc sticking through the back of the front seat, and into the rear cushion. The passenger airbag only made things worse. With incredible force, it burst from the padded area above the glovebox. Inflating upwards to the ceiling, it took the pipe and Nev with it. Her forehead slammed into the headliner with enough force to snap her neck.

Seven supplemental restraints enveloped Wynn on the driver's side. His feet flew up and under the dashboard. The seatbelt and shoulder harness prevented him from anything but minor injuries.

Braced against the upright portion of the front seat, Ahnim bounced around like a balloon. She came to rest on hands and knees on the rear cushion. Lifting her face from the velour, her gaze fell where the bloody pipe poked through from the front, exactly where Nev's heart would be.

A massive tool chest in the bed of the truck, weighing more than five hundred pounds, tore loose at the moment of impact. As the back end of the truck fell down from the rebound of the collision, the heavy steel box with all it's contents fell toward the windshield of the Peugeot. In a millisecond, Ahnim calculated its trajectory would bring it down on top of Wynn. It had to be stopped or redirected.

With focus, she pressed out against time and space within the confines of the car. Shards of glass came to a halt in midair. All sound and motion ceased. The spray of Nev's blood hung in a cone-shaped, crimson cloud. Ahnim moved at light-speed. Her blurred form reached the inside of the windshield before the roiling tool chest outside. With time stopped in the car, she couldn't reach her matter-energy reserves hidden in orbit above, where her true self floated in the shadow of the moon. She struck with what power she had on tap in the moment.

From outside the car, a searing white flash erupted outward from the glass. It vaporized the huge metal box and everything in it, around it, behind it. The last four feet of the truck turned to black smoke. A fireball of diesel fumes billowed skyward. The forward half of the bed and the quad-cab dropped to the street, tossing a shower of sparks.

A young family on the sidewalk flinched sideways at the nearby crunch of metal and plastic. They turned just in time for the silver car to smash into a long white truck. A small star exploded between the two, all in three-tenths of a second. The flash blinded them. Incapacitated for the moment, the father groped around, calling for his wife and child.

A minute later, the car drove up the street again, in a strangely prolonged déjà-vu.

*****

Nev leaned over close to Wynn. "Where did you find this nut, in a freakin' squirrel's nest?"

Ahnim let herself fall out the window. She tumbled onto her feet and dashed forward, in a super-human sprint to far ahead of the Peugeot.

"Oh, *crap!* She fell out the window!" Nev screamed. "Stop the car!"

Out Wynn's side window—no Ahnim. Nev stared wide-eyed straight ahead. The blonde in the purple jacket and white pants stood alone in the crosswalk, just at the intersection. A large plumbing service truck turned in right behind her. The driver had run the red light. Shaking her head with disdain, the swishing pile of gold hair bounced a half-tempo behind the back and forth swing of her dainty chin.

Wynn crept the car up to her, to stop just shy of her knees. Her lemon yellow shoe tapped with impatience on the asphalt.

"Are you insane?" Nev yelled out after her door lifted up.

Ahnim strode up to her, ducked down a bit inside of the car. In the center of the windshield, the glass warped. In the front of Nev's shirt, just between her breasts, a bloody hole matched the one in the back.

"Just so we're clear on this," Ahnim said, a petite thumb jabbed toward Wynn. "*He's* the one going to the brain bender. I just went along to make sure he didn't say or do anything crazy."

"What just happened?" Wynn asked. "Did I fall asleep? I swear we were just in a car accident. Did I dream that? The airbags went off and everything. My shins are sore. My face," he said, poking at his reddened cheeks and puffy lips, "feels like I took a good slap. And what is *up* with the windshield?"

"I'm not so good, actually," Nev said. "*Oh, no-no-no! I'm bleeding!*" She dabbed around the hole in her shirt, still a bit damp from the previous impalement and loss of her life's blood. Her eyes glazed over, and her head bobbled.

"I put everything back," Ahnim said to Nev. "There was a lot to do. May have gotten a few things out of order. Sorry. Are you in any pain? Try taking a few deep breaths."

"Ahnim?" Wynn asked. "What exactly happened just now?"

"See that truck with all the pipes and stuff hanging off the back—way up there at the next light?"

"Barely," Wynn said. He strained to focus at the quarter mile distance. "What about it?"

"Hey!" called a voice from behind Ahnim. The young couple pushed their baby stroller, stopping at the edge of the curb. The husband glanced at his wife. She held him tight around the elbow for a brief moment before letting go. He stepped down to the street to approach the car.

"Was that for real?" he asked. "I mean, that whole thing came out of a science fiction movie or something." He inched forward, his body tense as he peered in over Ahnim's shoulder. "You!" he said, pointing at Nev. "You should be dead! There's no way. There's no way."

"It's all right, sir," Ahnim said. The car behind them wanted to get through the green light. A few polite honks of the horn signaled them to wrap up the conversation.

"Oh no, it isn't okay," the pedestrian said. "This car got destroyed by some kind of bomb or something when it hit that truck. And then you," he said, now pointing at Ahnim. "You were the only thing left. You were standing right there, right where it exploded! You can't be—are you for real?"

"No!" Wynn yelled from his place in the driver's seat. "She's not! That's what I've been trying to tell everybody!"

Ahnim leaned back in over Nev. She caught Wynn's eye and they shared a long smile, a knowing look.

"Correction," Wynn continued, "she's the most real thing in the made-up world of Gordon Matalon."

The honk of the car horn behind them became a persistent howl. Satisfied that the hole in her shirt went no further, Nev reached for Ahnim.

"Anna, who are you...really?" she asked.

Ahnim turned toward the back of the car, waved her hand sharply at the driver to stop honking and just go around. He did. Distant sirens caught the attention of the three teens and the bystanders. Cars from the police and the GC-Four Counter Terrorism Unit rushed toward them.

Chapter Fourteen

Ahnim made a game of it. Wynn had told her, "Just comply with them. Don't do anything, you know—"

"—nuts," Nev finished for him, just as the three were separated in the hallway of the police station.

Ahnim sat alone in the interrogation room of the police department, handcuffed to the table. Not handcuffed in any true sense. She held up her wrists to where they'd be in view of the hidden cameras, then purposely destabilize the anti-photons in each forearm. The black ceramic cuffs dropped to her lap. She slipped her hands back in, and did it again.

With Wynn alone in the room down the hall, she copied herself and went to him. She remained invisible, even to him. Her hand reaching forward, she walked her finger tips up his arm. Shallow dimples in his flesh matched the slight pressure. At his elbow, she appeared to him in the frequency of light she'd used at his family's home.

"What's a boy like you doing in a place like this?" she asked.

"Very funny," he said. "They confiscated my Nish. Won't take much to hack it."

She appeared pensive, her eyes rolled up in her head. "They

haven't tried yet. It's still sitting on some guy's desk, next to Nev's."

"They scanned my prints already. You?" Wynn asked.

"They certainly tried," she said, laughing. "First, I made them all identical. Then, I randomly made one blank, then this one, then that one..."

"Not sticking to the whole 'don't do anything nuts'," he said.

"You should've seen their faces when they came back, *completely* irate," she said, satisfied.

"And why were the authorities irate with you, Ahnim?"

"When I finally *did* give them a full set of actual fingerprints, they were like, 'Now we're getting somewhere.' Then the guy says, 'Osama bin Laden! What the hell?'"

"You're playing with them," Wynn said. "Please don't. We're in enough trouble right now."

Ahnim moved past the table and wrapped her arms around his neck. She leaned her chin on his ear. Again, he lost himself in her natural perfume. A mix of fresh-baked breads changed to the faintest of exotic perfumes.

A click of the door handle broke him free of the trance. Ahnim disappeared.

"First," Detective Charles Lacour said, "I owe you an apology."

Lacour placed the flat digital e-folder down on the table with care. Then took his time to remove his suit coat, draping it over the back of the chair on his side.

"How's that?" Wynn asked.

"In truth, you are not Gordon Matalon, the accomplice, as I earlier presumed. You are in fact, Edwynn Dubroc. Previously under the care of the federal government's witness protection program as case number 3483457. Identity assignment is three of four, to be granted operational privilege, so as to remain safe...from what?"

"You'll have to tell me," Wynn said. "Not something we discussed at the dinner table. May I please have my Nish back? I'd like to contact my parents."

"We will make appropriate communications as necessary," Lacour said.

"So, that's a no—"

"Article 226, do you know what that is, Edwynn?" Lacour asked.

"No, sir."

"Under Russian law," Lacour said, "their intelligence community is bound by a document titled Criminal Procedure Law of the Federation of Russian States. Three hundred and forty-five pages in that manual. I had to read it, study it, be tested on it, to get my previous job. There are two hundred and twenty-five formal Articles in the document. Those articles explain what is, and what is not allowed by the staff, in the performance of their duties. If someone under that command violates any of the two hundred twenty-five rules, they are in deep trouble."

"I'm not following," Wynn said.

"However, it is known in that community, someone might take action against say, a foreign power, or a business with valuable information, or a family—an uncooperative family. They follow the rule *not* documented. And that my young man, is Article 226."

"Handy for them, I'd guess," Wynn said. "You mean like,

they get to write their own rules at that point?"

"Even better, they write Article 226 to fit what they might do, or what they've already done. One of their staff members travels out to another country. They complete their assignment, and things look a little rough around the edges. They need a legal precedent for their actions."

"As long as they keep it legal, right?" Wynn asked. "Who's to say it wasn't?"

"And that's the problem you have, young Mister Dubroc. They came here to discuss certain things with your father— Eric. He told them to take a long lick up the back of a hairy dog, as you kids might put it. Obviously, they expected some discretion from your father. When that didn't happen, they wrote another line in Article 226, a line with your name in it."

"The kidnapping," Wynn said. "That was the Chinese."

"Your father knew better than to trust the system with the safety of his family. All of the records and depositions he made were purposely falsified. Eric Dubroc made a fairly robust Plan-B."

"Why am I being held against my will?" Wynn asked.

"When someone is transferred into the Reboot, you can't interfere with them. It endangers their—"

"Exactly what we're doing, Edwynn, protecting you from danger," Lacour said.

"You mean from *her*."

The detective studied him long enough to give Wynn the creeps.

"You're in love with her," Lacour said. Wynn's ears turned a bright red. The detective leaned back in the chair. "You're a lucky man, Mister Dubroc, to have such an intelligent and attractive girlfriend. Why, when I was your age, if I had a girl like that, I would've done anything for her."

"She hasn't done anything," Wynn said. "You need to let us all go right now!"

"You and your sister, Geneva, your mother and father—you're renting a house in Lochiel. Your father also rents an apartment out of town, in Ohio. Doesn't he live with your mother? Are there marital problems between your parents?" Lacour asked.

What I don't get, Wynn thought, *is who they're after? What could Ahnim have done to attract so much attention? That's stupid. She probably can't tie her shoes without NASA picking it up on radar. Either she messed up something, or Lorenzo blew my cover.*

"They're married," Wynn said. He kept a straight face while staring down the portly detective. "They've argued about the same things for as long as I can remember. He forgets to take out the garbage. She spends too much on clothes. Marriage."

"And don't forget their son being kidnapped and held for ransom. And that ransom being the husband must divulge top-secret biotechnology to the Russian intelligence agency." Lacour let that sink in. "That would cause severe tension in the home. Your father moved out. He's working out of town? That kind of pressure would be enough to damage any marriage, the strongest, the most faithful. Indeed, even the most faithful of men might find himself lonely, under such circumstances. It would be hard to condemn a man should he become compromised."

"You don't know what you're talking about!" Wynn

snapped.

"Your sister," Lacour said, "she's not taking this too well. I gave her time to compose herself. But the day is getting late. Let's see what she knows about your girlfriend, Anna Lumiere. Perhaps, Geneva can explain how there is absolutely no trace of this person having ever existed before last week." He made as if to stand out of the chair, his eye on Wynn's reaction.

"Nev doesn't know anything about Ahnim," Wynn said, his head down nearly to the table top. "Nev only just met her today. She doesn't know any of it."

"Are you so sure about that? Nev might know more than she's letting on. Your sister may know more about this girl than you do. As they say, love is blind. Perhaps your Anna took the liberty of bringing Nev into her confidence about the plan."

"What? No, they've never been out of my sight since— what *plan*? There's no plan. We're just teenagers trying to make it through a new school in a crappy city, under new names. Somehow trying to be these new people. The only *plan* is to not flunk out of Mistez Plantain's SocioSpeak. Or get into it again with some girl's jealous ex-boyfriend."

"Lorenzo Flores," Lacour said.

"You know about that?" Wynn asked.

"We have the entire attack recorded, right here on our own lab equipment."

"Seriously? Seems a bit beneath you guys. Nothing more exciting than a high-school beat down? Has someone called my parents?"

"I know you and Mister Flores had a disagreement," Lacour said. "And that it escalated into violence. What bothers me,

Edwynn, you're not the type of person who would condone murder."

"Hey, I didn't kick him *that* hard! I mean, c'mon! What? What are you talking about?"

"So, you were there, too?" Lacour asked.

"Where? I was where? I was there when him and his wannabe thugs jumped me, yeah! In front of the gym, at the entrance to the locker rooms."

"I am talking about the other incident, Edwynn." Lacour leaned on his elbows, pushed himself halfway across the table to get as close to Wynn as possible. "I'm talking about you and your girlfriend *waiting* for him in his own home, *ambushed* him as he entered his bedroom. We have it all recorded, son. It's all too clear, your precious little Anna. She used a sword to impale Mister Flores through the stomach, then slice him to pieces. Almost like she enjoyed it. So, you weren't there? Maybe just out of view of the camera, hmmm? Perhaps you were the one to help her clean up the mess. Certainly did a good job of that. Not a trace of that poor young man. Not a single drop of blood in the entire murder scene! She does have you around her little finger, Mister Dubroc—yes she does. What else has she had you do for her?"

Wynn sat dumbfounded. He slumped down in the chair, all his energy gone. All his will power to stand up to this idiot and his ranting about Ahnim drained out of him. Perhaps he *was* insane. Maybe this was some hallucination, a delirium left over from the stress of the kidnapping.

"Did she have you plant the explosive at D-7?" Lacour asked. "Did she? You were right there in the Paramed's office, just a few minutes before. Did you smuggle the bomb into the school, and then she set the timer? Just like the one at the mall two weeks ago. Our lab took samples of both sites, Edwynn. The same type of device was used in both locations, in similar methods."

"But I don't know anything about any explosives!"

"And the other similarity, Mister Dubroc, your girlfriend — she was at both scenes immediately before the devices activated. *Something* blew a hole through the roof of the school medical office. You're in way over your head, son. She's manipulating you. You have no idea where she's from, who she was before a few months ago. I know you've been seeing a psychotherapist. Why is that? Are you tormented with guilt from doing things your conscience tells you is wrong? Stop protecting her, Edwynn."

Wynn experienced tunnel vision, his mind weary. The room darkened around Lacour. Then the lighting in the room changed. Beyond Lacour, the back wall brightened as the door to the hallway of the detective's wing swung all the way open. It bounced hard against the floor mounted door stop.

"Detective," Chief Tolleson called. "That's enough." The detective pursed his lips, rotated around in the chair. "As you wish," he said. Without another word, or so much as a glance back at Wynn, Lacour grabbed his coat from the back of the chair and made his exit.

"And detective," Tolleson said, "we're done with this. I've received a directive from the Commissioner that all three are to be turned over to the GC-Four CTU. This is out of our jurisdiction." He pulled Lacour out into the hall, closing the door on Wynn.

"Counter Terrorism Unit?" Lacour didn't bother to disguise his mistrust of the federal government's special heavyweights.

"This may be nothing at all," Tolleson said. "But you're onto something with the gamey little blonde. She's jerked us around since you first started tracking her. But whether or not her antics are at all related to Eric Dubroc, and his decision to mislead the Witness Reboot admin, has yet to be determined."

"You know," Lacour said, "the boy's the victim here. But he's already lost his head to her. Who knows? Maybe the whole 'lost at sea and rescued by an angel' story is part of the Russian ploy. Perhaps she planted that in his mind."

"And that's exactly why we're through with it. No one's saying your work and efforts are in vain, Charles. But the CTU has the reach where the Lochiel PD does not. You know that." Tolleson rested a hand on the detective's shoulder. It wouldn't do much to ease the sting of losing the case to the feds. "If this is nothing, then we'll know soon enough. The two Dubroc children will be released to their parents, and little Miss what —?"

"—Lumiere," Lacour said.

"Right—she can either explain her slight of hand to them, and her reasons for poking holes in rooftops, or she can enjoy a long vacation in their hotel on Cuba."

"And Eric Dubroc?" Lacour asked.

"Has he committed any crimes in this city?" Tolleson asked.

"None that I am aware of. Adultery has been removed from the code," Lacour said.

"Indiscretion is no longer a crime, Charles, as you say. And there's no evidence to show he did, anyway. Blurry images of a man entering a woman's home doesn't mean anything."

"You're the boss," Lacour said.

"Leave the girl alone. Don't even go down there. Colonel

Morse is in there already."

"Morse, of the CTU? Now I'll *never* get to find out—"

"You'll read their report, just like the rest of us," Tolleson said.

"Might as well watch for it on the evening news," Lacour said. He went to his desk, preparing to leave for the day.

*****

"So, Miss Lumiere," Morse said. "You have no identification, no birth certificate on record, no address, no Nish contract or TerraNet link assignment, no credit wire, no iris image from your day of birth, and your fingerprints change with the time of day."

Ahnim leaned back in the chair, tossed the useless handcuffs up onto the tabletop. Morse wanted so much to pick them up and inspect them. She'd somehow defeated this military grade pair. But that would distract him from the task at hand.

"I'd rather we just made friends anyway," he said. "I'd already asked them to take those off of you."

"Well, *Francis*," she said with a smirk, "you are without a doubt *the best* liar I've met on this planet so far."

Only two people left alive knew the name intended for Morse's original birth certificate. Himself, and his mother with advanced dementia. Miss Lumiere found her way into his head, and that concerned him.

"What reason would I have to lie to you?" he asked. Morse wore a long-sleeve plaid button down shirt and Levis. Oily hair fell straight down onto his shoulders. He resembled a trucker, or a bartender, anything but a Colonel in a department of the military.

"Thanks for directing Tolleson to call off that detective who was harassing Wynn," Ahnim said. "It's better he's not going to make it to me. I wouldn't have put up with that."

"With what, exactly?" Morse asked. Somehow, she knew what went on next door.

"Accusing Wynn of killing someone—he could never do anything like that," Ahnim said.

"Have you killed someone?" He might've asked whether she liked puppies or kittens.

"No…nothing that can't be put back together," Ahnim said.

"What, with surgery? A miracle from heaven?" Morse asked. "From what I saw, Lorenzo Flores was in at least six pieces when you carried him out through the window."

"As I said, nothing that can't be—"

"—be put back together, yeah. How are you going to do that, put Lorenzo Flores back together?" Morse asked. "I mean, his mom and dad are worried sick about him. As far as they know, he went up to his room after school, and...poof."

"Poof?" Ahnim asked.

"You know," Morse said, "never to be seen or heard from again. They'd like to get their child back."

"He was no child. He knew better," Ahnim said.

"Was? You said you didn't kill him. Is he alive or not. Anna?"

He will be, she thought. *When I'm good and ready, I'll reassemble him. First, there are preparations to be made.*

"Okay," Morse said, "let's start at the beginning."

"The Big Bang? I wasn't there."

"How about when you arrived here from the Russian Federation?" Morse asked.

Ahnim reached out with invisible probes. She inspected every instance of those words recorded in the building. With unrestrained vision, she flew up and down hallways, in and out of this man's computer, his written notes, files, and around in his mind. He'd gone bust trying to find a connection between this massive governmental entity and the Dubroc family.

"Where did you get your training," he asked, "Lubyanka?"

"You believe," Ahnim asked, "that I'm here to destroy lives, make people afraid?"

"I believe you're here to carry out an assignment. You've been directed to infiltrate the Dubroc family. You'll gather intel on Eric Dubroc and position yourself to leverage Edwynn. Against his will, if necessary, and to turn him against his father. Once you're in his pants and his head, maybe his heart if you're lucky, you'll coerce him to perform for the good of your leadership. If innocents are hurt along the way, too bad for them."

As Morse continued to speak, Ahnim understood their detainment was due to the authorities' paranoia, some evil remnant of hate left over from something called The Cold War. They believed her to be a spy, sent by one country to gain the advantage over the other.

Whoever this Russian Federation is, they're responsible for the horrible things that happened to Wynn.

"You are mistaken about who I am and why I'm here," Ahnim said.

"Please," Morse said, "enlighten me."

"I came here to prove to the others you were real. That there are beings on this water planet, and that I could—that I did — prove your existence. I admit," Ahnim continued, "that my being here was irresponsible. I shouldn't have come. I don't know if I've done more harm than good. Please believe me, I had no idea what would happen if I met someone like Wynn. If I'd have just stayed in the probe form, all this..."

Ahnim considered her created body, the organs, sensations, emotions. This fragment of Immini thought, held together in a shape of a human girl, contained more power than anything the planet had ever witnessed. Yet a greater force overcame her restraint. Her unbearable love for Wynn kept her at the limits of control.

"It was a mistake," she continued, "to assume the shape, the mind, feelings, and urges of humanity. You hurt each other so often. Each of you envy what you cannot have. And your desires are so strong, even to destroy each other."

"Or you to destroy the GC-Four?" Morse asked.

"What? No!" Ahnim snapped. "I don't have anything against this place, your country."

"Let's get back to reality, here, Miss Lumiere," Morse said. "You may have twisted poor Edwynn's brain with your artsy delusions, but I'm afraid you'll find me less willing to accept the zombies-from-space theory. Now listen, you're not going anywhere. We're going to get the answers one way or the other, right? So, why don't you save yourself the weariness of sleep deprivation. Or, I don't know, maybe a quick flight out to our friends in Lebanon, where they don't have any laws against enhanced techniques. Just tell me who sent you. Who's your handler?"

Ahnim's education grew further, faster. She used their own methods and turned it back upon them. She copied Morse's finger prints from the edge of the table. She found every place within the building he'd ever touched, each button, swipes on a screen. From her view within the hardware itself, Morse's face studied the text on the tablet he'd held last night in his hotel room. Every word he'd read in the past day, week, month.

"Comrade Vitaly Kryuchkov," she said. Ahnim met his gaze, her face as hard as stone. Morse moved at the statement. Ahnim spoke the exact name he'd hoped for. It quickened his pulse.

Ahnim leaned forward against the table. "He's the man you believe is ultimately responsible for the attack," she said.

"Okay, Anna," he said, "if you say so. Now tell me why the Committee Chairman would authorize the terrorist bombing of a women's clothing store, and the nurse's office at a high school in a do-nothing city like Lochiel."

"Bombings..." Ahnim scoured through the files kept by Morse and Lacour.

Bombings? Bombs. He's talking about the effect generated when I made an impromptu exit of the two facilities. "Wow, you guys sure do make a big deal of a girl slamming the door on the way out."

"You could've injured so many—" Morse countered.

"And precisely nobody was," she said. "You must believe I'm a real monster."

"Are you admitting to the—?"

"Oh, enough of the stupid bombs already! That's just a hydro-plasmic reaction to me making a hop." Ahnim reached out over the polished metal tabletop. She dipped her hand into and through it. While Morse stared in amazement, the layers of material melted out of her way to drip onto his feet underneath. She withdrew her arm to leave a gaping hole the diameter of a young woman's fist. "Sorry about the two rooftops. But that's just not at the top of my list of priorities right now."

All the blood drained out of Morse's face. Years of intensive training to deal with the most violent extremists didn't prepare him for the reality of Ahnimgoyothalia. She stood, and stepped right through the middle of the table. As tall as Morse was seated in the chair, she didn't bend over far to meet him eye to eye. One half of the table toppled to the floor with a thud. The other half tipped back to bang against the wall.

Her hands reached for him. He wanted to run, scream, at least shove her away. His bladder emptied as Ahnim's small hands wrapped over the tops of his shoulders. Heavy pounding outside the door did little to distract her from the task at hand.

"Now, Francis," Ahnim said, "you're going to show me what you know, every single detail in your mind about Kryuchkov. Who he is, where I might find him, and who he sent to hurt my Wynn. This...is *me* using advanced techniques."

*****

Nev woke from sleep on the floor of the police station lunch room. Her mother's voice echoed down the hall. Her left side ached where her ribs conformed to the flat surface over the past four hours. She gave herself some time to take the first good inhale.

"Mom! I'm back here in the kitchen!"

Brigitte and Wynn fast-stepped to the doorway. The lighting flicked on to bland gray walls and the remnants of yesterday's chocolate birthday cake for some officer in the precinct.

"You guys have had me worried sick!" Brigitte forced herself through a hesitation to hug her daughter. It had been a while since they'd cared enough to bother.

"Well," Nev said, "I've been to the mall, the library and the theater so much lately, I figured, 'hey, lessa feet-up at'n'd Badgie-bid'n.'"

"They say we can go," Wynn said. He turned to go but came face to face with another person in the hallway. The man blocked Wynn's path.

"What's the problem, officer?" Brigitte asked. "You told me —"

"I invited you to the station," Chief Tolleson said.

"And implied," Brigitte said, "my children needed me to pick them up."

"Your assumption," he said, then pointed a finger at Nev. "She has yet to be interviewed. And Edwynn is scheduled for a psychological evaluation by the department's forensic analyst. That won't happen until tomorrow."

"Now wait just a minute!" Brigitte snapped. "On what grounds are you holding them? They're minors. You can't hold them without my—"

"Protective custody," Tolleson said. "His girlfriend, Lumiere —she just escaped during an interrogation session. She assaulted a federal agent. He's on the way to the ER now."

"Ahnim would never hurt anybody," Wynn said. But even as he spoke it, he began to doubt. His mind became clouded about who she was, *what* she was.

In just a few days, he thought, *she's changed from a being — calm, and very much in control, to an irrational and moody example of some comic book superhero.*

"Who is this we're talking about?" Brigitte asked. "What the heck is a Loo-me-air?"

"His new girlfriend," Nev said.

"I understood her name was Michelle? John-something?"

"That lasted about half a day," Nev replied. "But hey, this nutty one comes in handy when you've been killed in a car accident."

"Wait," Brigitte said, her finger held up to shush her children. "This is not a conversation to have in public. What is your name, sir?"

"Chief Tolleson."

"I'd like to have a private conversation with my children. Not recorded, no eavesdropping."

"There's a small outdoor patio," Tolleson said, "on the north side of the building, with a picnic bench. You can go there for now. I'll have to post an officer to be with you at all times though, in case any of you get the urge to scale the fence. It's ten feet with barbed wire. But after today—and after how Lumiere did her thing—I'm not taking any chances with your black magic brood. No offense."

"Thanks, I think," Brigitte said.

Tolleson led them out the fire exit and around to the bedroom-sized cage, the 'fair-weather lounge' for his staff. One side short of a chain-link cube, broken asphalt surrounded a concrete table. Early morning starlight did nothing to mute the glare from the high-intensity lamp overhead.

"Give them some privacy, eh?" he said loud and clear to the posted officer. Tolleson directed the guard back to the far corner from the family. After Tolleson re-entered the building he spoke to him again secretly through the audio-implant in his ear canal.

"Listen up, Hemmings. We've set your body camera's microphone to the highest gain. The lens is running at ultra-def so we can merge with the lip reading app. Scratch your nose now if you're with me so far—good. Now here's what's at stake — Lacour is gone. He'd just left when Morse went in with the blonde. Can't get him on his Nish. We found his car rolling down the street about half a block away. Still in drive, tires rubbing along the curb. Understand? Charles is *missing*. We believe she took him. When she walked through the wall and out into the parking lot, she would've seen him driving off. I have absolutely no idea how she's doing this, but that's one dangerous little girl. This Dubroc kid is our best link to her."

*****

"So, do you think they're listening?" Wynn asked.

"Do you trust Tolleson?" Brigitte asked. Both Wynn and Nev shrugged. "Then does somebody want to tell me what is going on?"

"Where's dad?" Nev's blunt question brought Brigitte up short, unprepared to deal with that subject.

"He flew back to Ohio," Brigitte said.

"And you *let him*?" Nev asked. "You just let him leave without seeing us?"

"Since when does your father do anything except what he wants? Sorry."

Brigitte understood Nev couldn't bear the thought her father made the choice to ignore his children. Easier, and more convenient at the moment, was to blame the one parent there, the one who could accept the pain and offer comfort. But Brigitte kept a secret from her children. Eric found corruption and bribery at higher levels, above him and his leaders at the lab. Even within the Witness Reboot program, his family couldn't be truly safe. He randomized much of their personal details, to make it far more difficult for anyone to find them. Painfully, they were better off with him far away.

"I guess," Brigitte continued, "I could've argued with him, made him stay here with us."

"Dad makes his own choices," Wynn said, staring off past the fence. "He's doing more to protect us than we know."

He met his mother's understanding and appreciative gaze.

"All-righty then," Brigitte said, "tell me all about this nutty chick, and did you say car accident? Wait—*killed in* a car accident? Who the heck was killed in a car accident?"

Wynn pointed at Nev. Nev pointed at herself.

"Words would be helpful," Brigitte said, arms crossed over her chest, head cocked.

"I still had half a day left on the rental," Wynn said. "I took Ahnim—Anna—we'll get there in a minute—took her with me to the brain bender."

"Bad idea. Go on," Brigitte said.

"Turns out, the bender—"

"*Doctor* Fonteno," the mother corrected.

"—wanted to meet her," Wynn said.

"Her, who?" Brigitte asked.

"Anna," Nev said.

"Have I met her," Brigitte asked, "this Anna or Ahnim or which is it?"

"Pick one," Wynn said. "Trust me, it only gets more unpronounceable from there."

"And why would Doctor Fonteno want to meet this girl?" Brigitte asked. "Is this a girlfriend? Are you two doing something —?"

"No! We're not," Wynn said. "We haven't. Well, not really..."

"Not really what?" Nev asked. "Do tell!"

"Okay! We kissed, that's all," Wynn said.

"Skip to the part about Nev getting killed, please," Brigitte said.

"Afterward, we—me and Ahnim—picked up Nev at Tarjays. The car's acting weird from that code you downloaded into it."

"Define 'acting weird'?" Brigitte asked. Nev interjected before the long, drawn out, boyish explanation got up to speed.

"When you press the accelerator," she said, "the tires smoke and it hauls ass."

"Got it," Brigitte said. "You were driving aggressively."

"She was in the front," Wynn said, "Ahnim in the back. She —Ahnim climbed out her window…"

Nev and her mother wore matching facial expressions— eyebrows up, a sideways smirk.

"I looked back, *just for a second,* and there was this huge truck, with pipes sticking out, and a bumper as big as a piano, I guess? I mean, this thing had stuff everywhere. My foot jammed down on the brake pedal. It bent to the floor. After that, everything went white, or black, I don't know."

"I remember," Nev said, "turning back to Anna, then up at Wynn, this dorky grin on his face. I heard a pop. Something shoved me back into the seat. There were two pipes, and they went into me. My head hit the roof...ceiling. Heard a crack. I couldn't breathe. Like my body got paused, like in a game. My eyes worked, but nothing else. After a minute, it felt like I'd been holding my breath, you know? Like when you try to stay at the bottom of the swimming pool for as long as you can?" Wynn nodded. He gestured as if an object went in his chest and out his back. Nev took over nodding.

"This is for real?" Brigitte asked. "The car came in on the flatbed. They moved it from the impound lot to the garage here on the other side of the building. There isn't a scratch on it."

"That's because Anna erased the accident," Nev said.

"Erased...?" Brigitte waited for the punchline.

Nev opened her sweater to show Brigitte the blood stained hole in her t-shirt. Brigitte stared a long moment, then mouthed a four letter word. Nev continued to describe the events.

"I sat there, gasping, but not. Stuck in the middle of one big gasp, you know? Things hovered in mid-air, over my legs. Glass, dirt, pieces of plastic from the car, blood drops. Like they floated in a thick, clear liquid—submerged in hair gel or something. I saw a bright flash, right in front of the dashboard.

"My door opened," Nev continued. "Anna was there. She told me everything would be all right. She said she'd help me. Her hand...made the pipe disappear. She went to stick her fingers inside me, in the hole in my chest. I got scared. I tried to tell her to stop but my voice didn't work. She put me back together inside. My heart beat again. But she held my breath back while she held my neck."

"Your neck was broken, Nev," Wynn said, his eyes wide as the memories emerged.

"She healed my neck, mom," Nev said. "That sounds so stupid. But I swear, she did. I felt the bones moving and crunching, going back onto each other."

"This is all true," Brigitte said, stuttering, in disbelief. "You guys aren't making this up." It had to be a joke. Reality didn't allow for her children's explanation. Her tears welled over.

"Yeah, mom, it's true," Nev said. "Ahnim pressed her hand on me, holding me back from waking up, or from—I don't know —from restarting."

"From coming back to life," Wynn said. Brigitte looked back and forth between them.

"Yeah, like...I'm stuck in a single moment. She held one hand on me as she climbed between the seats and onto the back seat. She always kept one hand on me, touching, holding me back. That's when she laughed. And she let go of me."

"Laughed?" Brigitte asked. "Not so funny to me."

Nev busted up herself, tears spilling down her own cheeks to run around her chin.

"Yeah, no...but yeah, she let go of me and I came back. I took this huge breath, like I said, coming up out of the pool. The air real, not like liquid anymore. And I thought...I thought, 'this girl, Wynn's girlfriend—she's nuts!'"

"And then?" Brigitte asked.

"And then," Nev said, "she fell out of the window, right onto the freakin' street!"

Chapter Fifteen

"They're done," Officer Hemmings said. "The family wants to come in." Even the controlled whisper roared with the maximized amplification of his body camera's microphone transmitter. Tolleson winced as the words whistled from his earbud.

"All right," he said. "Bring them inside. The mom is feisty, so you might expect some resistance there. And beware the boy. Screw it. Just watch them all. SWAT just arrived to keep an eye out for their little blonde."

Wynn held the door open for his sister and mother as they re-entered the precinct building. Officer Hemmings stood stone-faced, his hand resting on the grip of his taser.

Something's wrong, Wynn thought. *Ahnim—she's really messed up this time. Why not just stay invisible? Why not just stay in my head? Now, everyone knows. Everyone knows she's real. If only she wasn't...*

Tolleson waited in the hallway. A calm smile and hands behind his back gave nothing away. Brigitte approached him first, pushing her way around her daughter in the cramped hallway.

"Chief," Brigitte said, "can we talk privately? I'm sure we can work this out. This 'friend' of my son has been playing some tricks. I can assure you—"

"Of course, right in here." Tolleson ushered her into an interrogation room. Two officers hidden behind the door took Brigitte by the wrists. Within a few seconds, they bent her over the table, arms behind her back.

"Hey, mom? Where'd you go?" Nev asked. Five officers piled out of the squad room. Two uniformed females took Nev by each arm. They lifted her up onto her toes and marched her around a corner.

This can't be happening, Wynn thought.

Brigitte cursed and yelled, demanding to be released. The first of Tolleson's officers to reach Wynn made a rookie mistake. He reached out with a straightened arm, to grab a fistful of the teen's shirt. Wynn's adrenaline got ahead of his judgement. He clamped his left hand down hard over the officer's fist to lock it in place, then rolled it over, exposing the man's hyperextended elbow. Wynn came across with the right palm to the underside of the cop's arm just as the other two rushed in. The crash of four bodies into a metal cabinet drowned out the crackle of torn ligaments.

"Wait!" Wynn yelled. "You can't do this! We haven't done anything!"

"Just stop resisting, Mister Dubroc," Tolleson said. "You're making this harder."

More faces peered from down the hallway. The two officers he struggled with failed to turn him around to face the wall. He whipped an elbow across, and blood splattered across the ceiling.

His determination to fend them off only added to the list of reasons why they should restrain him.

Over their shoulders, he picked out the face of Serene Fonteno. She stood behind a wall of blue uniforms blocking off the middle of the secured inner hallway.

"Doctor Fonteno!" Wynn screamed. "Tell them it's okay! Just tell them the truth about us—about Ahnim!"

Tolleson twisted to his left to catch Fonteno's eye.

"Just please don't hurt him," she said. "He's a very sick boy."

*****

"Privet, Irina," the baker said, in his native Russian. "Isn't it just a beautiful day today? Look at the sun!"

Snowfall spun outside the small shop. It melted on the warming sidewalk. A strong glow pushed through the overcast sky.

"Yes, it is!" she said. His weekly customer made a point of returning to the ornate doorway. She leaned close to the glass pane. "As soon as I stepped out the door this morning and saw the ground, I turned back. No galoshes for me on this fine day. Here's my new shoes I bought last month!"

Bright green slip-ons glittered under the lighting from the overhead lamps. Cold fluorescent gloom of the bread's showcase detracted from any pleasing effect.

"Fine shoes they are, my dear," Oleg said.

"Oh, spasibo," she replied. "I wanted to ask you, were you able to meet that person with butter and honey? You said it might take some doing to get on his list of trusted clients."

Oleg came around the counter with a brown paper bag. Golden brown tips peeked out the open top, a glimpse of the toasty treasure within.

"You know, Irina, there is a waiting list of people who just want to speak with that man. And even then, the price will be beyond the reach of someone like...like..."

Oleg watched through the glass of the front door. A young woman stood alone outside the shop. Underdressed for the weather, she appeared oblivious to the cold and the snowflakes caught in her curls.

"My goodness," he said, "she's going to freeze."

"Oleg, the butter and honey?" Irina asked.

"Surely you understand, my dear. There is no more honey. All that's left was stored from the previous years, Here, take your bread. The bees are gone, Irina. Those idiot, pot-smoking Americans are destroying the world. What—does she want to come inside?"

Irina leaned forward to peer around the wide bicep coated in flour dust.

"For heaven's sake, Oleg...beauty, but no brains. Call her inside."

Jingle bells wiggled out their three-note harmony. The door yanked open to swing wide for the baker. He put on his best face for the pretty moron in the snow.

"Eh, mogu ya vom pomoch?"

Ahnim blinked twice during her three-second absorption of the entire Russian language.

"Da, vy mozhete pomoch' mne?" she replied.

Oleg turned back to Irina, puzzled. "Didn't I just ask her

that?"

"Brainless," Irina said.

Oleg heaved himself down the few steps to the cracked cement of the walk. He rested a gentle and caring hand on the small shoulder, ushering the girl out of the snowfall. She complied in a childlike way. It didn't occur to Oleg there was no steamy exhale from his guest.

"Please," he continued in Russian, "come in out of the cold, my dear. I'll get you a nice, hot tea."

Irina constructed her most polite smile for Ahnim, who stood wide-eyed at the sights and smells in the neighborhood shop.

"This is a delightful place," Ahnim said. "I didn't expect this. You don't have war machines here?"

"I have bread," Oleg stated. "Please, sit." He moved to behind the counter and retrieved a dainty cup and a teapot. He poured her a serving, which she stared at, pondering the wisp of steam. He returned again with a slice warm and fresh from the oven.

Ahnim met his eyes in disbelief. She'd expected a battlefield, filled with brutish, evil warriors, each one hell-bent on the destruction of everything good.

"That is kind of you. Thank you," Ahnim said.

"Hello, my sweet," Irina said, her gloved hand extended in friendship. "Are you from Otradnoye?"

"No, I'm just visiting." Ahnim picked up the slice of bread between her finger and thumb, held it up to her nose.

"My name is Irina Yuryev—and yours?"

"Ahnimgoyothalia," she said.

"Oh! Well, I have a niece your age. Her name is Nimi. I'll call you Nimi."

Ahnim smiled big, invited Irina to sit. "Would you like to share my bread?"

"Thank you, I have plenty," Irina said, with a pat of her hand on the paper bag. "How long will you be in Moscow?"

"Long?" Ahnim asked.

"Yes, how long...a week, a month? How long?" Irina turned her face sideways to Oleg. She made a face in jest of the idiot with the coveted tresses and big words.

"Oh, I understand now," Ahnim said. "I'm just waiting for someone."

A black limousine rolled down Samarskya Road. Its damp brakes squealed to a stop in front of the bakery.

"Oh, a boy, I hope?" Irina asked. "Is your true love a handsome boy?"

Ahnim smiled, remembering Wynn. The concept of 'true love' brought out her first embarrassed giggles. She absentmindedly stuffed a wad of fluffy white bread into her mouth. By all standards of human attraction, Wynn's features rated just above average. Yet she perceived an odd adjustment within. It drove her to disregard the data as blatantly false. Even the memory of his face caused her emulations of human behavior to flush her cheeks and twinkle her eyes.

There is no person as beautiful as Edwynn Dubroc, not in all of this galaxy, anyway.

The singing of bells announced another visitor to the shop. Two men in floor-length trench coats invaded the cozy space. Their menacing scan of the interior pushed Irina's face down into the bag with her loaves. A minute later, a third man in similar dress made his way up the steps. Taking his time, he checked the view up and down the street.

"A good morning to you, comrade," Oleg said, his tone professional.

The neatly trimmed goatee and mink fur hat gave evidence to this being a person of means. The man offered no reply.

Vitaly Kryuchkov pulled off one glove, leaned over, and surveyed the entirety of items in the display case. He tapped once on the glass in front of the basket of sushki. Oleg readied himself on the other side. He stood with his back against the wall, attentive, but out of the way.

Oleg placed three bagels wrapped in wax paper just so in a medium sized, white bag. He set it on the counter closest to the shorter of the two bodyguards. Vitaly turned to make his exit and walk down the steps.

Ahnim waited for the moment when the chauffeur held open the right-rear passenger door to make her move. In a blur, she streaked through the shop door and into the back of Vitaly, slamming into him. She knocked him across the back seat, headfirst into the panel of the door on the driver's side. The hard-chromed metal of the inside door handle split his scalp where his expensive ushanka had flown off.

Guns drawn, the two bodyguards stumbled together to the sidewalk, desperate to secure their boss. No amount of yanking or beating would release the car's door latches. Bulletproof glass ignored their pathetic attempts to pound with the butt of their pistols.

Vitaly spun on the seat to face his adversary. His pistol in hand, he fired all nineteen rounds at point blank range. When the smoke cleared, he gathered himself and tried to get out through the door behind him. The handle didn't budge.

"Calm yourself, Mister Kryuchkov," Ahnim said. "I have some questions to ask you. I'd prefer it if you'd try to cooperate." Controlling her irritation, she sat in a relaxed posture, legs crossed, and hands folded in her lap.

In a futile attempt, the chauffeur in the driver's seat grabbed a fully automatic submachine gun, pointing it at Ahnim's head. Before the trigger fired the first round, she swiped the air with a hand, as if to shoo a fly. The Kalashnikov crumbled into fine black dust, every atom having lost cohesion to its surrounding matrix. A scattered mess of useless bullets rolled across the seat. Another swish of her hand and the man froze in place like a wax statue.

"What are you," Vitaly muttered, "a witch?"

"Depends on who you ask, I suppose," Ahnim said. "I can think of a few who find my attention...maleficent."

"What do you want with me?" he asked.

"Information," she said.

"I'll tell you nothing!"

He fumbled to pull the Eastern version of a NowSeeHear out of a coat pocket. He'd hoped to call in a drone strike on his own location, a missile to dive on his GPS coordinates.

With a glance from Ahnim, the aluminum frame and its attached microcircuitry vaporized into a small cloud. It drifted down into his lap.

"You *will* end up telling me...showing me everything I need to know, human. I'm not going to take no for an answer."

Vitaly's muscles tightened in prelude to another attack. This time, he came directly at her with the double-edged knife inched up out of his boot.

In a black flash of negative light her left arm shot out as a dark spear. It pinned his torso to the door behind him. Vitaly flailed his fists toward her. His kicks went through her legs and knees like air, with zero effect. He caught the gaze of his bodyguard through the windshield, gave a hand signal to fire his weapon directly into the glass. The nine millimeter round nosed bullets left small spatters as they bounced off.

The second bodyguard used a key from his pocket to open the trunk of the limo. From within, he produced a semiautomatic shotgun loaded with armor piercing slugs. With a harsh slam of the trunk lid, he took aim on Ahnim's head. The rounds tore through the glass, the back seat, the floor, and finally to smack hard into the street below.

"Hey!" the guard in front screamed, "Vitaly gave order two-five-two!"

From behind the limo, the thumb-sized bullets roared into the car again, this time walking across from the middle to where Vitaly was seated.

"Oh, no you don't!" Ahnim said.

In a sudden eruption from within the car, a black crystalline hemisphere tore upwards through its roof. The limo's metal ripped backwards, to fold itself down upon the bodyguard. The rock hard surface crushed the entire vehicle from the inside out, as it enveloped everything for twenty feet around.

A few seconds later, the center of the obsidian dome erupted at the topmost of the arch, to shower the neighborhood with shards of the darkest hail. To the frightened bystanders, someone or something carried an armload of Vitaly Kryuchkov parts up into the gray sky, and onward into space.

Deathly quiet crept in. Oleg forced himself to peek out the glass of the front door. Residents and nearby shopkeepers ventured out. They gawked at the giant black ball sunk halfway into their street.

"Irina?" he asked. "Are you out here? Irina? I told you to stay in the shop."

Where the solid concrete steps girded the entrance to the bakery, a deep red stain spread to the foundation. With it, an ugly green shoe sparkled as the sun broke through the thinning clouds.

*****

"Where am I?" Vitaly asked.

"With me...in me," she said.

"That is nonsense. What is this place?"

The Chairman either floated in water or hovered in air. All around him, the deepest black stretched on forever. Ahnim leaned close, herself one with the darkness.

"What are you afraid of, Vitaly Kryuchkov?" Ahnim asked.

"I am not afraid of you," he said, though he stammered.

"Wrong answer. And I don't care if you're afraid of me or not. That is not the question. Now, what are you afraid of?"

"So you can wield your witchcraft to use that against me? You have much to learn about how to extract information. You pathetic little girl. Spiders and snakes only clog the pathways to the memories locked inside the brain. You have no idea what you are doing. Wherever you've taken me—this is where I do my best work."

Ahnim probed deep into his mind. He did indeed have much experience at forced interrogation.

"Vitaly, you should know something," Ahnim said. "Me finding out from you who kidnapped Edwynn Dubroc, and the coercion you ordered against his family—that has nothing to do with you and your fears. Here, let me show you."

Ahnim took him back to when he was just a four year old boy. He lived on a rural farm in Vstrecha with his mother, two sisters, and a violent stepfather.

"How are you doing this?" Vitaly asked. His adult mind visualized the rest of him, somehow back in time—back to the worst period of his life.

"You're correct, Vitaly," she said. "It's the memories, they are the key. No use in trying to scare a grown up like you." Pain in his arm stung and burned. The iron grip of the new daddy twisted his young skin and bent the soft bones.

"Let me go!" he squealed. Short legs hurried through the tall grass to keep up. "You're not Daddy! Daddy make you stop!"

"Your foolish father is long dead, boy," the wrinkled scowl far above said. "It's time you learned what it means to respect your mother's husband."

"No," Vitaly said, "please don't take the child there...not again."

"I'm not," Ahnim said, "it's you who is taking *me* there. This is your memory, Vitaly, not mine."

"Why are we going? Ouch!" the little boy asked. "Why are we going to the wood shed? We have plenty of wood for the fire already. Let go of me! That hurts!"

"You shall soon see, lichinka," stepfather said. "And you will never forget today, I assure you."

"You are a witch from hell," Vitaly said.

"We're just walking to the woodshed," Ahnim said.

"Just kill me, witch. Take what you want from my head and kill me."

"I don't kill people," she said. "That's what you do, isn't it? I can see your plan. It's right there in the front of your mind: Project Strelyat Pervy—Shoot First. You're going to launch a pre-emptive missile strike against your enemies. Beyond all the faces, all the people that did your bidding when you attacked Eric Dubroc and his poor family. I see them all now. But you're going to do so much worse. Your plan is to bring the GC-Four to its knees."

"You can destroy me if you want, or you can keep me here in this otherworldly dungeon. It matters not. But the Russian Federation is going to rule over this planet. With or without me, this is going to happen, witch. And you cannot stop it, even with your powers of illusion. You won't be able to make the people you care so much about come back to life, once we have ground them to dust."

"You aren't planning to irradiate them all," Ahnim said. "You're just going to cripple their military, their ability to trade, to import the food they need."

Where Vitaly's fears failed to leverage his will, pride turned the key, unlocking the many secrets. He blathered on while Ahnim sifted through his mind.

"They will gladly accept us as their new masters," Vitaly said, "when their children wither away from starvation. People will follow whoever has the food. They have done this to themselves. America sold off their farms, gave away their ability to grow their own food. In a single day, we will crack their perfect little egg. All the life will drain out.

"It's so simple," Vitaly continued, the flood of words one step ahead of his will to shut up. "First we attack them with a dozen or so stealth missiles, to ruin their ports and coastal cities. The population goes hungry, the weak die off. Lazy ones and the many psychopaths will murder each other for whatever is left. When only the strong are hiding in corners, the new Russia will replace the previous warlike government. We will arrive in America with a loving, caring, benevolent image of pacifists.

"Our planes will drop baskets of food to save the Americans. They will fling open their gates to us. We will roll in with so much love, they will trip over each other to kiss our feet. Our many soldiers can take over the management of three hundred million slaves. We won't require so much as a pistol."

Ahnim calculated that this plan, by the only other country to survive the Cold War, might work. The industrial age once brought together many diverse cultures and rallied the various ethnic groups under one banner—invention. But it had long ago been replaced by the age of personalized entertainment.

This is a good plan for world domination, she thought.

"The Chinese," Ahnim said, "have satisfied the American's appetite for violence with games. Harmless toys played from the comfort of their couches. So many people are addicted. They aren't even aware of what's happening to the rest of their world."

"And we won't take that away from them," Vitaly said. "Oh no, we'll let them play war all they wish. As long as they trade their deadly sidearms for another meal. They've already been trained as slaves to the corporate greed of their employers, and bankers, and insurance companies. They won't even notice a difference. They will work for the betterment of the lives of the Russian people. And they will go back to their apartments to play their games."

"No one should be a slave to anyone else," Ahnim said.

"Wrong! They are slaves and do not even know it. Only their masters will change. The Chinese had this idea decades ago. Too timid to push the button. They never started the sequence of events that would've led them to sure success."

"But you have," Ahnim said.

"It's on automatic, now," Vitaly said. "In case we might change our minds, we started the countdown. It's out of the hands of anyone in the Kremlin. A thousand computer systems are synchronized. Any one of them can fire the missiles. It cannot fail."

"Vitaly Kryuchkov," she said, "there's one thing you didn't plan for."

"And what is that, little witch?"

"A woman's scorn."

"There is no woman on Earth who can stop this," he said.

"I don't disagree there, Vitaly," she said. "But then, you're not dealing with a woman from Earth."

Vitaly's mind opened like a flower blossom for her, to reveal all of his secrets, every name, location, and ruthless intent. She found those who plotted to harm her beloved Wynn. She would focus her own expression of hate against a thousand clocks.

*****

Brigitte stood at the command of the court bailiff. Her defense attorney, appointed by the state, took some time getting her wide bottom extricated from the narrow arms of the old chair.

"Honorable Dwight Zaborsky presiding," the bailiff said. The judge took his place behind the bench and the court staff eased down. A dozen or so others in the oak paneled room did likewise.

"We stay standing this time," Brigitte's lawyer whispered.

"Brigitte Dubroc," the judge said, "this court finds you guilty of aiding and abetting a terrorist. As the legal guardian of the minor child Edwynn Dubroc, who did in effect carry out such acts, you were personally responsible. The conviction will be on your record. However, as your records are sealed by the GC-Four Witness Reboot Program, that is a moot point. You are free to submit to the government a request to re-enter the program should you wish to. Your attorney can assist with arrangements for your new identity to be listed as next of kin, to your son, Edwynn, as he is confined to the Southeastern Regional Psychiatric Hospital."

Brigitte's mouth made to form the words 'thank you'.

"Hey," her attorney said, "you're free. There's not going to be a penal hearing. And now you can go visit your kid."

The judge rambled on. Brigitte gave up trying to track both conversations, her mind and soul wearied from constant interrogations and depositions.

"Furthermore," the judge said, "this court is willing to request that the Child Protective Services Agency extend leniency toward you. You may perhaps regain custody of your daughter, Geneva Dubroc, from the State. Of course, I have no jurisdiction there. I would caution you, ma'am, to have no further contact with the person Anna Lumiere. In fact, your best defense would be to let the authorities know if you see her again."

I've never even met her, Brigitte thought. *But I've told you all that a hundred times. I don't even know who this person is, only that she's destroyed what was left of my family.*

"Mrs. Dubroc?" the judge asked. "Am I clear on that?" She managed a nod.

"Yes, she is, Your Honor," the attorney said.

"Very well," the judge said, "then I hereby remand you to the State of Louisiana, to answer for the charges made by their Department of Transportation. 'Of knowingly tampering with the safety and control systems of a motor vehicle', and 'knowingly and deliberately falsifying a rental contract for a motor vehicle', and 'permitting an unauthorized minor child to operate a rental vehicle', and lastly, 'knowingly and deliberately putting a minor child in harm', which of course stems from the use of the tampered vehicle by Edwynn Dubroc."

His words faded into the background of her mind. Brigitte retreated once again to the place where the bad things, the terrible things, stood silent along the walls. All the rest waited in line outside the door. The next bottle of wine guarded the only entrance.

An odd tapping distracted her from the compressed numbness of alcoholism.

Drip. Drip. Splat.

She opened her eyes. Tears puddled on the papered surface of the table below her.

"Your Honor," the attorney said, "Mrs. Dubroc would wish to thank you for your generosity today and during the trial. She is prepared to work closely with the Louisiana courts to work out a remediation."

"Yes, please do that," he replied, modest in the use of a gavel. A sideways glance at his staff brought the session to a close.

"Court is adjourned," the bailiff announced.

"You should go home and get some rest," the attorney said.

"Take me to Wynn," Brigitte said. "I want to see my son."

"We should have the—"

"Take me now. Or I'll call a cab and go myself."

Chapter Sixteen

Ahnim used the power of her ship-self to embrace the moon, like a small child holding a butterfly.

"I'm sorry, little rock, but I'm a bit rusty with firing my blaze emitter. I'm in need of some practice." Her massive stellar body flexed slightly. The gravity organ held her in place on the side opposite from Earth.

I'll need something to target. What's that?

Her shape, an enormous pyramid six hundred miles from corner to corner, rotated around. Her uppermost point took aim with its blaze emitter at the dusty surface of the moon. A dark impression resembling the human heart encircled a tall mountain in the middle. Using her finned sensory system, Ahnim touched the moon's prominence with energy waves.

Tsiolkovsky Crater—how fitting. She pushed herself away until this feature appeared as an oblong smudge against the chalky glare. *That peak in the center is about the size of Russia's capital, Moscow. I'll need to narrow my beam quite a bit.*

From within the gap between the nine shutters embedded into her peak, more lenses pressed outward diagonally to the edge of the boxed fins. One by one, they constricted until the blaze emitter closed to a fourth of its original size. To Ahnim, the sensation would be similar to a person blowing out a match. Though instead, she'd use nuclear fire to set alight something cold and inflammable.

A liquid stream of superheated hydrogen and helium burst through the lenses. It set space aglow in the two seconds it took to reach the enormous depression on the moon. Ahnim's skill at use of the Immini's only defensive weapon was well executed. A black square the size of Hawaii smoldered where a mountain once towered. As the molten rock cooled, a new glassy plain reflected starlight with a ragged twinkle.

"That should do," Ahnim said aloud to herself. The English words rumbled and rang throughout the caverns and hollowed depths of her living mechanisms and metallic tissues. "A thousand of those won't begin to tax my reserves. I could do that all day."

All day—that's funny. I'm beginning to talk about time like a human.

A gentle tug on the eastern horizon pulled her around. Ahnim placed her ship-self in orbit directly above Mother Russia. It took a modest effort to plot out the many targets stretching from Europe to several floating oil platforms in the Bering Sea.

*****

"Yes, of course, Mrs. Dubroc," the attendant said. "Edwynn's been asking for you. He'll be delighted to know you've finally come."

"It wasn't my fault," Brigitte said. "I wasn't allowed to

come."

But the woman already turned from her service window at the lobby to make arrangements for the incarcerated patient. Wynn would need to be given a stimulant and the summary admonishment against any behavior considered disruptive. Patients who broke the rules received a week in a dank isolation cell. The hospital's visitors often created more of a problem than they would ever know.

The axles of the wheelchair chirped with the weight of the muscled orderly adding to that of the gaunt young man in the seat. Brigitte held her tongue while the ward employee delivered rules and warnings in a practiced oration. Once he returned to his tasks, she needed only to reign in her nervousness.

Oh, my baby, look at you, Brigitte thought, *at what they've done to you—at what I've let them do to you. How could I permit this to happen? My beautiful son—I'll never forgive myself.*

"Hey, are you up for a visit?" She rubbed Wynn's arm with the tips of her fingers, testing for a reaction to her presence. It took all her willpower to not pull him up and cradle him.

"Mom? Is that you?" His chin rested on his chest. He rolled his eyes to his forehead as far as he could, appearing all the more mentally disturbed.

"Yeah, baby, it's me, it's mom. I'm here." Her caress grew to a firm grasp.

"Oh, wow," he said. "I've missed you...everyone. Where's dad and Nev?"

"It's just me today, Wynn," Brigitte said.

"How long have I been here? Why won't they let me call you guys?"

"I don't know the reason, Wynn. It's just the rules. You've been here for a month. Baby, I'm so sorry."

"It's not your fault, mom. Not your fault. No, I just couldn't hide her anymore. She's real, mom. It was lying to hide her from you. It's me that's sorry. I should've told you right away, when she came to me as a real person."

"Wynn, please." Brigitte said. "please don't, son. I hoped by now you would've—"

"Would've what, mom? Been cured of my insanity?" Wynn asked.

"No, Wynn, that's not what I meant," Brigitte said.

"You want...you've always wanted...ever since she brought me back from that boat...that horrible day on the boat. You and dad wished I would tell you something else, something believable, about how I got home. In the hospital, I tried to show you my finger, but you didn't—*wouldn't* even look at it."

Wynn forced his head up to meet his mother's sorrowful gaze. Losing hope, he quit trying.

"Wynn, please," Brigitte said. "You're breaking my heart. If you would just let go of all that."

"Let go of the truth? What do you think kept me together all this time?"

"You call this together, son? You're in a mental institution. I understand the kidnapping warped your perception. It would mess *anyone* up. But you can overcome this. Wynn, she was an illusion, created by your tortured mind, to get you through something. Can't you see? That's over now. You can let go of that. Let go of her."

"Let go of what's real? It's *you* who doesn't see," Wynn said.

"If it wasn't for Ahnim to pull me out of that hell—off the boat, away from those evil men—you wouldn't be visiting me in some prison, mom. You'd be at my grave."

Perhaps Wynn is in the right place, Brigitte thought. *Maybe this is for the best.*

Brigitte didn't want to say anything else to rouse his anger. She watched for that flick of his eyes whenever *she* was nearby.

But then there's that girl in the police station. Real to Nev, real to the police. How did she get into my son's head? How did she fit into all this? Are they somehow the same person? Perhaps, he imagined her first, and then he latched onto the first girl that looked like her. That's it. Doctor Fonteno was right. Two people experiencing one psychosis.

I don't want my son to be insane. I cannot live with that.

"I'm glad you're here, that you came," Wynn said. "I don't want to argue."

"No arguments, Wynn—let's just be together, okay? We don't have to say anything."

"What's up with...how's Nev?" he asked.

"Better," she said, "back at school now—a new school—making new friends. She's says she likes it."

"Dad?"

"He's working in Ohio…still..."

"Do you talk to him?" Wynn asked.

"Sometimes…" A long silence followed the only questions that mattered.

She held his hand, stroking it, as she did when he was a toddler.

"How long can you stay?" Wynn asked.

A signboard taped to the wall of the game room listed the rules next to an old clock.

"About another forty-five minutes," Brigitte said.

Wynn strained to focus on her, the fog of the day's meds wearing off. Dark circles under her eyes were worse than he remembered. Makeup hastily applied. Gray spread far along where she combed it back.

"Wynn," she asked, "would you like the vids or the news?"

He watched vids and news twelve hours a day.

"Sure, why not?" he said.

Brigitte glanced up to the left corner of her periphery. Icons for any links to computers or TerraNet hubs should've been ready on the display of her Nish. She smirked, remembering they confiscated her Nish in the visitor's lobby. She'd have to actually stand up and locate a handheld remote control, push the buttons herself.

Immediately, a loud and excited newscast blared from the overhead speakers. The voice rained down apocalyptic jargon with fervor.

"Again, this is actual video from our affiliate in Volgograd, forwarding a vid-stream down from the northern border of Russia and Finland. There's the rooftop of the Marriott Vasilievsky in Saint Petersburg. The entire western half of the city is nothing but charred ruins. In fact, the entire area is flattened...worse than flattened. It's been melted down at least several hundred feet below street level. Listen to this audio byte from our reporter on scene, James Dornan. 'The radiation is terrible. Our skin is tingling and hot, like a bad sunburn. Only battery operated devices are working. There's no power in the hotel, or in any part

of the city as far as we can see. So much smoke and ash in the air.'
Again, that was from our reporter on the scene in Russia."

Brigitte sat with her hand still holding the remote, pointing it
at the old flat-screen monitor. Several of the staff came out from
behind the front desk. One of them kept an eye out for the shift
supervisor. He crouched in his office, tuned to the same channel.

"What could do that?" Wynn asked.

"I suppose," Brigitte said, "a volcano or some other kind of
eruption might. But I don't remember there being any that far
inside the mainland. Volcanoes in Russia are along the far eastern
coast, near the Pacific ocean."

The newsfeed continued. Air-raid sirens and wails of
emergency vehicles replaced the usual mood music typical of
American broadcasts.

"Eyewitnesses report seeing a large object in the sky only
minutes before the fires and explosions occurred. Speculations of
a meteorite or a small asteroid that hit Russia head on. We go now
to our reporter on the street, speaking with a witness. Jim? Jim,
can you hear us? You're live."

"Yes, Jane," the reporter said. "but only just."

"Can you get an eyewitness account of his experience
today?" the news anchor asked.

"Yes, Jane. He's right here with me. Hold on, is he mic'd up
yet? Here we go..."

The hospital's flatscreen speakers rumbled as nervous hands
struggled to clip on a wireless lapel microphone.

"I'm here with comrade Sergei Romanovich, a citizen of
Saint Petersburg. He and his family were taking the bus."

"A double-decker bus," Sergei said. "We were on the roof.

It's not covered."

"Thank you, Sergei. Can you describe for us what first caught your attention?"

"I was admiring the view when I noticed a glow in the sky directly above us, far away. I expected it was another meteor, as we are prone to experience in our country. That the red streak would move across the sky from one side to the other. But it didn't move. It was tremendous, like a mountain. Yes, a crystal blue mountain, upside down in the sky. It stretched all the way from one horizon to the other. It filled the sky. The center of it started to burn. The red glow became larger, and I saw the huge mountain behind it. At first, I thought it would all fall down upon us. But it stayed, hanging in the sky."

"And then what did you see? How did it change?" Jim Dornan asked.

"There was a bright flame...like the purest fire...that came down. Like a giant ribbon of flame, or many ribbons. But each one as wide as the city. Where the ribbons struck the ground, everything broke apart—the buildings, the streets, automobiles, people. It was madness. Everything just turned to ashes, right there before me."

"Would you say something red fell down from the sky and crashed into the city?"

"Oh no," Sergei said, "that's not it." His wife nodded her head in agreement. "The only thing that fell down were the flaming ribbons. But the object up in the sky sent the ribbons down. It stayed where it was, like I said. It was a frightful thing, and we were miles away from the destruction. I cannot imagine what it must've been like for those poor souls down there. To be trapped between the layers—the ribbons of flame—until one of them got you."

Back in the hospital with Wynn, Brigitte turned to the orderly who'd come to stand with them. Together, they took in the scenes of horror and chaos. She leaned closer to Wynn to catch his attention.

"Are you okay?" she asked. "Okay watching this?"

"It's like a game," he said.

The ticker tape across the bottom of the newsfeed stated another attack just occurred to the northeast, in Petrozavodsk, on the shore of Lake Onega. The entire city and the population of a quarter-million reduced to cinders. The northern half of the lake boiled away. The rest rushed down to fill the emptiness.

"As you can see," the news anchor said, "reports of a massive object in the upper atmosphere over various cities in Russia are followed by tales of utter destruction, and innumerable casualties. Is this war? Has China attacked their former ally? We've just received confirmation from the GC-Four military, they have *not* fired at Russia. Radar shows no missiles outbound to Russia. At this point in the broadcast, we have not learned who, or what, has declared war, or for that matter, whether they intend to attack all of the countries in GC-Six."

"Mom?" Wynn asked. "Is this for real?"

If it is, how is Wynn going to understand reality? He believes so vehemently in his imaginary friend.

"Let's pray that doesn't happen here," she said.

The newsfeed broke into sections on the screen. All down the right side of the vid, a red box listed the cities and remote locations where an attack had been observed. For the larger metropolitan areas, a number representing the last census count followed the city name. A running total at the bottom of the list ticked up to well over two million.

"For those of you who may have just joined us," the news anchor continued, "for this breaking news story out of the northeastern hemisphere. War from space spreads across the Russian landscape. Twenty-two ground strikes confirmed. Also, two instances of large military aircraft, believed to be Antonov cargo planes used for electronic warfare. An unidentified source in the Russian Air Force advised both aircraft were assigned to patrol the border, as part of a group of twenty-four. They disappeared from radar moments after the pilots radioed they were under attack. Wait. All right, I'm told we are going now to our affiliate station in Moscow."

The orderly behind Brigitte barked out an expletive. Brigitte rotated in her chair. The white-clad man stomped and paced behind them, shouting more profanity.

"That's it!" he yelled. "It's all over! It's the end of the world. We might as well just go light some long blunt. Be flyin' high when it hits, y'all."

"Just so you know, mom," Wynn said, "I've never done that."

Brigitte managed a warm smile for her son, glad to be the one he called mom.

"How about you?" he asked.

"Oh, just a little—"

"That's okay," he said. He hoped to hide his surprise.

"Lots of people try—"

"—over about four and a half years," Brigitte said.

Wynn held his head steady to stare sideways at his mother.

"That must've been one big joint," he said.

"Yes," Brigitte said past a wicked grin. "Yes, it was." The monitor changed to a different image, one of clouds and mountaintops. Whoever held the shaky camera fought to narrow down the visual subject for the viewers.

"This is Jane Monroe with Net Now News. Tracking the story out of Russia. Chaos…panic…entire cities decimated. Bringing you amateur video now from Lyubertsy, a suburb just ten miles from central Moscow. As you can see, most clearly at nineteen seconds into the one minute video. Something visible above the clouds. So tremendously wide, it takes up the entire shot, as the citizen pans his Nish cam from left to right. Right there! Can we pause there? Yes, you can see this object. Obviously some kind of UFO, though it boggles the mind how something so huge could possibly fly. Moving forward…now at thirty seconds…the familiar red glow mentioned in other reports."

The monitor in the hospital visiting area went blank for a moment. It came back with the annoying growl and tonal shriek of the Emergency Alert System, used just prior to any important announcement from the government.

"This is not a test. This is an emergency alert. The GC-Four Military has directed the Emergency Alert System to advise all citizens of the southern region to remain indoors until further notice. Do not panic. Do not attempt to drive a motor vehicle. Remain where you are. Locate a basement or other protected area of the building. If you are on the road now, drive to the nearest school or designated terrorism shelter. Tune your NowSeeHear or other TerraNet linked device to the EAS frequency for further instructions. This message will repeat. This is not a test. This is an emergency alert—"

"Yep!" The orderly boomed from down the hall. "It'll all be over in a minute!"

"And here I hoped to stop at Buckster's for a grande caramel machiatto," Brigitte said. Wynn gave no sign of appreciating the humor.

Brigitte stood and moved to the service window of the nurses station, opposite the one from the lobby. It took several minutes for one of the two women to tear her gaze away from the newsfeed playing on her computer.

"Is there a coffee machine?" Brigitte asked.

"I'm sorry, visiting hours are over in ten minutes," the nurse said.

"Okay, well, they just said on the alert that no one's supposed to leave the building they're in. So, do you have a coffee machine or—?"

"Rules is rules," the nurse said.

"Don't be an idiot, Cheryl!" the second nurse snapped from the other end of the room. "She's obviously going to stay here as long as whatever, or until they tell us otherwise."

Brigitte forced a smile for the two women, both now angry.

Hope I haven't started a problem. Especially if we're all stuck together in this horrible place for who knows how long. At least I'm with one of my children—the one who needs me the most.

"C'mon, sugar," the nursing supervisor said, waving to Brigitte from the other end. "Follow me. We'll get you something from the lunchroom. Then we'll see if there ain't a spare bed we can push into Edwynn's room for the night. Just in case, you know?"

"Thank you. That's very thoughtful."

"You know, sugar," the supervisor said, "if this is the end, you gonna be here forever."

Chapter Seventeen

In the days after the exchange of nuclear warheads by fearful governments, what remained of the citizens of Russia, China, and the GC-Four crawled out from under the rubble, or emerged from their bomb shelters. They discovered how to live out their lives in the undamaged gaps between the polka dot wounds in the land. Survivors found the odor of decomposition inescapable.

On this particular day, the utter stillness of the previous four weeks broke with distant thunder, a roar in the sky above the wilted meadow. An older boy whistled to his younger brother to halt their hunt for rabbits. Already late morning, any creatures roaming about in the radiation did so before sun-up anyway.

Donny squinted through the smokey gray of the seared sky. He pointed a grimy finger up towards the fiery trail left by something in a fall to Earth.

"Is that another one?" Donny asked. "I thought the war was done."

"It's supposed to be," Ronny said. "They called it quits when they figured out it wasn't neither sides doin'."

"What's that then? Sure looks like one of 'em comin' in for a blast."

Ahnim slammed to the ground with excessive force several miles from the rabbit hunters. With a few steps up out of the crater, she noticed the nearest of the cars in the parking lot covered in fresh debris. A cloud of dust above her rolled and spiraled. She strolled past the line of inoperable vehicles. Any foreign particles whisked away to leave a perfect sheen on the renewed paint.

She found the main entrance of the hospital locked when she gave a polite pull on the door handle. Ahnim morphed through the glass with hopes to not frighten anyone. As it turned out, the lobby and attendant rooms sat empty. It took a moment to find Wynn in the building. She smelled his photons. They emanated out from under a single door at the darker end of the wing's wide hallway.

"Hey," she whispered, "wake up, sleepyhead." She sat down next to where he laid.

Wynn yawned and rubbed at his eyelids. Her aroma— cookies and fresh baked bread mixed with sandalwood.

"Ahnim?" Wynn sat up, leaning his back against the wall. He checked the second bed, the one Brigitte used since the attack. She'd gone for a walk, or to visit old Mrs. Hatchet in the women's wing.

"Are you visible right now?" he asked.

"Do you want me to be?"

Good question, Wynn thought. *If they catch me talking to the air, they'll figure it's because I'm crazy. Hence my being confined to a mental hospital. If they can see her, then it proves I was telling the truth.*

"Invisible is fine for now, thanks. That explosion outside was you?"

"Yeah, sorry," she said. "I searched everywhere for you. Once I zeroed in on where you were, I got a little anxious. What is this place anyway?"

"A hospital, a prison—a place where they put you when they aren't quite sure what to do with you. Most of the food stinks, but they do have decent apple pie."

"Who is 'they' exactly?" she asked.

"Wish I could say," Wynn said. "I went through four hearings. They charged me with county crimes, state crimes, federal crimes, terrorism, disrupting an educational institution...talking to an invisible girl from another part of the galaxy..."

"Why is it so dark in here?" she asked. "And hot—don't they usually have a place like this kept cool for you?"

"There's no electricity, Ahnim. There's a generator. But they only run it for the walk-in cooler in the kitchen. Wait a bit and it'll start up."

"I can make some power for this place if you want me to."

"No! Please, don't. We're good. Getting used to it," Wynn said.

"Well," she said, wrapping her arms around his neck, "I don't want you to get used to a place like this. I want us to go somewhere better."

"They aren't going to let me leave, you know," Wynn said.

"Who's going to stop us?" Ahnim asked. "Trust me, there isn't anyone left. There's no one who's going to harm you, or any of your family. You are free to be Wynn Dubroc, anywhere you choose."

"What do you mean, 'isn't anyone left'?" Wynn asked.

Ahnim smiled big, pretending it didn't bother her. But here and now, so close to the one who drew out her evolved human emotions, the guilt sat like a rock where a stomach had formed.

"I found the people who were after your family, Wynn. They cornered your father before, and when they couldn't get him to do the things they wanted, they kidnapped you, to force him to do it."

"That's kind of old news," Wynn said. "The guy who masterminded that is in prison."

"No, he...well...sort of. But he was just the one they pinned it on. Anyway, he and all the others are out of the way."

"Tell me exactly what you did, Ahnim." Wynn worried she might've done something to bring what was left of the law down upon him, his sister and mother. There'd been no word from his dad since one of the retaliatory Russian missiles struck the Ravenna site in Ohio. He assumed his father dead.

"When we were all in the police station," she said, "I found some information about who kidnapped you and hurt you. I wanted to make sure they never did anything to you, or anyone else again. They were around the other side. I went there as...myself."

"Around the other side of what?" Wynn asked.

"The Earth—around the other side. They were all in that place—Russia."

"That was you. Oh, please no—tell me you didn't!"

"I had to, Wynn," she said. "I had to. I'd never let anything bad happen to you. They were planning things, awful things. They were going to send missiles over here to—"

"They did send the missiles! Can't you see?" Wynn asked.

"What are you talking about?" Ahnim asked. "I destroyed the linked systems, every one of them. There was a countdown. I made sure each of the sites was destroyed before the count down to the launch date. You don't understand. He told me."

"Who told you, Ahnim? Who told you what?"

"The leader, Kryuchkov—he told me. I saw it in his mind, the secret plan. They set the countdown on automatic, so even they couldn't stop it. He's the head of the Russian spies."

"Ahnim, you asked the leader of the Russian spies to show you their plan?"

"Yes," Ahnim said, "he had to. It's all in his head. It had to be the truth."

"No, Ahnim. Oh, no! That was a trick. He was brainwashed, programmed. Those guys get their minds filled with plans that are real and many that aren't. That way, if they're ever caught, they say things that are truth to them, but aren't anything at all. He probably believed what he told you. You had no way of knowing it was a trap."

"How was it a trap?" Ahnim asked.

"When you attacked them, that activated their *real* plan, the one that causes mutual annihilation. It's the doomsday plan, Ahnim. As soon as they realized they were going to lose against whoever attacked them, they launched everything at us anyway."

Ahnim searched out every trace of information of what transpired since she'd walked through the wall of the police station, to set off on her vengeful journey. Her mind reached out from within the hospital, across the suburban landscape, and up to her ship-self in a high orbit overhead. With her fury vented and her focus on his planet's condition, she detected the global spread of the terrible isotopes. They ate away at the land, the trees, and the people. She understood now that during her mad destruction of the guilty, there were repercussions for the innocent. It was murder, to end a life, whether they deserved it or not.

Worse, her actions made Wynn's life all the more desperate. Her flames seared his Earth, bringing down a god's wrath upon the little someones she once wished to save, and the one she dared to love.

And the awful truth—her kiss had stolen away his grasp on reality.

"Oh, no! Please, Wynn!" she cried. "I'm so sorry! I didn't know!"

"No, of course you didn't. How could you? You're just a space girl in fashionable clothing. Whatever you are, my sweet Ahnimgoyothalia, you are innocent."

"I've ruined everything," she said. Her bottom lip quivered, curling out, uncontrolled.

Wynn pulled her close. She laid down on top of him, wrapped herself into and around his arms and legs. With her face buried in his shoulder, she cried actual tears. As the sparkling liquid dripped from her face, it did not disappear in a flash. No matter how small or insignificant her particles, Ahnim evolved to become real for Wynn. He held her tight as she sobbed at the realization of all she had done to this poor little water planet, and to the life of this one amazing person.

"Who's crying?" asked Brigitte. "Wynn, what's going on?"

She'd been outside the open door, listening to the conversation.

"Wow. Hi, mom." Wynn pointed down toward the invisible girl on his bed, on him.

"Wynn, what *the heck* is going on?" Brigitte demanded.

He whispered into the ear hiding under the invisible golden mop. A fog of nothingness parted to reveal a girl.

Ahnim turned over. She wiped the tears and boogers from under her nose.

"Hi, Mrs. Dubroc," she said.

Brigitte fell back against the hard wall. She slid down to her butt.

"Mom," Wynn said, "I'd like you to meet Ahnim. This is the one, you know—her."

"No..." Brigitte mouthed. She had little air in her lungs to form a word. "You aren't real. You aren't...can't be real. He was just seeing things."

"Mom, I wanted so much to show you the truth—the truth of my life. This is my reality, mom. She's real. She's as real as you or me."

Brigitte held her hands flat against the sides of her head, an instinct, to shield her mind from the impossibility seated before her.

"What...are...you?" she asked.

"I am an Immini. We live out in what you would describe as the space between the stars. There's actually a lot going on out there you cannot see. But yes, Brigitte, I'm real. I mean, like *this* I am. I choose this form because I want Wynn to appreciate me. Just like you pick out your clothes, fix your hair, paint your eyelids. I put on...Anna."

Brigitte's compulsion to protect her child swept aside the

imposed reality, the rush of inevitability, and the face of frightening truth. She no longer cared about real or unreal. She found the thing...the enemy...the invader.

"You're the reason my son is in this prison," Brigitte said.

The words sunk into Ahnim like a punch to the gut. She tried to gain control over her quivering bottom lip, but found it too human. More tears streamed down her cheeks, fell from her jaw and onto the glossed leather.

"I'm so sorry," Ahnim said. "I never meant for this to happen...for any of these things to happen. I just—he was there and—"

"I want you..." Brigitte stood, leaned down over the diminutive girl now sitting on the bed. "I want you to leave him —*my son*—leave him alone. You go back to wherever it is you came from. And you forget you ever met him. Do you understand me?"

"Yes. No! Can I—?"

"You can march yourself right out of here, right now. You leave him alone!"

Rage welled up inside Ahnim. If this were any other person, any other than the woman who gave birth to Wynn, she would slice them into handy chunks and cast the bits into hell itself. But at Wynn's deepest level, half of him resided in all of this mother's cells. Humanity grew as a tree of life. Brigitte represented Wynn's branch, his Joining.

"Please," Ahnim said, "can't we find a way for this to work? I want to be your friend."

"*No friend!*...would do the things you've done." Brigitte said, an inch closer. She stood ready to lash out with a murderous blow to some soft body part, should it come to that. She would stop at no extreme to derail this mad scheme of a demon from space.

"How long?" Ahnim wanted to show Wynn that she'd learned what that meant—that how long was about time—that she wouldn't harm his mother. She would wait.

Brigitte blurted out the first thing that came to mind. "Fifty years ought to do it."

"Fifty—?" Ahnim asked.

"Promise me!"

"I promise," Ahnim said. Without another word, the girl from space walked from the room, out of the sight of the fuming mother, and back into the world she'd only wanted to prove wasn't her imagination.

*****

As she walked out into the gritty wasteland, Ahnim's manifestation dissolved into the wind. She awoke as her ship-self in orbit above the blue planet. Immediately, she detected the presence of others in space, surrounding her. Four Immini, all Defenders, floated in formation behind her.

"Have you come to take me back?" she asked.

"Are you ready to return?" asked Donthel, the leader of the rescue party.

Ready? No, I'm not ready to leave Wynn. How can I just abandon him?

"I don't wish to leave," she said. "But I've done more harm than good."

"You've learned something out on your own." Donthel

coasted around to rub his edge along Ahnim's massive pyramid. She accepted the brotherly caress.

"Yes, I did," Ahnim said. "I can envision this entire world at once, even a few minutes into its future. Yet my viewpoint is limited."

"By what?" he asked.

"By what I wish to be true."

Donthel led her away from the remaining three. Ahnim followed him around in a slow fly-by of Earth.

"I detect much damage below," he said. "Your doing?"

"Some," Ahnim replied. "They did the rest themselves." A smokey haze stained the swirling clouds below, blanketing the blue and green. She turned her soul away from the evidence. "Will you force me to come back to the Joining?"

"They sent us to watch after you, to make sure you didn't come to any harm."

Ahnim flew silent, sorting out the pain, longing for Wynn. On the planet below, leaves turned to rusty hues. Snow fell deep, frost melted. Where the surface healed, green sprouts pushed through burnt soil to reach for the sun. Under the patient gaze of two Immini, Earth aged half a year.

"I met someone," she said.

"Tell me about them," Donthel said.

"On their world, he's shaped as an adult, though his thoughts are still young."

"Like you."

"Yes, I suppose so." *My beautiful Wynn, how can I ever make this right?*

"And what did you give to him?" Donthel asked.

"What? I didn't give him anything. I brought pain into his life, and very nearly destroyed his planet."

"Of course you gave him something. What did he need when you met him? What did he receive from you?"

Ahnim considered the boat, the evil men, Wynn's fate.

"At that moment, his situation seemed hopeless," she said.

"And you gave him hope," Donthel said.

I guess I did. As bad as it got, it could've ended much worse. I cannot imagine life without Wynn. He must stay alive, no matter what.

"Ahnim?"

"Yes, Donthel?"

"What is his name?"

"Wynn—Edwynn Dubroc." Her mind filled with copies of him, his voice, the smoothness of his skin, his fingers combing through her hair.

"And this Edwynn Dubroc," Donthel asked, "what did he give to you?"

Love. He gave me love.

"It's hard to put into words," she said. "The humans bind together in a pairing, as opposites. For such small creatures their physiology—"

"Not an analysis, Ahnim. Just tell me what he *gave* you."

"He gave me love, Donthel. They call it love." Ahnim watched for a reaction, waited for the question.

"You should know something, Ahnim," Donthel said.

"I know, relationships with Externals are forbidden. I shouldn't have gone down—"

"On each of the inhabited planets the Immini have

encountered, we find love."

What? What is he saying?

"Donthel, are you telling me the Joining visited other planets like this one? They've met the people, interacted with them?"

"No, I'm saying you aren't the first one to break the rule."

I'm not the first to escape the Joining? There were others?

Donthel pressed his ship-self against Ahnim's. He transmitted memories over to her mind, where forever grows out of unbreakable moments together. In disbelief, Ahnim absorbed the images, and the strong emotions which accompanied the dance through time.

You had a girl. Donthel knew a girl!

"She was green, with fangs?" Ahnim asked, amused at the mental scene.

"It took me a while to get used to her bite."

You can't experience love without pain. To have someone, to truly be one with them, requires a sacrifice. Maybe that's what the Immini hoped to protect me from. My own Joining couldn't lose me to another.

Ahnim reached into Donthel's memories, seeking more. But he withdrew, coasting away in the direction of the waiting Defenders in high orbit. Ahnim held onto the last thought from Donthel and the mate he'd found, coiled together in past's forbidden embrace. She indulged in a fantasy, that he'd broken the most serious of Immini laws: to bring an External within your internal self.

Could you do that, Donthel? Did you find a way for your slithery mate to come inside?

Ahnim flew towards him, but stopped halfway.

I'm not letting go of my Wynn. Now that I've found him, we will be together forever. And I'll make this right. I've come this far, and learned so much. Until now, I've never had a true purpose to make my inner world.

"The Elders were right, Donthel," Ahnim said, calling to him. "You all were right. And I'm sorry. It was wrong to impose myself upon humanity. I see now what harm I've brought to them. But I've decided to stay for now. Before I leave, there's something I need to take care of. I'll catch up. I promise."

"I understand," Donthel said.

Yes, I believe you do.

*****

The sweet smell of apple pie wafted on the hot wind. It pulled the old man from his slumber. With a hard shove, he managed to free the heavy cement wedge. He used it to seal himself in during the nights under the highway's bridge. With enough concrete piled around him, he kept windblown debris from infiltrating his makeshift tent.

The sun barely up, the temperature climbed to well over a hundred degrees.

"So much for a nuclear winter. Idiots."

He shrugged off the lice-ridden blankets, and ventured out where sunlight poured in on one side of the overpass. Bones ached. Teeth and hair had long since fallen out from radiation poisoning. The bloody stools hadn't worsened in months. He figured this might be as bad as it gets.

And the pie. Everyday, cool and tender apple pie. He never

quite caught her leaving it. A shadow crossed his periphery, or a stirring in his soul. And whether the new plate and the fresh slice of pie was his imagination or reality, he didn't care. He'd find it on the post of the railing, ants and flies held back by some unseen force. A sterling silver fork laid just so on bright linen. A tall glass of clean, cool water stood ready to wash it down.

Under the bridge, he'd stacked the empty china, one for each day, over eighteen thousand. The piles leaned, some crashed over. Pure gold filigree sparkled where sunbeams reached in.

Wynn trudged up the dusty embankment to the street level. The sun's brightness added to his confusion. With caution, he moved closer.

In the middle of the two lane road sat a table for two. A red and white checkered tablecloth covered the circular surface. Two gold-rimmed plates each held a big slice of the best apple pie. Seated in one of two chairs, a young woman, her hair blonde and crazy. Blue eyes sparkled like his dreams of the ocean. She wore a burgundy leather jacket, pink pants and bright yellow sneakers.

Hands folded neatly on her lap, she awaited his arrival.

"New outfit?" he asked.

"Got it today, just for the occasion," she said.

"And what might the occasion be?"

"Our fiftieth year, don't you remember?"

Was it fifty years? Wynn wondered.

So long he counted the days and months since Brigitte chased her away. Later, when the administrator of the prison hospital died, the rest of the staff abandoned their posts, one by one. Finally, the last nurse unlocked every door. She unshackled each patient before taking her own life, swallowing a handful of the remaining pills.

Afterward, the passage of time became difficult to manage. Especially for a homeless man living under a useless bridge on the edge of a crumbling city. Seventy years old and half dead from the war's aftereffects, Wynn clung to the barest of hope. One day, he would meet that girl again. She'd come back down to him, if she was ever truly there.

She did live in the heavens, right? Perhaps I died last night and this is heaven.

Her darling face made a good start on the afterlife.

"You forgot the forks," he said. His shadow stumbled along with him as he approached the table. Wynn dipped a dusty finger into the sweet drippings.

"You are correct, Mister Dubroc. I forgot the forks." She stood, pulled him close to look up into his eyes. "However, I do know where to find some."

"Do you?" he asked.

"Yes, and I would like to take you there," Ahnim said.

Wynn released a long and tired sigh. It washed the pain, doubt and weariness from his body.

The girl wasn't my imagination, after all.

"Miss Ahnimgoyothalia, I'm ready to go wherever you want to take me."

"Come on, then," she said.

Ahnim held him tight as their bodies erupted into a light so terrifying, it left a permanent shadow of a table and chairs on the broken asphalt. Like lightning, they became one, and that one tore through the day to join with the deep darkness far above.

Chapter Eighteen

"She's coming," Donthel said to Johoram. "Ahnim is pulling to us now."

The four converged near a point in space not far from where she'd once left them. Red glow of a nearby star warped and depressed with the pressure of her gravity. Ahnim appeared as space settled back into its normal state of nothingness and now.

"Hey, brothers," she said. "Anna's back!"

She circled around behind them. They crowded in with gentle bumps and cosmic collisions. Like a micro-Joining, her Immini siblings surrounded her on all sides.

"Okay-okay!" she said. "Does this mean I'm not going to be banished for my unapproved absence?"

Johoram gave her an Immini kiss. It left a mile wide blush on her top side.

"Have you changed your name, now, too?" he asked. "What is an Anna?"

"Long story," she said, "but worth every moment."

"You can tell us on the way to catch up with the Joining," Johoram said.

"Which is where?" she asked. "They chose not to wait?"

The five colossal living vessels linked together in diamond formation. They focused their combined gravitational organs into a lens. It located the greater mass of the Immini so many light years away.

"The Joining is just around to the far side of the little star cluster, just there," Donthel said. "They detected several fresh singularities deep inside the cloud."

"Am I to be replaced then?" Ahnim asked. "Another newborn already?"

"Yes, Ahnim," he said. "We need to replace the baby in the family."

If the Immini could smile in their stellar state, Ahnim would have.

"Thanks," she said.

"We love you, too," one or two of her brothers said.

Though not her first time in the cozy embrace of a micro-Joining, Ahnim never experienced the incredible surge of energy that occurred when everyone had their own light-speed engine. She didn't even have to pull on the distant stars, tired from the long journey back. She hummed along, the frequency of her own willingness merged with theirs.

Time and distance ignored, the trip across the eleven parsecs to the lush garden of a hundred stars ended too soon for her. With a rumble, the Joining broke loose its seams and segments to make room for the returning group. They jostled and pushed their way into the layers to find their place on the surface of the blue-green globe.

"Ahnim?"

"Is that you Brecca?" she asked.

"Did you miss me?"

"As it turns out," she said, "yes, Brecca, I did miss you."

"What did you find, exactly?" Brecca asked.

"I found there's a girl with a lot to learn."

"You must've had quite the experience. I presume you went back to the water world?"

"Of course," Ahnim said. "I had to know for certain."

"And?" Brecca inquired. "Are there many tiny someones on it?"

*****

During her voyage back from the faraway star system, she'd practiced what to say, how to answer the questions when they came. Faced with the moment of truth, the reality of all the harm she'd done to Earth, her well-crafted explanation fell short. Even with her vast mind and ability to create nearly anything with just a thought, no words could express the delight, pain, and joy of the humans' relationship known as marriage.

Wynn permeated every cell of her being. That perfect face smiling back at her, or his anger bringing an inner burn, his animal lust pushing aside her fears, merging with her in all ways. Part of her now, inescapable. By any Immini calculation, this speck of flesh and blood would be inconsequential at most.

And yet, here he stood, youthful again...and so alive.

The muscles in his arms became firm to pull her close. She pretended to resist. His warm, soft lips found a place on her neck, that place connected to something deeper. Wherever they touched, oneness. The boundaries faded where her anti-photonic self met his physical being. Once a pair, now only man and wife, a single entity with tolerable polarity.

They fell together on the couch. It slid into the end table. An antique lamp rocked back against the creamy white wall of their living room. Giggling, she reached over his head to save the burnished brass fixture from further risk.

"See what happens when you get frisky with me on the couch?" Ahnim chided.

"Oh, that's nothing," Wynn said. "I remember what happened last time we scooted the couch too much."

"What?" she asked.

"What what? Don't give me that. You know!"

Laying over him, Ahnim pushed herself up on her elbows, embarrassed. "I know very little about what goes on in that wacky brain you carry around, sir."

"C'mon, I suppose I have to remind you, then," he said.

Wynn rolled the two of them onto the tasseled rug beneath the rustic coffee table. They scrambled like children, on hands and knees over to the screen door. The couple peered out from between the wooden slats onto the grassy front yard.

A cute little girl, around three years old, enjoyed a chat with her two imaginary friends, all seated at a small dinette. She asked if they needed a refill on their tea, or another sweet biscuit.

"She did," Wynn said.

"She did what?"

"She happened, after we scooted—you know, on the couch."

Ahnim stared out at their daughter. Wynn's dark face, with her crazy hair and crystal-blue eyes.

"One plus one equals three," Ahnim said.

Unimaginary 289

Wynn's own eyes twinkled agreement.

A programmed breeze rustled the leaves of the apple trees at each corner of the yard. Perfect white paint on the picket fence sparkled in the sunlight, as directed by the flowing script and the mechanisms within her ship-self.

The cavernous, four-dimensional studio over fifty miles across, featured a domed ceiling to capture Earth's starry nights with near perfect simulation. A golden sun warmed the artificial days as it crawled across the canvas. Ahnim created the hollow places inside her own massive body, written the lines of bio-code herself, and brought to life an entire lifetime for the two of them to live out.

And now, amazingly, the three of us, she thought.

Wynn's love for her imprinted upon the dark matter choreography. It manifested itself in the little girl, born into Ahnim's conjured existence. The adorable Dahlia Dubroc brought a whole new layer of joy to a perfect life.

Ahnim wondered if Wynn knew the truth. That he was in fact, trapped inside a created inner-world, made real by Ahnim and her immeasurable powers, and her uncontainable fixation on him.

*****

While Ahnimgoyothalia streaked through the heavens, her image racing to catch up, Earth orbited, rolled, and spun as it always had. Left behind in the warmth of Sol, the little water world counted the years as the few remaining tiny someones struggled to survive. But she rescued Wynn. She'd rescued each member of the Dubrocs, having made ready a place for them inside herself, a grand existence for his entire family.

Wynn awakened to a glorious day, one he might've dreamt about. The voices of the three females downstairs in the kitchen, fussing over how to cook for the men. Ahnim there, laughing with his mom and sister. Nev and Brigitte loved her as family.

She belonged.

In a nearby park, he gazed up at her from bended knee. Her delicate finger encircled.

She would.

The roar of the Hammond organ in the church balcony thrummed in his chest. But all around him the halo of tunnel vision framed her beauty. With magnetic charm she held him.

She does.

Throughout a dozen cities of twenty-first century Europe, hotel beds ravaged.

Exhaustive perfection.

To today, if truly a day, or even any measurement of time or space or reality, there sat the exquisite Dahlia, so careful as the magical hostess to the empty plastic chairs.

Wynn focused his eyes on the minute cracks in the varnish of the screen door, finding dust in them. A green praying mantis hung on the outside of the metal screen. Ahnim's warm shoulder leaned up against his, the pressure of the wood floor against the skin of his elbows, his daughter's sing-song way of explaining a dandelion.

How is this not real? Wynn asked himself.

He didn't want to know. He'd gladly live out this existence here with them, or maybe a thousand lives, if Ahnim wished it. From deep within his boyhood dreams, he experienced the adulthood he would've created for himself. Whether on his planet, in a single night's dream, or on some incomprehensible voyage, they were together, and they were delirious with joy.

*****

Beyond the trees, the tiny town, lush fields beyond, and the horses and hills, more caverns awaited. Each held its own lifetime, or eternity, to be lived out as prescribed.

Detective Charles Lacour scoured the empty streets of downtown Lochiel, searching for someone. Just around the corner—footsteps, or laughter. The entire city deserted, Lacour wandered alone, accompanied only by his unquenchable desire to find that person. If he could only remember who.

For the man, Dwayne Large, it would be dogs. Bitten as a child by a rabid stray, the sensation of four canine teeth piercing his skin, the wicked eyes of the mad beast haunted him. Brutal pain from the rabies injections at the emergency room stabbed deep into the abdomen. His arms and legs pinned to the hospital bed by uncaring hands. Needle removed, the dog returned. Unrelenting, the vicious animal and the excruciating medical procedures filled the moments, one into the next. Forever the child, wounds healed, only to be ripped open yet again. Cramps subsided, only to be attacked by the faceless doctors. Despite the treatment, madness ensued.

His hand shaking, Sonny Conde gripped the bloody handle of the dull kitchen knife. His feet slipped on the wooden floor made slick with the red fluid dripping from his elbows. He stole a harried glance out the window of the boat. The maelstrom swirled and spun the small craft in ever tighter circles, never reaching the center. Just the pinky remained on his other hand. He grit his teeth and began to saw away at the joint halfway to his knuckle. Searing pain tore at his sanity.

Back and forth, back and forth, the tiny serrations did their work with slow and deliberate monotony. Until at last he severed all four fingers, again. Sucking in a ragged breath, the obsession to remove one more finger consumed him. The knife passed to the mutilated hand, four fingers miraculously regrew. He took hold of the knife, to resume the grizzly task of amputating the digits of the right hand, for the nineteen-thousandth time.

Doctor Serene Fonteno sat, entranced by the minute hand of the antique clock. Nine minutes after three. Well into nine minutes after three. In the quiet of her dreary office, the clock's tiny motor groaned. It strained to turn the gears and move the hand around to the next mark.

"I'll give that boy one more minute," Fonteno said. "Then I'm charging his parents for another wasted hour of my time."

Any second now. But it was always just nine minutes after three.

*****

"There, all finished," said Michelle Jean-Terese. "Now, I'm the prettiest girl ever."

She rested the small bottle on the vanity's surface. Wiped her hands with a towel.

All done. Perfect, she thought.

Michelle enjoyed herself in the reflection. No need to apply more. She sat back, relaxed for now. The essence of beauty, she perched like a candle flame atop a faraway peak. But the harsh light grew strong from the two dozen bulbs framing the mirror. Waves of incandescent heat brought a trail of perspiration to run down from her temple. It meandered through the platinum strands, along the jaw to her powdery chin. She wrung her hands in horror as the makeup peeled and wrinkled along the jagged path. The bead of sweat dripped to spatter beige tones on the French provincial desk.

"Argghh! Not again!" she roared.

In a fury, the teenage girl grabbed another towel from the pile. She scrubbed at her face to wipe away the garish colors, thick black lines, and caked on mess. Michelle's bare skin now exposed—swollen, red, and painful. Towel thrown to the side, the mound below her to the right of the desk slid away into terry cloth infinity.

Not again...not again...no-no-no! I refuse! I am in control of myself!

With her forearm, she swept the surface free of the many bottles, jars, brushes, and towels. The rattles and clanks of bouncing glass echoed from the deep, gray canyon far below.

Her composure regained, Michelle admired her natural form in the polished glass.

"You *are* pretty enough for Gordon Matalon, my dear," she told herself. "Far prettier than that freckled boy stealer, Anna. Oh, how I love to hate that person. Even without any makeup, I will always be prettier than her. I am the prettiest girl ever."

Deep breaths calmed her anger. Poise brought temperance and controlled relaxation.

I will not do this again, she thought.

Michelle clutched her hands together on her lap. She maintained a deliberate smile, demure, but confident. Her gaze steadied in the mirror, focusing on the eyes. She must stay focused on the eyes. Hours passed, if there were hours. Star after star rushed past the distant transparent wall. Deep coldness filled the canyon's curve. Fog blanketed the mountain within. Alone, she sat at the top, just a girl at her makeup table. A queen on her hovering throne to preside over a kingdom of futility and hatred.

Don't look. I am strong enough to resist. I will not do this again. I can just sit here calmly. I am in control of myself.

The blank wall behind her glowed as pure white milk. From beneath the vertical surface floated a doorframe, a door. The chromed knob turned. Parting hinges sleeved in silence. In the mirror, Michelle noticed her, the nemesis. A hand couched in red leather. But she refused to focus on it, or acknowledge the other's presence in the emptiness.

You are not real. This is not real. This is imaginary. Please, God. Only a dream.

Encouraging hands wrapped from behind over Michelle's bare shoulders. The other, bending down, always there, always the same.

I will not. I will not. Michelle argued. I am strong enough to resist. I must resist.

A whisper flooded into her ear, the breath warm and sure.

Those words—not again.

The other's hand pointed into the mirror.

As with the wall behind, the surface of the vanity morphed to liquid. A stack of fresh towels, clean and white, lifted up from nowhere. Endless bottles of makeup appeared in neat rows, sorted by shade, every conceivable shade.

Do not look. I will resist. I will not look.

Green painted fingernails drummed satisfaction on Michelle's collarbone. Hands slipped away. The other's footsteps, relaxed and confident, retreated across the virtual floor. The door shut in silence. Within the frame, it sank into white nothing, to leave Michelle alone in her purgatory.

I am...I am the prettiest girl ever.

Muscles in Michelle's neck stiffened. Her gaze locked onto the reflection of her own blue eyes. As long as she stayed steady on the eyes, and not turn away.

Do not waver. I can resist. I am...I am...the prettiest girl... ever...

She noticed a spot on her cheek. A small place, still youthful and glowing.

Almost pretty enough, but not quite.

The End

But wait...there's more!

Dear Reader,

Thank you for purchasing Unimaginary. I know you could choose any book, and I sincerely hope you enjoyed the story. Share it now, by going to Amazon Books, Goodreads, or your favorite social media site to leave a review. It would mean so much to me.

Please consider my two-book sci-fi series, Wisdom & Rebellion. They are available through links on my website www.patricktylee.com, also on Amazon, and Apple iBooks.

Using her brother's telescope, an orphaned Arab girl is first to spot an alien ship bound for Earth. She's befriended by the person from the vessel, but he hides a terrible secret. His promise of peace is a trick. When she dies in an accident, his cloning technology restores her life. Now her mind is a copy of his, and she knows the truth.

Go to my website and watch the Wisdom Trailer. Fans at every author event say they love it. I know you'll be hooked. Please share the YouTube link with your friends. Read Chapter One of Wisdom on the following pages of this book!

If you know of a 4th or 5th grade reader who might enjoy their first taste of science fiction, check out my mid-grade novelette, Mrs. Tricker is Not Herself.

And thank you again!

Patrick

WISDOM

by

Patrick Tylee

Obedient Sand
2470 CE
Polaris Ab4 *(Alruccabah)*

I've existed for centuries, though never as a child. Yet within me
is this childlike awe of things which sometimes seem so
insignificant. In my travels across the Orion Arm, I've witnessed
events to cheer or to abhor, along with the science, nature and the
glory of a thousand worlds. But I stand transfixed by this delicate
sensation. Here's this one thing, to see and feel these tiny grains
of Earth's Cooperative Sand as they trickle between my toes.

Balanced back on the heels of my blue silicone feet, I lift up
another little pile of fine, brown silica on the tops of my toes. The
lens of my eyes zoom my field of view down to only a few
millimeters, right where the crest of a micro-dune is supported by
one or two grains at the bottom edge. If I had lungs, I'd hold my
breath. The breeze cooperates so as to prevent any slight
disturbance to my silly game. I watch the microscopic grains
press together. They strain against each other as the weight of the

ones higher up presses down. The miniature slope has settled to a state of perfect equilibrium. I feel anxious, like a real human. I wait for the moment of release when chance brings just one crystal of silica to the brink. There's nothing but the whirring hum from my moto-vascular servos deep within my chest.

Any moment now...

"Daddy!"

Instinctively, I blink. The crest heaves as hundreds of grains topple over the edge. The avalanche rushes down the slope, to accelerate across the vertical centimeter. It jumps into space and away in freefall. The shadow of my big toe swallows the crash of the crystals within my tiny personal cataclysm.

She did that on purpose. She's always done things like that on purpose. It's a human trait. I saw it on Earth many times.

"Catch me, Daddy!"

Her symphonic voice goes right through me. I can't stay mad. She bounds up the dune with a grace and speed as only cybernetic legs will do.

"Hello, my darling," I say. From four meters away she launches herself into the air, straight at me. Oh, this is going to hurt. I can hear her metallic laughter even before she slams into my outstretched arms. We fall backward together down the windward slope of the dune, tumbling, tumbling, tumbling. This is the best. I hear more laughter and realize it's my own. Finally, we reach the bottom. Somehow I've managed to hold onto her, and all of our appendages are still attached as they're meant to be. I stand up from my seated landing and hoist her higher to a more comfortable position in my arms. "Oh, my, you're getting heavier every day! Do you ever stop growing?"

"Now, Daddy," she scolds, "you know very well my weight hasn't changed a single bit in ever. I'm exactly the same as when they grew me again."

True, of course. Except for the new polygold hair, she's still my perfect little Elmyrah, my...adopted daughter from Earth. Even after five reconstructions, with much of her biological self replaced, she's so beautiful, so exquisite. I'll have her forever, my forever child.

"I know," I say, "but on your planet, daddies say that to their little girls quite often."

"Carry me back," she says.

"That's a long way, Em—"

"Do it," she whispers, her warm face against my cold cheek. "Do it or...you know."

We begin to slog up the face of the dune, indeed remittance for the previous amusement. On the hike to the landing site, she doesn't say a word, her face stony. I worry sometimes how she has taken to worrying. Another example of how she's become more like me. Or more like her, like Wisdom.

Programs aren't supposed to act like that. They're designed to help you. Elmyrah has gone through enough already. I see now how I should've kept them apart.

Perhaps it was an error in judgment on my part to involve Elmyrah in certain distasteful errands, so long ago. And having her bodily mass reanimated, along with some much needed improvements, of course. I'm not convinced she would've chosen this path for herself. She's lost many of her friends to age and time, an unfortunate consequence of immortality. The guilt of this impossible situation can have a terrible stranglehold upon a person, even an artificial person like me. My own guilt is burden enough, for the things I've done, for the things I've failed to do. You can make a lot of mistakes in the course of four hundred years.

I envy Elmyrah when I catch her crying. At least she can. The part of my programming that causes me to learn and discern truth from my surroundings, from the emotions and thoughts of others, also brought to my mind the realities of love and hate, joy and pain. I'd hoped that my inner turmoil would be vented in that one moment when I pressed the Fire button and sent that immeasurable nuclear wrath upon my enemy. We watched their ships melt in my conjured furnace of hell, hanging weightless in the heavens. The churning surface of their home world brought to a boil, dissolving, a cindered mist blowing away in a puff of stellar wind. *If it was me that did that.*

I was there. But we were all there, the three of us.

There was no satisfactory feeling to the recompense. No feeling. Just...observation. They needed to die, all of them. And now, that's done.

Well, perhaps my darling Elmyrah can cry enough for both of us.

My weight pressing on the ship's first step, it groans and creaks loudly, in a pouty kind of way. Elmyrah and I look at each other with matching smirks.

"Are you ever going to have that fixed?" she asks.

"That's not a problem. That's a feature!" I give her a gentle, tickly poke in the rib cage before we climb aboard our opulent landable star-craft, Abandon. I admire how the knurled titanium railing transitions to interior platinum and zebra-wood. Aloe-snail upholstery flows in streams over the bama cushions and piles of pillows in several shades of purple. Not just transportation, this is living in luxury while you have to be on the way to someplace else.

When I took delivery of the new TransWave vessel from the Deneb system, the shipwright's representative asked what name they should engrave on the cockpit placard. I looked at my First Officer, Gemmeck, who'd accompanied me.

"What do you think, Gemmie? What shall we call her?"

He shrugged, to avoid my potential displeasure.

"C'mon," I pressed, "use your imagination. What's the last word you'd ever want to see next to the word 'ship'?" We all roared with laughter at his well- timed punch line, and it stuck.

Abandon Ship, it shall be.

Elmyrah jumps out of my arms and trots down the aisle to paw through her stowage, likely to pick out a couple of Flight Buddies - cozy, stuffed characters to keep her company during the long trip to Lupus' KeKouan. If she falls asleep, I'll busy myself writing in my journal titled, 'Note to Self'. An ink pen on actual paper is my expensive indulgence, much like my printed photo scrapbook.

Lift thrusters begin to raise their howl against the ground below. Elmyrah leans close to rest her head on my shoulder. I figure she'll be asleep by the time we climb out of Alruccabah's pink sky and into the deep blue of space. I'll just pass the time performing a mental edit of my newest sales pitch that I've reserved for the Twin Princes of KeKouan. But who can resist? The marble-sized crystals of Obedient Sand are like magic to most, but merely a natural geologic Jovian phenomenon. I mean, really, doesn't everyone have sand that comes alive and responds to your every command? Not yet anyway.

Anomalous, it exists in one star system, Sol. And who has the monopoly on the Obedient Sand of Jupiter? Who has the exclusive rights to the Cooperative Sand of Earth? Yours truly....just forward your nics to—

"Daddy? Tell me the story again about how you saved Earth, how you were made and found me for us to be together forever. And about the Prawl-Tang monster that would've destroyed everyone. Tell me the story, please?"

"My perfect girl," I say, "you don't want to hear that all over again, do you?" I can feel her head nod with enthusiasm against my shoulder. When she behaves childish this way, it almost seems like acting, pretense. Though, in what do we not pretend? She is no child. I am no father. I know that deep within her lurks a reality. She hides it well.

"How many times is it that I've told you the story...hmmm? Ten or twenty, I bet, no?"

"Five hundred, thirty-seven," she whispers into the furry face of Omni-Pooh, the polyester filled Flight Buddy.

Yes, I'm sure that's correct. Of course it's correct. With a brain like hers, mass-optimized and converted into the oxyserum chamber above her pelvis, could she ever be incorrect? I can only imagine how much more intelligent and process capable she is than I will ever be, no matter how many upgrades I get. It's a good thing I bought all those spares. There should be enough extra me and me parts to last...a lifetime. Well, another millennia anyway, if I don't get killed too often like in the early days. Oh, yes, speaking of...

"Okay, my daughter, I'll tell you the story. But nobody was going to destroy us, now, don't be silly. You know better. They just wanted to harvest the Earth."

How can I even say that without stammering?

Memories of those awful days push their way from the archive to my visual cortex, a very human thing to happen, it seems. I am the only patron of a haunted theater, watching the most gruesome, gut wrenching history projected inside my head.

Just harvest the Earth...of everyone...of everything...animal, vegetable and mineral. Doesn't sound so bad if you're billions of miles away and going fast in the opposite direction, Brothers! But I *was* there. I should have been long gone, but I stayed behind, wanting everything to be just so. What if this happened instead? Maybe I will do this and not that. Maybe I will screw everything up.

Boy, did I screw everything up. All I was supposed to do was deliver the message. It shouldn't have been anything fancy or unplanned. Just go there and deliver The Great Deception to the people of Earth. Heck, I could've told them I was Jesus or something and half of them would've volunteered to drop dead for Heaven. Well, the transparent skin over bluish-chrome meat was a sure giveaway.

I don't think Jesus had transparent skin.

I hear her snort a little snore - perfect. Well, I really didn't want to tell it again anyway.

Who am I kidding? I would tell the story twice to a mirror. Here goes number five hundred, thirty-seven.

"In the beginning...wait...not *my* beginning, and not even *the* beginning. But you know, as far as the Sand is concerned...it all started one day when the sensors on a lost Prawl-Tang ship detected a high probability of a large concentration of hydrogen on a planet in a star system not too terribly far away."